Vicious

A Garrison Family Saga

By MJ Boshers

Dedicated to my family.
Family is everything.

First Edition

1

The moonlight reflects off the bayou as Marilee lies back in the boat Jamie bought them. She loves to stargaze. As she looks up, she fiddles with the diamond ring on her left finger that Jamie gave her almost a year ago. She can't believe all her dreams are coming true. Jamie is the father of her child and now they are about to get married, that is, if she can ever come up with a date. Though she won't admit it, she is a bit scared to be married to the King of New Orleans. Will she ever be able to hold up to everyone's expectations? She is only a country girl, after all. The only thing she knows she is good at is cooking. She silently wishes Frank was here to see everything they've accomplished.

As she closes her eyes, the wind blows a familiar scent her way and she smiles. Jamie's cologne always makes her smile. "I can always find you out here," he says.

"It's so peaceful," she replies.

"Even with the mosquitos?" he asks, laying down beside her.

"They aren't that bad yet," she says. "Plus, I sprayed some repellant on. They aren't coming near that stuff." Jamie cuddles up next to her and sighs. "Tired?"

"Yep," he says. "Another busy day tomorrow too. Only three more days until the grand opening of the Jackson Bayou Lodge."

"I can't believe it's been almost a year since we have been here. Are you sure you want to go with that name?" Marilee asks. "We can always go with Garrison."

"I told you that name is great. Your dad needs his name on something. Plus, if we used Garrison we might as well put a big bullseye on our front door. Besides it is too late to change it or the restaurant's name."

"Well, I love the restaurant's name. Celia's is perfect."

"It is, isn't it?" Jamie says, kissing her cheek. "Just like you."

"So are you," she says, giving him a peck on the lips.

"Then why haven't you set a date?" he asks.

She sighs with irritation and looks up at the stars again. "Jamie, we've talked about this. I want to make sure everything with the lodge is settled and things with the Family are good."

"I told you the Family is fine. Something else is worrying you. What is it?"

"Nothing," she says. "Stop pushing!" She stands up and brushes herself off. "I'm going to check on Celia." Jamie sighs as she walks away from the conversation. His heart aches for a moment wishing he knew what was wrong. He just don't know why she won't talk to him.

~

Marilee walks into the nursery and picks up Celia. "Hey, Miss—"

"Sonya," Marilee says. "I thought I told you to call me Marilee."

"Sorry," the nanny replies.

"No, I'm sorry. I'm on edge."

"No problem," Sonya says. "I was just about to give Celia a bath."

"I'll do it," Marilee says. "You go get settled into your room."

"Yes, ma'am," she says. "Ma'am?"

"Yeah," Marilee says.

"Are you okay?"

"Yes, thanks, Sonya. I've been so busy and I've missed Celia."

"Oh, of course," Sonya says. "I'll leave you to it." She walks out as Jamie walks in."

"Hello, Mr. Garrison."

"Hello, Sonya."

"Call me when you need me."

"Thank you," Marilee replies. Jamie smiles as Celia reaches out to him.

"Hey, Sunshine," he says as Marilee hands her to him with a smile.

"I'm going to run her a bath," Marilee says. As she starts to turn away he pulls her back by the arm.

"Hey," he says. She looks at her arm and back up to him. "I love you."

"I love you too," she says and kisses him on the cheek.

"I won't ask again," he says.

"What do you mean?"

"The date is all up to you, however long."

"Thank you," she says. "And don't go and get Celia all riled up before bed." She pokes him in the chest playfully.

As Jamie holds Celia in his arms, he realizes just how big she is getting. It seems like yesterday that he found out about her. He plays with her for a moment until his phone rings. Hearing the phone, Marilee comes back to get Celia.

"Hello," Jamie says. As he hears William's voice, he swallows. "Can you hold for a minute?" he drops the phone to his side and breathes. "I'm going to take this in the office downstairs, Marilee. It's William."

"Oh, okay," she says, biting her lip. "Good luck." She gives him a light smile, knowing that

William must have found out about Arianna's and Jamie's divorce.

"Thanks," he replies, rolling his eyes at her. He hasn't talked to William since he left the lodge seven months ago. When Jamie found out about William's knowledge about Frank still being alive, he wanted to kill him that night, but now he is glad he never got the chance. Arianna and Will would never forgive him for that. "Yes, William," Jamie says, walking out of the apartment. He walks downstairs to the manager's office. "Jamie," William says with a calm tone. "Have you been well?"

"Yes, sir, and you?"

"Well, I have to say..." William starts and sighs. "I was a bit disappointed to hear about you and Arianna's divorce."

"It was mutual, sir," Jamie says as he reaches the office. He regretted this conversation since they signed the papers. He finds the liquor cabinet and pours himself a drink.

"Yes, yes, I know," William says. "I just wanted to call and make sure we are good."

"Us?" Jamie snickers. "I suppose we are good but,"

"But?" William says with a tense tone.

"Are you coming to the grand opening party?"

"That is another reason I called," William says. "I'm actually in town."

"Really?" Jamie ask, peeking out the window.

"Yeah, and I was wondering if you had any rooms ready yet?"

Jamie spots William by the dock and he gives a chuckle. "Come on in, Sir." Sliding his phone back in his pocket, he chugs his drink and goes to open the front door. Taking a breath, he opens the door hoping his anger for William doesn't come back.

Arianna, Will, and Devin rush at him before he even opens the door completely. "What are you guys doing here?" he says trying not to fall over. "I thought y'all weren't coming in until this weekend."

"We couldn't wait," Arianna says. "Plus, we thought you may need some help, but I guess I was wrong." She looks around the lodge with amazement. "Jamie, this place looks amazing."

"Thanks, but it was all Marilee," he says.

"I think I had some help," Marilee says, running down the stairs to meet them for a group hug. "Oh my God, I'm glad I came down here after all. It is great to see you guys again!"

"Where is Celia?" Devin asks. "I've been dying to see her."

"Sonya just got her in the bath, but y'all come on up," Marilee says. She looks up at William, still not sure about her feelings toward him, especially now that he knows about the divorce. "Hello, William."

"Marilee," he says with a nod. "Arianna is right, this place is exquisite."

"Thank you," she replies.

"Marilee," Jamie says, grabbing her arm. "Why don't you guys go on up and see Celia. I'll be up in a bit. I need to talk with William." She presses her lips in a hard line, not liking the idea of the two of them being alone, but Will, Arianna, and Devin push her up the stairs.

Jamie motions for William to go into the office. "Would you like a drink, sir?"

"Sure, Jamie," William says. "What is this about?"

"Just wanted to talk about something." Jamie pours them both a drink. "You know, sir, I really do respect you."

"Well, thank you, but, Jamie, I told you we are good. You don't have to—"

"Yes, sir, I think I do," Jamie says. They both take a sip of their drinks. "You know I love Arianna, just as I love Will, and when you get passed his sarcasm, Devin too. They are my family and I will always protect them with my life."

"That is good to know, Jamie, but—"

"But they are not what holds are two Families together."

"Oh?" William raises an eyebrow. "What is holding us together, son?"

"You and me," Jamie says. "The head of the Families are what holds them together."

William laughs. "Are you proposing to me?" Jamie chuckles at his comment.

"My grandfather never got this either. He was all about Family. Family first, blah, blah, but he never trusted anyone. He always had to have leverage."

"Leverage can be a very effective tool," William says, finishing off his drink.

"Not at the expense of people we love. Maybe he didn't care about the people, but—"

"That is one thing you are wrong about, boy," William says, standing up to face Jamie. "He cared too much."

"Is that why he left Marilee and Celia with a stranger to keep them safe," Jamie says, glaring at William.

William's eyes widen, but he tries to play off his surprise. "What are you talking about?"

"William," Jamie sighs, exhausted from all the lies. "Frank told me you knew about everything. You even helped him pull it off."

"When did he tell you this?"

Jamie narrows his eyes at William. "Right after I poisoned his whiskey," he says.

William's head slowly turns to the empty glass on the table. He falls back down in his chair, thinking he has been poisoned, and sighs. As he laughs at his predicament, he places his hands on his forehead. "I didn't know he was going to go crazy there at the end, you know. He was supposed to just hide-out and play it safe...retire, but he just couldn't let it go."

"Let what go?" Jamie asks, folding his arms over his chest and sitting down on the table.

"The game—you and him—he was obsessed with beating you."

"What about Monroe?"

William looks up at Jamie. "I knew nothing about that until after and then I lost contact with him. I promise I would not have destroyed all the Families like that."

"I know," Jamie says, walking behind him and patting him on the shoulder. "That is why you're whiskey is clean." As William turns his head, thankful he has not been poisoned, Will walks in the room.

"Really, Dad?" Will says. Realizing his son is disappointed in him, William turns away. Jamie walks back to his desk.

"I'm not my grandfather, William," Jamie says.

William looks down with a chuckle. "You are more alike than you realize." William sees the contempt in Jamie's eyes. He didn't like the comment. "You're methods may be different, but you both want the same thing."

"And what is that?"

"Power."

"I don't want power," Jamie says, making William laugh.

"Yes, you do. You want it because you don't trust anyone else to have it."

Jamie sighs. "Well, either way, I have it. Frank is not here anymore." He bites his jaw and looks to Will. Stroking his hair, Will gives him a nod. "William, maybe it is time for you to hand over the reins."

"What?" William says, looking at his son, but knowing it could be a good idea to finally retire. "Retire?"

"Things are going to get messy," Jamie says. "The other Families are not going to want me to take over. A man half their age telling them what to do. You know I'm right."

"What about Scott? Didn't he take over?" William says. "That was the plan."

"Well, he has other priorities right now and he put me in charge. I will be the new King of the US territories."

"I see." William lowers his head for a moment. "Do you mind if I have another drink?" He walks over to pour it himself.

"I just think if you retire it may persuade the others."

"That is asking a lot, Jamie," William says. "Head of Families usually don't just retire. They are in it for life."

"I know, but I am going to be making some changes and the older ones are not going to like it."

"What changes?"

"Rules and stuff, things my grandfather was blind to," Jamie says.

"They may not go without a fight," William says.

"Can't you just talk to them, Dad, please?" asks Will.

William turns to his son and takes a sip of his drink. "Son, are you sure you want this?"

"Dad, I can handle it," Will says.

"I didn't ask you if you could handle it, I know you can." William places his glass on the desk and walks to his son. He places his hands on his shoulders and looks him in the eye. "What I am asking you is, do you want to handle it?" Jamie and Will exchange puzzled looks. "Those are two separate things. Do you want this?" Will bites his jaw, thinking. He looks to his dad and then back to Jamie. "If you are not sure—"

"I'm sure," Will says. "I want this."

"Well," William says, giving his son a hug and kissing his cheek. "Then so be it. Just remember those words when you come to blame me one day."

"For what?" Will asks.

"There will be something," William says. "Now if you'll excuse me," William straightens his clothes, "I think I'll go to bed. We can talk more tomorrow." He turns back toward Jamie. "I sure hope you know what you are doing."

"Me too," Will says, following his father out the door.

When they both leave the room Jamie sighs. "Me three," he says as he sits down and strokes his hair with worry. After a few drinks, Dylan comes in the room and lingers in the doorway.

"We are back," he says, noticing Jamie sulking. "What is wrong?" he says, closing the door to give them privacy.

"William came early," Jamie says, burying his face in his hands.

"Oh, did you tell him?"

"Yes, but I don't know if this—"

"Jamie, this is the right thing. You know I would take it if Dad wanted me to, but he wants you."

"I'm sorry, Dylan," Jamie says, looking into his eyes.

"No, don't be," Dylan says, regretting his statement. "I finally get to be King of New Orleans. I'm good."

"But to be King of it all—"

Dylan chuckles. "Well, let's not get carried away. It isn't exactly King of it all," Dylan says.

"You know what I mean," Jamie says. Marilee—"

"She will understand."

"I don't even know how to tell her," Jamie says. "She is already on the fence. She won't even set a date. What if this pushes her over the edge?"

"Marilee loves you. I think it will take more than this to push her to leave, but she will be pissed if she finds out from someone else. Take her on the boat and tell her. At least she can't run away."

Jamie laughs knowing that Marilee does like to run away during an argument.

2

After Marilee puts Celia to bed, Jamie grabs her by the hand. “Let’s take a ride.”

“A ride?” she asks, raising her eyebrow. “Where?”

“Just somewhere so we can talk,” he says.

“About what?” she asks, folding her arms over her chest. “You said you weren’t going to ask about that anymore?”

“No,” he says, grabbing her hand again. “But it is important.

“Okay, you’re scaring me.”

“No, look,” he says, shaking a waving a wine bottle in her face. “I have wine. Just you, me, wine on the boat.”

“Well, that sounds romantic,” she says with a giggle. “I’m in.”

~

They climb aboard the luxury pontoon boat and set out onto the bayou. After he gets a little way from the lodge he turns off the motor and lets the boat drift. After opening the wine, he gives her a wink and pours some into their glasses. Marilee mouth turns upward. She can tell he is nervous and she is almost scared to ask, but she does anyway. “So, what is this about?” Jamie’s head lowers to his glass of Chianti.

“Marilee, I’ve been trying to find a way to tell you something.”

“Tell me what?” Her eyes narrow as he tries to get his words out the right way.

“You know how Missy has been having major improvements on walking?”

"Yeah, Charlotte told me she could be walking on her own by the end of the year," she says, grabbing his hand.

"Yeah, it's great, but Dad wants to be there every moment for her..."

Her smile fades. "But he can't be there and do Frank's job too," she says, finishing his sentence.

"Exactly," he says with a sigh.

"They want you to take over the whole thing?" she says, biting her lip. "Jamie, you just became the King of New Orleans."

"I know," he says, noticing the growing disappointment on her face. "Look, if you don't want me to, I won't. I'll tell Dad to get Dylan to and—"

Marilee begins to laugh. "Thanks for the gesture, but you know, as well as I do, that somehow you'd end up there anyway. As bad as this life can be," she sighs, "I think you belong here." She strokes his cheek. "Do you want this?"

"I think I do," he says, as his teeth bare down on his bottom lip. "I think I can change things."

"I think so too," she says, leaning in and pressing her soft lips to his cheek. "I will support you in whatever you decide. Whether Scott comes back or not. We are in this together."

"I love you so much," he says, reminding himself again how special she is.

"I love you, too." After kissing a moment, he starts to laugh. "What is it?" she asks.

"This didn't go how I thought it would."

"Then why did...Oh my God," she says, hitting him in the arm. "You thought I would run, didn't you?"

"No, I didn't," he says, laughing. "Dylan did."

"Oh, ye of little faith," she shakes her head. "And here I thought you just wanted to get me all alone."

"Well, maybe I did," he says, leaning her back slowly.

"Oh..." she giggles.

~

They stay there until almost daylight, tangled up together. "We better get back," Marilee says. "Celia will be up soon and we have a big day of finishing the lodge."

"Yeah, we probably should have slept some," Jamie says.

"It was worth it," she says.

"Let's see if you think that later." He laughs and starts the boat to head back to the lodge. When they pull up to the dock, Jamie notices Marilee pouting. "What is wrong?"

"It's just...how long have you known about taking over for Scott?"

Jamie sighs. "About a month." He rolls his eyes at her. "I know, I should have told you sooner, but I was...I'm sorry."

"I get it," she says. "But, Jamie, you have to trust that I will be here for you whenever you need me. I want you to promise me, no more secrets. I don't care how bad it is; just promise that you will tell me." Jamie doesn't know how to respond. This would be the perfect time to tell her about Frank, but he just doesn't want to hurt her.

"I promise," he says. The corner of his mouth tilts up, but he is dying inside.

As they walk back up to the lodge, Jamie surveys the area as the sun is coming up. "This place is so peaceful," he says.

"Yeah, it is," Marilee says. "I'm glad we found it by chance."

"Do you really think it was by chance?"

"Probably not," Marilee says.

"So," Jamie says with a yawn. "What is first on the list today?"

"First?" Marilee bites her lip, thinking. "I think the guy comes in to put in the wheelchair ramp and to fix the elevator. It was supposed to already be done by now."

"I'll have a chat with him," Jamie says.

"Also, we might have some last minute painting to do, the applicants come in at lunch to train, and the food arrives at three along with our new chefs." Marilee takes a breath. "Oh, and the decorator comes today to look at the place. I think that is everything today. Tomorrow is pretty much all training and preparing the menus."

"Relax," Jamie says as they reach the front door. "You are doing an amazing job."

"You don't think this place is too...cozy, do you?" she asks. "I mean for the Family. I know they like things to be...elegant."

"Don't worry about them. This is supposed to feel homey, inviting, and comfy. You did outstanding." He opens the doors and kisses her forehead. "Besides, it is a lodge not a hotel and it is the best looking lodge I have ever seen."

"Have you even ever been to a lodge before?"

"As a matter of fact, I have," he says, clearing his throat. "They have an upscale lodge in England that Arianna and I visited and they don't hold a candle to this place." He brings her to the middle of the lobby. "Look around," he says. "Look at that massive stone fireplace, that huge A-framed window, look up at those beams, but you know what my favorite part is?"

"What?"

He turns her toward the restaurant. “That...Celia’s. That is the best part of the lodge and that is what everyone is going to be talking about.”

“You really think so?” she asks.

“Of course, now let’s get upstairs and check on our other Celia.”

~

Around seven o’clock there is a tapping on their door. Marilee opens it to see Charlotte. “Hey,” Marilee says as she grabs her for a hug. “Why were you knocking so low? I barely heard you. Come on in.” Charlotte comes in and Dylan comes in behind her. “Dylan,” Marilee shrieks and gives him a hug too.

“We didn’t want to wake Celia up,” Charlotte says as her and Dylan walk through the doorway.

“Oh, that girl sleeps through anything,” Jamie says, walking in the room dressed in his best suit. Marilee bites her lip, catching the squeal before it comes out.

“Wow,” Charlotte says. “Dressed like a king.” Dylan slaps her on the arm.

“Ouch,” she says, biting her lip and remembering they don’t know if Jamie has told her about being king yet. “Sorry.”

“It’s okay,” Jamie says. “We are good.”

“Yes, we are,” Marilee says. Charlotte slaps Dylan back while Jamie gives Marilee a goodbye kiss.

“I’ll be back after lunch to help with things,” Jamie says.

“And I’ll be here to help you all day,” Charlotte says.

“Thank you,” Marilee says. As the guys walk out the door, Marilee watches Jamie walk out with a smile. She turns to Charlotte. “Coffee?”

Charlotte notices and laughs. “Y’all are too cute.”

“So what is the meeting about today?” Marilee asks as they sit at the kitchen island.

“Well, since you agreed for him to be king, he has to meet with the others and tell them his plans, if any. Speaking of plans,” Charlotte says. “I have some news.” She holds out her hand to show her a diamond ring.

“Oh my God! Charlotte, I’m so happy for you.” As they hug, someone knocks on the door. Before she can open it, Arianna opens it and peeks her head in.

“I didn’t wake up Celia, did I?” she asks.

“No, come on in,” Marilee says.

“I heard squealing,” Arianna says.

“Charlotte just showed me her ring.”

“Isn’t it beautiful?” Arianna says.

“Gorgeous,” Marilee says.

“I didn’t want to take your engagement bliss away,” Charlotte says. “But since Dylan is becoming King of New Orleans, I have to get him married.”

“What do you mean,” Marilee asks, narrowing her eyes at Charlotte. Arianna laughs.

“The women in this Family are vultures,” Charlotte says. “If they see a man go up in rank, they are all over them.”

“Yeah, it is the same in London,” Arianna says. “Will is going to have fun, since he is taking over for Dad.”

“Will is taking over England?” Marilee asks.

“Yep, as soon as Dad gets some things in order.”

“Wow, there is a lot happening,” Marilee says, pouring them some coffee.

“Yes, and not to be a bad friend or anything, but I know you love Jamie so why won’t you set a date?" Charlotte says. Marilee rolls her eyes at the comment. "If you don't put your stamp on him someone will try to take him away; not that you have to worry about that, but still these women are piranhas."

"My stamp?" Marilee laughs.

"Yes," Arianna says. "These leaders have daughters too. If someone decides they want their daughter to be with king—"

"Round and round we go," Charlotte says. "Set a date."

"Maybe we need to show her what kind of girls she will have to deal with," Arianna says.

"Tonight we can have a girl's night out," Charlotte says.

"Guys, you're being silly," Marilee says. "Nobody came after him last time." They both widen their eyes at her comment and laugh.

"Hello," Arianna says, acknowledging herself.

"Well, besides you."

"Oh, yes they did sweetie, you just weren't paying attention. Do you really want to go through all of that drama again because you are scared?"

"I'm not scared," Marilee says. Arianna and Charlotte look at each other and then back to Marilee. They both fold their arms over their chest and give a sigh. "Okay," she says. "I'm terrified, but I'm not going to be forced into setting a date."

"Oh, Lord," Charlotte says. "Here comes that Jackson stubbornness."

"What?" Marilee says. "I am not stubborn." They all giggle. "Fine, girl's night out."

~

As Jamie and the guys' walk into the room, it is empty. "They are usually here before us," Dylan says, reaching for his phone. "Jack, where are you guys?" Dylan rolls his eyes. "Jack, tell them they are being ridiculous." Jamie grabs the phone from Dylan.

"Jack, tell them to be here in an hour. I will not be disrespected twice." He paces back and forth after handing the phone back to Dylan. "Will, did you talk to your father?"

"Yes, he said he is working on it," Will says, shaking his head and placing his hands in his pockets. He takes a long sigh and gets out his phone to call his dad.

"Jamie, they want to vote you out," Dylan says.

"Of course they do," Jamie smirks. "Did you think this would be easy?"

"But they can vote you out," Dylan says.

"Not without just cause," Devin chimes in. "That is the law in every faction."

"Yes, it is yours by birthright," Will agrees.

"If they do vote against you it still has to go through all the factions including the international ones. These four voting against you, means nothing."

"Good to know," Jamie says.

"And you are king as soon as everyone signs. So if you want to relieve anyone of their duties you can."

"They have to sign first," Jamie says. "You are quite useful today, Devin."

"I aim to please, your Royalness," Devin says as he bows.

"Shut up," Jamie says, slapping him on the chest. "Okay, this is how it is going to go. I don't care if it matters or not, I want them to sign. I can't have them going against me. We need intel, any information we can use against these jerks," Jamie says, getting out his phone. "We need to let them know that I will not tolerate their actions...Charlotte," Jamie says.

"Yeah, what's up?"

"We need you to dig some dirt on some people."

"Of course," Charlotte says.

"I'll text you the names," he says and he starts to hang up the phone. "Oh, Charlotte, congratulations."

"Thanks," she says.

"Okay, so I'll send Charlotte Stan and Jack and we can handle Reece and Patrick. We need businesses, family, bank accounts, enemies, properties...I want it all."

~

"Who was that?" Marilee asks.

"Jamie," Charlotte responds. "I don't think their meeting is going well."

"Oh?"

"He wants me to dig up some dirt on some people. That usually means he needs to blackmail someone."

"Can I help?"

"What about the lodge?" Charlotte says.

"It's okay," Marilee says. "Nothing is going on until after lunch. I'm just waiting for that guy to finish fixing the elevator. He has been at it a while. I'll meet you guys in the office. I'll go get my computer from the kitchen. We can get more done with three computers."

"Sounds good," Charlotte says, packing her stuff up to go meet in the office. "Be down in a minute."

Marilee runs down to the restaurant kitchen and grabs her laptop. As she turns to leave, someone places their hand over her mouth. "This won't hurt a bit, sweetheart," the man says. She struggles a bit, and by the stench of his cologne, she can tell it is the electrician. The snap of his knife opening tells her that his grip on her isn't as strong and she is able to escape his grasp.

"Charlotte!" Marilee yells. Charlotte and Arianna hear Marilee scream and they run as fast as they can. Their eyes widen when they see the man with a knife. Marilee runs to them as they enter the dining room.

"Are you okay?" Charlotte asks as the man comes toward them all. Arianna pulls out her gun and the man stops in his tracks, his eyes widen.

"No, guys," Marilee pleas, trying to catch her breath. "No blood, it took forever to get this place perfect. Just try to do this quickly with minimal damage, please."

"On it," Charlotte says, going after the man. Arianna puts her gun back in its holster and she smiles.

"This should be fun," she says as Charlotte takes her stance to fight the man. He shows his slightly crooked teeth and runs at her. She knocks him out in less than a minute without any bloodshed.

"Thanks," Marilee says, feeling like a helpless child. She wishes she had the skills her friends have.

~

Jamie's phone buzzes. "Yeah," he says a bit agitated. He jumps up immediately. "On our way," he says.

"What is it?" Dylan asks.

"Girls were attacked," he says. "Cancel the meeting. We got to go." They gather all the info they have and rush out as quickly as they can.

On the way back to the lodge, everyone is worried about the girls. Jamie uses this time to get security for the lodge. He's pissed that this wasn't his first priority. "This should've been handled months ago," Jamie says, clenching his fist. "Yes, this is Jamie," he says into the phone. "I need twelve of our best and most loyal for security detail. Tell them to be at the lodge within the hour." Dylan's eyes dart to the rearview mirror. He knows Jamie is beating himself up inside.

"I didn't think about it either, Jamie," he says. "Nobody did."

"We were just stupidly happy, I guess," Jamie says with a huff. "Nothing has happened in so long we just assumed that it wouldn't. Where is William?"

"He left early this morning to meet with Dad," Dylan says. "What about the meeting?"

"We'll worry about that when I know the girls are okay," Jamie says. They pull up to the lodge and Jamie hops out before the car even stops.

3

Jamie runs inside the lodge yelling for Marilee. "She is upstairs," Arianna says. Running up the stairs as fast as he can, he feels like a thousand knives are stabbing him. He bursts through the door. "Marilee!"

"In the bathroom," she shouts.

After racing to the bathroom, he sighs with relief when he sees her taking a bubble bath. "Are you okay?" he asks, sitting on the edge of the tub, a bit out of breath.

"Yes."

"Where is Celia?"

"Sonya took her to Dad's."

"What happened?" he asks, grabbing her soapy hand. Marilee hasn't cried all day since it happened, but seeing Jamie so worried makes her break down. "Hey...it's okay." He pulls her out of the bathtub and sits her on his lap. Soapy water pools in the floor and on Jamie.

"No, I'm sorry," she says. "I made you miss your first big meeting and now I'm getting your suit all wet."

"Don't worry about that," Jamie says. "Did he hurt you?"

"No," she pouts. "Just my pride. I barely got away and Charlotte comes in and knocks him out in two seconds."

"Marilee, Charlotte has been trained for that," he says with a snicker. He brushes his fingers across her face. "Are you sure you are okay?"

"Yes," she says with a smile. "I'm sorry you had to worry about me."

"Don't be," he says. "I will always worry about you. You are the love of my life." He kisses her and puts her back in the tub. "Okay, I need to take care of things downstairs."

"I'll be out in a bit," she says.

"Don't be too long, we have people coming," Jamie says.

"Oh my God, I forgot," she says with her hands over her face. "The decorator, the chef, the food—"

"Calm down," he says. "It is only 10:30. You have time." He closes the door behind him and leans against the wall to take a breath and to thank God to himself that she didn't get hurt. After a moment, the gravity of the situation hits him. This could have been so much worse. He grinds his teeth and heads downstairs.

~

Jamie is pissed and he is ready to kill the man who tried to take Marilee's life. As he walks down the hill toward the dock, he sees Devin, Dylan, and Will beating him, but he is still standing and conscious. They see Jamie coming so they stop and wait for him. "He isn't talking, but he is no professional," Charlotte says. "I could tell by the way he fought." Jamie is silent, but they can tell he is furious. He bites his jaw as he scowls at the man.

"You going to talk?" he asks the man. The man is silent, but spits in Jamie's face. Charlotte quickly hands him a handkerchief and notices the look in his eyes. She has seen it many times so she glances at Dylan.

"Maybe you girls should go back and check on Marilee," Dylan says. They nod and start back up the hill toward the lodge. As soon as they are up the hill, Jamie starts beating the man. As he falls to the ground, Jamie asks again, "One last time." He kicks the man in the face. “Are you going to talk, asshole?”

The man looks up at him with swollen, bloody eyes and says, “Fuck you,” spitting blood on the ground. Jamie kicks him one more time and nods to Dylan.

“Take him for a ride,” Jamie says. “Dump the van.”

“I got the van,” Devin says as Will and Dylan grab the man and dump him in the boat.

As Jamie walks up the hill toward the lodge, he sees a car pull up. He worries for a moment until he realizes it is his security team. He turns and sees the boat pull away. Wiping the blood off his hands, he continues up the hill to greet his men. Most of them he knows. A stalky man walks to shake his hand. “Mr. Garrison,” he says.

“Blake,” Jamie says, shaking his hand. “Nice to see you again.”

“Sorry about the circumstances,” Blake says.

“I’m hoping you see to it that there are no more circumstances.”

“Yes, sir,” Blake responds and walks over to the men.

“These are your best?” Jamie asks.

“Of course,” Blake says. “You wanted the best.”

Jamie motions for Blake to follow him. “Blake, some of these men were under my grandfather.”

“Yes,” Blake says. “They were very loyal to him, therefore, they will be loyal to you.”

Skeptical that this will end well, Jamie raises an eyebrow to Blake. “You know me and Frank did not get along?”

"Well aware, Mr. Garrison, but I assure you these are the best men for the job." Blake sighs. "But if you would like me to find others—"

"No, no," Jamie says. "It will be fine. I trust you. Just don't let me down."

"Yes, sir," Blake says. "We will survey the property. Anything I should know?"

"There is a side entrance as well as a basement and the third floor is our apartment. Only those with security clearance should be anywhere near there."

"Of course, sir."

"I'll leave you to it then," Jamie says. He gives the men a nod and goes back up to check on Marilee. On his way, he wonders if Frank was right about others not approving of Marilee.

"Marilee?" Jamie calls as he opens the door to the apartment. Marilee, Arianna, and Charlotte are drinking coffee in the kitchen. "How's it going?" he asks, propping up against the archway.

"I'm better, thanks," Marilee replies, noticing a bit of blood on his hand that the handkerchief must have missed. She quickly looks back down to her coffee mug. "I'm going to go clean up," he says. Seeing her reaction to it makes him question his actions. He looks at himself in the mirror and shakes the feeling off. Coming back after he cleans up, he find Marilee alone. "Hey," he says, pouring himself a cup of coffee. "Where did the girls go?"

Arianna went to finish some painting and Charlotte went to take a stab at fixing the elevator."

"Okay," he sighs. "Are you sure you're fine?"

"Yeah," she says. "I'm better." She assures him with a smile. "What would you think about me getting some training from Charlotte, at least enough so I can defend myself?"

"I would actually love that," he says. "Because this won't be the last time someone tries to kill you. I'm sorry, I will understand if you want to take Celia and—"

"Would you?" she asks with a smirk.

"No," he says, shaking his head. "I'd be miserable, but—"

"Look, I can't live without you so if I have to endure a little inconvenience of being attacked every day," she says, shrugging her shoulders, "then so be it."

He laughs. "You are amazing, you know that?"

"Yes, but listen," she says. "We are going to have to get some security around here. I don't want anyone getting to Celia."

"It is already in place," Jamie says.

"Good. I mean I want a bodyguard on her at all times."

"Yes, ma'am," Jamie says, leaning in for a kiss, but Marilee's phone buzzes.

"Crap, the food is here," she says.

"Is Sonya on her way back with Celia?" Jamie asks.

"Yes, I told her to come back as soon as possible," Marilee says.

"Great, are you ready?"

"Yep," she says, grabbing his hand. With butterflies in her stomach, she takes a breath and they head downstairs.

~

The rest of the day is pretty busy and it takes Marilee's mind off of recent events. She checks her to-do list as she sits in the lobby. "Food...check," she says under her breath. As she looks up out the window, she sees Jamie greeting a woman. Jealousy starts to creep up her spine and she gets up to get a better view. Arianna comes to stand beside her. “What is she doing here?”

“You know her?” Marilee asks.

“Yeah, her name is Ruby. She is an interior decorator.”

“Oh, Ruby Brown. I hired her,” Marilee says. Arianna folds her arms over her chest. “To decorate the lodge for the party.” She notices Arianna still giving her a look of confusion. “What? She came highly recommended.”

“Yeah, by mostly men,” Charlotte adds to the conversation.

“I can’t believe you hired her, Marilee,” Arianna says. “She is one of the biggest piranhas around.”

“Well, thanks for the heads up, guys. Y’all knew I was looking for a decorator.”

“Sorry,” Arianna says. “She’s also had her eyes on Jamie for a long time.”

“Who?” Dylan asks. “What are you girls doing?”

Devin comes over and peers out the window as well. “Oh my,” Will says, peeking over Devin. “What is she doing here?”

“Do I have to screen everyone before I hire them to make sure they don’t have a crush on my fiancé,” Marilee says with frustration.

“If you did that you would never hire anyone,” Arianna says.

“Marilee Jackson, are you jealous?” Will teases.

“No...” she folds her arms and pouts. “Okay...yes, but look at her. Blond hair, tan, and showing her legs off in that skirt. He doesn’t even flinch when she touches him. Crap.” They all try to hide as Jamie looks up. He laughs when he realizes they are watching them.

"Come on," Jamie says. "I'll introduce you." He brings her inside and toward Marilee.

"Marilee, this is Ruby, the designer you hired."

"Nice to meet you Ms. Brown," Marilee says, reaching out to shake her hand.

"Actually," Ruby says. "It's Brown-Taylor now." She shakes Marilee's hand, but still concentrating on Jamie. Marilee let's out a noticeable sigh of relief.

"Oh, congratulations," Marilee says.

"Well, I had to do something," Ruby says, placing her hand on Jamie's shoulder. "Since this one is taking himself off the market again." Jamie blushes, but Marilee doesn't think the comment was funny or charming. She sees Arianna holding Charlotte back from interfering. "I told you," Arianna mouths. Charlotte returns to fixing the elevator so she doesn't do anything she may regret.

Before Marilee can get out her response, Ruby laughs. "Just kidding, she says. "I heard y'all were engaged. Congratulations, when is the big day?"

"Uh, Ruby," Jamie chimes in. "Why don't you start in the dining room. We have trainees coming soon."

"Okay, great," Ruby says. "I'll go get started. It was great to meet you in person, Marilee."

"You too," Marilee says through gritted teeth.

"I'll show you where it is," Jamie says, gesturing her to go first. He takes his hand and places it on the small of her back. This strikes a nerve in Marilee and the girls can tell. Arianna comes rushing over to her.

"Marilee, he is just being nice."

"I know," she says. Deep down, she is still jealous though. She takes out her notebook. "Decorator, check."

"Plus, they have a history," Dylan says.

"History?" Marilee folds her arms in annoyance.

"Well, let's just say she has been after him for a while." Dylan notices Marilee's eyebrow arch. "But he has never shown her any interest, I promise." He holds his hands in the air and smiles.

"I fixed it!" Charlotte says. "I told you I could."

"That's my girl," Dylan says giving Marilee a wink. The light above the elevator pops on and the door opens.

"Awesome!" Marilee says. "Thanks, Charlotte."

"Great," Arianna says as the chefs and the trainees start to arrive.

"Oh, got to go, but I'll see y'all tonight." She walks off with a hint of nausea, thinking about Jamie and Ruby.

4

Marilee has been going non-stop all day and looking forward to a girls' night out. She has finished training and met with the chefs. Everything is checked off the list. While soaking in another well-deserved hot bath, she thinks about the decorator earlier. "Ruby," she says with distain. Trying to take her mind off of it, she grabs her earphones to listen to some music. As she relaxes in the bath for a bit, she senses someone. She opens her eyes and jumps as a figure walks by the door. "Jamie?" she says and waits for a reply, but nothing. With chills going down her spine, she steps out of the tub and puts her bathrobe on. Tip-toeing out of the bathroom, she walks through her bedroom, biting her lip. "Hello," she says, trying not to shout because Sonya should be putting Celia to bed. "Jamie?" She looks at the clock and it shows eight o'clock. "Where are you, Jamie?" He was supposed to come up before they left for girls' night. Peeking into the office, she sees a silhouette of a man in front of the open window. She jumps as lightning flashes on his face. It isn't Jamie. She runs as he starts toward her, but she trips over one of Celia's toys. As the man reaches her, she hears the front door close. He runs for the open window as Jamie turns the corner. "What the hell?" he says, running to her. She points toward the window.

"There was a man," she says, her voice shaking.

Running to the window, Jamie takes out his phone and dials security. "Back side of the house...intruder came through the window. He just left. I urge you to find him." He starts to head out the door.

"Wait," Marilee says. "Don't leave." Jamie starts to picks her up. "No, go check on Celia first." He does as he is told and a minute later he's back at her side.

"She is fine...sound asleep with Sonya." He picks her up and takes her to bed.

"Where were you?" she asks, making him feel horrible for not being here when she needed him.

"I was having drinks downstairs," he says, stroking her cheek.

"With who?" she asks.

Jamie hesitates and feels even worse than before. "Okay, but before you get mad, it was just a few drinks and she insisted and I didn't want to be rude."

"She who?" she says, narrowing her eyes, but knowing the answer.

Jamie knows this isn't going to end well. "Ruby, the decorator you hired," he says.

"Oh..." Marilee says with disappointment. "Why?" she asks, making sure to show no jealousy at all.

"She left some papers so when she came back to get them she asked if she could have a drink. I accommodated her. We got to talking and time slipped by."

"Did it now?" she says, now with a jealous tone.

"I'm sorry I wasn't here," Jamie says.

"You can go if you need to," she says, lying back in bed. "I'll be fine." She turns her back to him and he sighs. He doesn't know if there is anything he could say right now to make it better so he starts to leave. "Can you tell the girls that I won't be going out tonight after all?"

"Yeah, get some rest," he says and leaving noticing the wet footprints on the floor. He grinds his teeth thinking of the man watching her in the bathtub and dials security again. "Did you find him?"

"No, sir," Randy says. "Keep at it. I don't care if it takes you until morning, call back, and just get me something."

"Yes, sir," Randy says.

The phone buzzes again. "What?" Jamie shouts.

"Jeez," Charley says. "That is a warm how-do-ya-do."

"Sorry," Jamie says. "A little tense."

"Okay, bad time to say we are waiting outside in the rain?"

"No, actually," Jamie says. "Your timing is impeccable. On my way down." He runs downstairs to open the door. Charley and Betty run in as soon as it opens and almost knock him down. "Hey," he says. "I thought y'all weren't coming until tomorrow night?"

"Well, you know Betty," Charley says. "Impatient."

"Hey," Betty says, slapping Charley on the shoulder. "But he's right. Where is Marilee?"

"She is upstairs," Jamie says with a sigh.

"What did you do?" Betty asks, folding her arms over her chest. "Is she okay after today? We came as soon as Charlotte called us."

"She is fine and I didn't do anything, on purpose." Charley and Betty smirk at each other. "Look, after the earlier attack," Jamie says. "Marilee had an appointment with the decorator for the party. She also happens to be a very influential person within the family."

"She?" Betty says.

"Yes, and later on she forgot something. When she came back she asked for a drink. I couldn't tell her no."

"You could have asked Marilee if she minded though," Betty says.

"Good point," Jamie says. "Thank you, Betty." He rolls his eyes at her. "Anyway, while we were having drinks, Marilee was attacked again."

"What?" Charley shouts. "Are her and Celia okay?"

"Yes, they are fine, but Marilee is a bit pissed that I wasn't there."

"How did they even get in?" Charley asks. "I saw the guards outside."

"The window in the office was opened, conveniently."

"So you're thinking inside job?" Betty asks.

"Yep, and there is only one person here that we don't know well enough to trust one hundred percent yet."

"Who?"

"The nanny," Jamie says. "Time for an interrogation. Want to come?"

"Sure," Charley says, rubbing his hands together. "I kind of missed all the action."

"Well, come on. Marilee will be thrilled to see you. Maybe you can take some heat off me."

"She's not mad at you for not being there, Jamie," Betty says. "She is mad at who you were with when it happened."

"Makes sense. I'm mad at myself too."

"You didn't do anything wrong," Charley says. "But don't tell her I told you."

They laugh as they go upstairs. “Marilee,” Betty whispers, making Marilee jump.

“God!” she shrieks. When she realizes it is Betty she hugs her. “You about scared me to death,” she says.

“Sorry,” Betty says.

“I didn’t think you were coming until tomorrow.”

“Are you kidding?” Betty says. “As soon as we heard about the attack we packed our bags and now we just heard you were attacked again. Are you okay?”

“Yes, I’m fine,” Marilee says, hearing a commotion in the hallway. “What is going on out there?” She jumps out of the bed to check it out and Betty follows. Jamie and Dylan have Sonya by the arm.

“I think it’s about your nanny,” Betty says.

“Why?”

“Jamie thinks it was her who left the window open,” Betty says.

“Why would she do that?” Marilee asks, shaking her head in confusion.

“Who knows?” Betty says. “Maybe she wants Jamie for herself.”

Marilee scrunches her nose. “I have never got that vibe from her.”

“You never know with people,” Betty says. “Most just want the power and the money.”

“Arianna and Charlotte were saying how all the women in this family would want him, but I just don’t think Sonya. Oh my God!”

“What?”

“It wasn’t Sonya,” Marilee says, running out the door. She runs out of the lodge and down the hill. She sees Jamie point the gun to Sonya’s head.

She yells at Jamie to stop. Everyone turns their way.

"Marilee?" Jamie says, putting his gun to his side. "Is everything okay?"

"No," she says. "Sonya didn't do it."

"What?" Jamie raises an eyebrow and chuckles. "Marilee, go back—"

"I did it, I left the window open," she says.

"You don't know what you are talking about," Jamie says. "She—"

"Didn't do it!" Marilee says. "Stop being so stubborn!"

"You were almost killed, Marilee."

"Yeah, I know and you're mad, but you can't go around and kill everyone!"

"Yes, I can," he says. "I will kill anyone who puts you in danger, including our nanny."

"James Garrison," Marilee says. "I'm telling you that I left that window open!"

"And you are lying to me!" Jamie says, making Marilee flinch a bit, giving him a hurt expression.

"And you're becoming exactly the kind of man you told me not to let you become," she says. Jamie yells in frustration. "Why don't you use that anger and find the man who actually tried to kill me?" Jamie glares at her and she glares right back. Suddenly, he cracks a smile.

"Very well," he says. "You win. Sonya you are free to go."

Sonya looks up to Marilee and cries. "Thank you."

Quickly Marilee grabs her hand and pulls her up before Jamie changes his mind. "Come on," she says. "Let's get you some coffee." The girls head back to the lodge. "Betty, call Arianna and Charlotte. Tell them to meet us in the apartment."

"Okay," Betty say with her hands shaking. "Oh my God. That was intense."

~

"Do I even want to know what that was about?" Charley asks.

"I think my soon to be wife was challenging me," Jamie says with a hint of laughter.

"So she actually thought you would kill her nanny?" Dylan asks.

"I guess so." Jamie says.

"Wait," Charley says. "So, you weren't going to kill her?"

"No," Jamie says. "Sonya is a part of the Family and we don't kill Family, anymore."

"Oh," Charley says. "I'm so confused."

"I just needed to scare her to see if she knew anything." Jamie laughs and they all tease Charley a bit.

"I didn't know. I've been gone a while."

~

"Are you okay, Sonya?" Marilee asks, pouring her a cup of coffee.

"Yes," she says.

"I really don't know what Jamie was thinking," Marilee says, shaking her head.

"He was trying to get answers," Charlotte says.

"Yeah, but killing our nanny is going a bit too far, don't you think?"

Charlotte and Arianna begin to laugh. Betty, Sonya, and Marilee glance at each other with narrowed eyes. "Did you guys forget the one rule Jamie is enforcing within the Family?" Charlotte says. After a moment of silence, Arianna rolls her eyes.

"We don't kill each other," Arianna says.

"So..." Marilee holds her hands out for an explanation.

"He just needed info," Arianna says, trying to contain her laughter.

"Seriously?" Sonya says. "That was so mean."

"He even called your dad to let him know."

"Oh my God," Sonya says, jumping up. "I have to call my dad." She runs to her room cursing.

"I forgot how crazy this place can get," Betty says, sitting next to Marilee. "Are you okay?"

"I'm fine," she says.

"Okay, next question," Betty says. "Why did you lie to Jamie?"

"You lied?" Charlotte asks with a gasp. "About what?"

"Well, I had to tell him I opened the window so he wouldn't kill Sonya."

"What?" Arianna asks.

"I knew she didn't do it," Marilee presses.

"Well, then who did?" Sonya asks, coming back into the room.

"It had to be Ruby," Marilee says. "She was here earlier today right after the first attack and then another just happens right at the time she was having drinks with Jamie...it just seems fishy. And it was before they stationed a guard at the door. Sonya and Celia were gone to Dad's all day. Ruby could have come up here and opened that window at any time."

"We still need to tell Jamie so he can take care of her," Arianna says.

"No," Marilee says. "I want to take care of this myself. If I can get her to back off, maybe the others will get the picture. I need to let them know that I'm not going anywhere."

"Okay, then," Arianna says. "What is the plan?"

"Tomorrow night is the party so she will be here to decorate," Marilee says. "I'll be busy so I'll need y'all's help. Sonya, you'll still be our nanny, right?"

"I guess," she says. "As long as y'all get that winch that made me make a fool of myself."

"I intend to," I say.

"Oh, in front of Will too!" she says, falling down in the chair. "He probably thinks I'm such a loser."

"Why do you care what Will thinks?" Arianna says with a grin.

"Ah..." Sonya's eyes widen. "No reason," she says. "I'm going to go check on Celia." We give each other a smile as Sonya runs out of the room.

5

Marilee wakes up early to make breakfast. Jamie came in late this morning so she lets him sleep. After kissing him on the cheek, she throws the cover off and heads to the bathroom for her shower. She lets the hot water run over her, relaxing her body. After a moment, Jamie opens the door and makes her jump. He steps in the shower with his pajama pants on. "Jamie, what are you doing?"

"You lied to me!" he says, with a creased brow.

"I'm going to kill Charlotte," Marilee says, assuming it was her that told him.

"Nobody told me, Marilee, I could tell on my own. How could you lie to me?"

"I had to," she says. "I thought you were going to kill her and I knew she didn't do it."

"How?" he says. "Who did it then? You just said yesterday morning for us not to keep secrets from one another, but you are—"

"You're right," she interrupts his rant.

"What?" he says as he comes closer to her.

"I said you're right," she says. "That wasn't fair of me. I'll tell you, but you have to let me handle it." He hesitates to agree. "Promise."

"I already know it's Ruby, Marilee," he says with a grin. She was the only one here that day."

"Oh..." Marilee sighs thinking she knew something Jamie didn't.

"Don't worry," he says. "I'll promise not to interfere, but you have to let me know if you need my help."

"I promise," she says, biting her lip and tugging at his pants. "Your turn."

"Fine, I promise not to interfere if you let me know when you need my help. But don't ever lie to me again," he says, lifting her chin.

"Deal, no more secrets, from either of us. Now will you take your clothes off?"

He laughs. "Just one more thing, Marilee."

"What?"

"Just be careful. Sometimes the women in this Family can be more vicious than the men. Promise me that you will watch your back."

'I promise. Now where are we on that clothes situation?"

"Well, I do aim to please, Ms. Jackson."

~

Marilee hops out of the shower to let Jamie finish his. "I'll go put some coffee on," she says.

"Great, I'll be out in a minute." After a moment, he gets a feeling that he is being watched. He turns the water off and listens. Wrapping a towel around his waist he walks around the room scanning it to see if anything is out of place. He sighs as everything seems to be in order. "Maybe I'm getting paranoid," he says with a laugh and shuts off the light. He stops abruptly as he notices a tiny shimmer on one of the bathroom sconces by the vanity. As he struts over to investigate he squints his eyes. "Very clever," he says, rubbing the screw cap. Someone has put a tiny camera inside the sconce. He goes to retrieve his knife from his pants and pops the cap off. Extracting the camera from inside, he thinks about recent activities. He looks to the shower wondering if someone was watching them. Suddenly, he lets out his anger and shoves his hand through the mirror.

Marilee comes running in the bathroom after hearing the glass break. "What the hell?" she says seeing all the blood on Jamie's hand.

"I'm alright," he says.

"No," she says, grabbing a wash cloth. "You're not alright." She wets the cloth and looks back to him. "Do you want to tell me what happened?" Jamie bites his jaw, but nods to the device lying on the counter. "What is that?"

"It's a camera," he says, grabbing the wash rag from her and placing it around his hand. He winces, but tries not to acknowledge the pain. "It was hidden in the light."

Her eyes widen. "In here?" she says. After thinking about it for a minute, she sighs. "Oh my God, Jamie!"

"I know," he says, holding up his cut hand. "Hence the bleeding."

"What kind of pervert would do that?" she asks. Jamie rolls his eyes at her for not thinking of the obvious. "Really, you think it was Ruby?"

"Well, I would ask her, but someone wants me to stay out of it."

"I know, but I need to handle this myself."

"Well, you need to handle it fast, before she goes too far."

"I think she has already passed too far, but I'll handle it. Just keep charming her up."

He looks down and smiles. "Charming her up?"

"I see you with her James Garrison. You know you put on that Southern charm."

"Oh, is that so? Well, first things first, we have to have this whole place swept for more cameras, new background checks on all employees—"

"And you need to get to the doctor."

"I'll get the doctor to come here. You need to get downstairs to meet with staff."

"Oh yeah," She kisses him on the cheek and runs to get her stuff together. As she proceeds down the stairs she sees Ruby walk in. "Keep it together," she whispers. Jamie walks passed her and smacks her on the behind and gives her a wink. He continues to Ruby and kisses her on the cheek. "I told him to charm her," she says. She takes out her phone and texts the girls to meet her in the dining room.

"So," Charlotte says. "What is the plan?" Marilee tells them about the camera.

"Ewe," Arianna says. "She is clearly obsessed with Jamie."

"Or Marilee," Betty says with a laugh.

"I'm going to go with Jamie," Marilee says. "Okay, we have about six or seven hours before people arrive for the party."

"So what are we going to do?" Betty asks.

"I have no idea," Marilee sighs. "Maybe I can just talk to her." Charlotte and Arianna begin to laugh. "What? Why not?"

"You can't talk to people like her, Marilee," Arianna says. "It will make her want him even more. It is a game to her."

"Well, I have to try something."

"Watch your back," Arianna says.

"That is what I have you guys for," Marilee says. "Stay close." She starts toward Ruby who is telling people where to place the decorations. What is she supposed to say to a woman who is trying to take her man? "Ruby?"

"Looks great, right?" Ruby says.

"Sure, we need to talk," Marilee says and turns to go to the bar. Ruby arches her brow, but follows behind her.

Marilee goes behind the counter to fix a drink. "A bit early isn't it?" Ruby says.

"Not at all," Marilee says. "Would you like one?"

"No thanks," Ruby says. "What is it that you need Ms. Jackson? I really do need to get back to work."

"That is what I want to talk about," Marilee says.

"Oh?"

"Yes, I really do love your work," Marilee says, taking a sip of her drink to give her the courage to say what comes next.

"Well, thank you," Ruby says.

"But if you keep hitting on my fiancé, I'm going to have to fire you."

"I don't know what you're talking about."

Marilee laughs. "Please, don't, I'm not stupid."

"Fine," Ruby says, shrugging her shoulders. "I admit it." Marilee shows her surprise.

"You do?"

"Yeah, and I'll admit this to," Ruby says as she stands to look Marilee in the eye. "You're not Queen Bee yet and I don't have to bow to you. If Jamie doesn't like my advances he is a big boy. He can tell me himself."

"Jamie belongs to me, he doesn't want you," Marilee says trying not to throw her drink at Ruby. "Leave him alone."

"Believe me," Ruby says. "He wants me. I can see it in his eyes and I felt it in his lips." Marilee rolls her eyes because she knows Ruby is lying. "You don't believe me?" She laughs. "Quite alright, only time will tell you what you don't want to hear and I'm pretty much done with the job anyway. But just a word of advice...I'm not the only piranha out there. Just the only one you should worry about. Jamie deserves a better Queen than you."

"Me and Jamie have been through a lot together, you know."

"Oh, I am quite aware of the history," Ruby says.

"Good, then you know that nothing you could possibly do will come between us."

"Then why are we here?" Ruby narrows her eyes as Marilee bites her jaw. "If I wasn't a threat...we wouldn't be having this conversation. Even if we didn't have that amazing kiss last night, I'd still be a threat." Marilee now wonders if she is telling the truth about the kiss and her facial expression shows it. "I was sure he would tell you about it. I guess I had a bigger effect on him than I thought."

"Get out!" Marilee shouts. "And stay away from him."

"Jamie is a big boy and he is my King. So whatever Jamie wants he will get and it doesn't matter if you become Queen or not." Ruby starts to leave, but turns around. "He is still a man, sweetie. Eventually, he will take advantage of the power he holds within his fingers. If it's not me now, it will be another sooner or later. I'll see you tonight then," Ruby says. She realizes she has had the last word as Marilee stands before her speechless so she walks out of the room with a smirk. With a scowl, Marilee downs the rest of her drink wondering if she really wants to be Queen of this so-called Family. She slams her glass down and goes to find Jamie.

As Jamie waits for the doctor in the lodge office, Ruby walks by and gives him a wink. He gives her a nod as Marilee walks in and slams the door shut. "You kissed her!" Jamie looks away and sighs. "How could you?"

"Come here," he says calmly and reaches for her hand.

"What?"

"Come here," he says again. She pouts, but takes his hand.

"Now, do you really think that I would kiss her?"

"No, but—

"The truth is she kissed me, but I pushed her away and told her never to do it again."

"Why didn't you tell me?" she asks a bit hurt.

"You were just attacked. It was trivial at the time. Plus, I felt bad enough that I wasn't there."

"You should have told me."

"I know and I was going to later, I promise. She just beat me to it. Do you forgive me?"

"Maybe," she giggles as someone knocks on the door.

"Jamie?" Charlotte opens the door. "The doctor is here." Marilee jumps off Jamie's lap as the doctor walks in. The doctor is a beautiful, blond, and tall. Jamie beams as he sees her. She stares as Jamie's eyes widen and he stands face to face with her.

"Hello, Jamie," she says.

"Vanessa?" Jamie says as he pulls her into his arms. Marilee looks to Charlotte and she shrugs her shoulders, clueless to who this woman is. "What are you doing here?" Jamie asks.

"I came back here after the shooting," the woman says. "I just couldn't stay."

"I'm so sorry, Vanessa," Jamie says, hugging her again. He notices the look on Marilee's face. "Oh, I'm sorry, this is Marilee and Charlotte."

"It's so nice to meet you both."

"Marilee, this is Vanessa, Marcel's wife," Jamie says. Marilee remembers quickly how Marcel and Jamie were close friends, but he was shot and killed when the look-a-like Jamie went on a killing spree almost a year ago.

"Oh," Marilee says. "I am so sorry for your loss." Her jealousy fades as she shakes her hand.

"Thank you," she says. "Now, what have you done to yourself, Jamie?" She puts her bag down and grabs his hand.

"A mirror pissed him off," Marilee says.

Vanessa laughs. "That doesn't surprise me."

"So how long have you two known each other," Charlotte asks, surprised she has never seen this woman.

"Marilee?" Arianna says, poking her head in the room. "The caterers are here."

"Okay," Marilee says, a bit disappointed. She really wants to stay to hear this story. "Well, it was really nice to meet you, Vanessa. Don't take it easy on him." She kisses Jamie's cheek and leaves.

Jamie notices Charlotte waiting for an answer. "We've known each other since we were kids," he says.

"Oh, so before the orphanage," Charlotte replies.

"Yes," he replies.

Feeling a bit awkward now, Charlotte dismisses herself and decides she can just ask Dylan anything she wants to know.

After a moment of silence, Jamie coughs. "So how are you holding up?"

"I'm okay," she says, finishing up with Jamie's hand. "You didn't cut it too deep...you should be fine."

"Thanks," he says. "Hey, why don't we get some lunch and catch up a bit?" She looks away and starts to clean up the bloody bandages.

"Oh, I don't know. Don't you have a lot to do?"

"Right, the party," he says with a sigh. "Well, you're coming then. Tonight at seven."

"I don't know," she says.

"That is a yes, then," Jamie says. "I just so happen to have one room left."

"You don't have to. I'm staying with my parents and I have a bedroom at my office."

"Nonsense," he says. "You'll stay here tonight. Dylan will have to catch up too."

"I guess I have no choice, your majesty," she says.

"Good, then I guess we'll see you tonight," he says, giving her another hug. "It is really awesome to see you again, Vanessa."

"You too," she says. As she walks out Jamie is still smiling. He can't believe after all these years she is back in their lives. The last time he saw her was at Marcel's wedding. As she walks out the door Dylan comes rushing in.

"Is it true?" he says. "Was that Vanessa?"

"Yep," Jamie says.

"Oh my God," Dylan say. "I'm going to catch her!" He rushes out the door and Jamie laughs as he looks out the window and sees Dylan pick her up and swing her around.

Charlotte comes to stand beside him. "Can you please wipe that look off your face long enough to go tell your fiancé that she has nothing to worry about?"

"What?" He sighs. "God, this whole jealousy thing is going to get old."

"James Garrison!" Charlotte shouts. "You stop being an ass and go make her feel better. I remember when you used to be jealous too. What if this were the other way around, would you feel the same way?"

“Okay, okay,” he says, throwing his hands up in the air and walking away.

“She is in the kitchen,” she yells. She looks back out the window at Dylan and this beautiful woman. She isn’t jealous of the Goddess with tattoos slightly peeking out of her classy outfit. She just has this feeling that she is going to be trouble, whether she means to be or not.

6

Jamie heads to the kitchen to set things right with Marilee, but when he gets there she is pretty busy. "Can I help?" he says.

"Yes, please," she says. "We need to set up the tables and centerpieces or you could help unload the truck."

"Are you okay?"

"Yeah, just busy, you?" she asks.

"Yeah," he says kissing her forehead. "I'll help unload the truck." About an hour later, Jamie comes in and falls down into a chair. "I am exhausted," he says.

Marilee laughs. "I gave you the opportunity to set up the tables."

"I didn't know how much work it was going to be," he says. "We have two more hours to spare. Want to go take a nap?" He raises his eyebrow at her and she laughs.

"You have two hours to spare," she says. "I still have a ton of things to do and still get ready."

"Where is everyone else?"

"Busy," she says. "Charlotte and Dylan are getting the bar area ready."

"I bet they are," Jamie says with a laugh.

Marilee smiles at his joke. "The cleaning lady never showed so Betty and Charley are getting the rooms ready and Arianna and Devin are checking in with security. Dad and my brothers can't make it because they are sick. I guess I'm going to have to run the front desk." Jamie can tell she is stressed so he takes her by the shoulders to calm her.

"Hey, don't stress," he says. "Go and get ready...I will take care of everything."

"What? No, I can—"

"I know you can, but you don't have to. I'm here to help so go."

"Okay, thank you," she says, giving him a kiss.

"No problem," he says. "I have a dress waiting on the bed. I sent out for one earlier...I knew you wouldn't have time."

"You're the best," she says. She gives him another kiss.

"You better go before I decide to follow you."

"Going," she says as she rushes out of the dining room. She quickly comes back to remind him. "The band."

"Got it!" he says, taking his phone out to call for back up.

"Be there in ten with a crew, Mr. Garrison." As he hangs up, he walks into the lobby and runs into Ruby.

"Oh, hey," she says. "Can I get you to look at the decorations and sign off on them?"

"Sure, but let us chat a bit first," he says. "Do you have a room here tonight?"

"Yes," she says. "Room 132, why?"

"When is your husband due back?"

"Not until about eight or nine, I think," she says with a smile.

"I'll meet you up there in ten," he says. He walks away leaving Ruby speechless and excited. He starts checking off Marilee's to-do list as the crew arrives. He assigns the jobs quickly and goes to check on the gang. "Dylan," he says walking into the bar. "Office." He walks away quickly and Dylan follows.

"What's up?" Dylan asks, shutting the door.

"Remember the plan we had?" Jamie pours himself a drink.

"Yes," Dylan says. "The stupid one."

"Yeah, I don't see any way around it. I've been racking my brain. If I want to be voted King, I have to do something."

"Jamie, I'll stand by any decision you make, you know that, but if you cross that line...you can't go back."

"Don't you think I know that?" Jamie shouts. "I just don't see any other way."

"Alright then," Dylan says. "I'm behind you."

"Just make sure nobody sees me come in or out of that room," Jamie says. He chugs his drink, straightens his clothes, and starts towards Ruby's room. Thinking about how angry he is at her for almost getting Marilee killed and how this still may be a bit excessive, he knocks on the door with knots in his stomach. So many things could go wrong with this plan. He starts to lose his nerve when the door opens. It is too late to go back now so he enters the room. Knowing this is the only way he can assure that he becomes King he closes the door behind him. Ruby jumps in his arms and starts kissing him and he kisses her back. After a few seconds he stops her. "I can't do this," he says. The plan was to give Ruby what she wanted in exchange for something he wanted, but he can't bring himself to do it. It isn't worth losing Marilee. He decides to go with another option. Which is what he should have done to begin with. To play her. "Why not?" she says taking his shirt off. She kisses his neck as she digs her nails in his back. He pushes her away, but guilt sets in that this girl is getting to him. He isn't shocked. She is beautiful after all. But he thought he had a bit more willpower than what he is feeling right now. The look on his face make Ruby smile. He struggles with his thoughts as she takes her dress and drops it to the ground. It feels like he is punched in the gut. He takes a breath as she comes toward him. As she starts kissing him again, he decides to take another approach and think about this woman almost getting Marilee killed. It works and he backs away. “What?” she says. “I know you want me.” He grabs her by the throat and pushes her against the wall.

“Yes,” he says. “I do, very much, but I know that you are the one who tried to kill Marilee.”

“And yet, here you are,” she says. “What does that tell you?” He squeezes harder and her eyes widen.

“I’m here because I need something from you,” he says. She bites her lip as he releases her.

“You can have whatever you want,” she says. He rolls his eyes, but laughs under his breath at the comment. “So what is it then?” she says as he lets her go.

“There are four men who could ruin things for me and this family.”

“How so?” Ruby asks as she puts her robe on.

“They want me out and I’m sure they have something planned, but I need you to find a way to persuade them to bow out.”

“How am I supposed to do that?”

“You are a very creative and beautiful woman. I think you can come up with something. Blackmail seems to work well for you.” He walks to the television and pulls the hidden camera down. “I suggest if you have any more, you hand them over.” She goes over to the bed side table and pulls out another.

“Thank you,” he says. “I’m willing to forget the whole thing about trying to kill my fiancé, but you have to do this for me.”

“Who are the targets?” she asks folding her arms across her chest.

"I'll send them to you soon. We need to hurry and get ready for the party." He looks at his phone. "Your husband will be here soon."

"What if I don't want to play this game? Maybe I want something from you too."

"Maybe I kill you here and now," Jamie says coming closer to her.

"Then kill me," she says pressing her body up against his. "You can't preach about not killing family and then threaten their life." She laughs. Jamie looks at the time. He has to speed this up.

"Just do it," he says with a growl.

"Make me," she says as they square off face to face. She kisses him again and he loses his willpower.

Getting it back, he pushes her away. "Fine. You do this for me and we will revisit this."

"Deal," she says. "I guess I will see you downstairs." Jamie starts to leave, but he thinks he better stress something to her.

"Ruby," he says without turning around. "If anyone finds out about this, I will take back my oath and I will kill you." There is a moment of silence and he turns his head slightly to provoke an answer from her.

"Of course," she says with a hint of uncertainty in her voice. He walks out of the room hoping nobody has seen him leave. He runs up to the apartment and runs into Marilee.

"Where have you been?" she asks. He can't even look at her after what he has just done.

"Just getting some last minute things taken care of."

"Is everything okay?" she asks, placing a hand on his shoulder.

"Yes, just in a bit of a hurry," he says. "I delegated a few jobs to people. Did you get your dress?"

"Yes," she says. "I'm about to go put it on now."

"Great," he says. "We better hurry up and get ready. I need to clean up a bit first." He feels like such an ass as he lets the scalding water wash over him. When he gets out, Dylan is waiting on him in the bedroom. "Where is Marilee?"

"She is already downstairs. So..."

Jamie sighs and shuts the bedroom door. "I couldn't go through with it. I'm such an asshole."

"But you didn't..."

"No, but, I wanted to," he says, stroking his hair in aggravation.

"That just means your human," Dylan says with a laugh as he slaps him on the back. "So where does that leave us?"

"She is still going to do it," Jamie says.

"How did you manage that?"

"I threatened her, but that didn't work. So I told her we would revisit the situation."

"Oh, Jamie," Dylan says. "This is not going to end well."

"I know," Jamie says, falling on the bed with his hands covering his face. Dylan walks to the closet and picks out a suit and throws it to Jamie.

"Well, at least she is going through with it and you will be king soon."

"Maybe."

"Come on, get dressed. Everyone is here."

"Okay, I'll meet you downstairs." As Dylan leaves, Jamie looks in the mirror wondering what kind of man he is turning into.

~

Marilee looks around with pride and what they have accomplished. Celia is working the crowd with her cuteness so she decides to find the girls. "Hey," she says, finding them in the bar beside the awesome stone fireplace. They hand her a glass of her favorite red wine.

"Congratulations, Marilee," Will says. "This place is remarkable."

"Thanks," she replies.

Dylan comes to join them. "Well," he says. "This has to be the best looking table here. You ladies look amazing.

"Thanks, Dylan," Marilee says. "Where is Jamie?"

"I just left him upstairs," Dylan says. "That man takes longer to get ready than any woman I know." They all laugh and Will pours another round of wine.

~

As Jamie walks down the stairs everyone turns to stare at him...the almost new King. He ignores their stares as he spots Ruby. She gives him a wink, but he continues to scan the room. He is frozen as he spots Vanessa walk through the crowd. She smiles as she meets him at the bottom of the stairs. "You look..."

"You too," she says.

Jamie turns to see Marilee watching them. He sighs feeling her jealousy hit him in the gut. *These women are going to be the death of him yet.* "I need a drink," he says. "Join us." He pulls Vanessa over to Marilee. "Hey, babe," he says. "Let's get a drink." He grabs her by the arm. "You look remarkable," he says as he kisses her ear, making her blush.

"Thank you," she says.

"Back so soon," Will says to Marilee.

"I had to go find my fiancé," she says. "Can't leave him for too long."

Jamie laughs and rolls his eyes. "So how long have you two known each other, Vanessa?" Will asks.

"We knew each other pre-orphanage," Jamie says.

"Oh, you were just kids then," Marilee says.

"Yeah," Jamie says. "We all grew up together. We were like the three musketeers."

"Until Ron came and screwed it up," Vanessa says. The table become quite.

"Will, why don't you go and introduce Vanessa to everyone?" Arianna says.

"I would enjoy that," Will says. "My lady." He holds his hand out and takes her away from the table.

"Thank you, kind sir," she says with a giggle.

"Sonya isn't going to like that," Betty says with a snicker.

"I know," Arianna says.

"You know she is like a sister to me, right?" Jamie whispers in Marilee's ear.

"Really?" Marilee says.

He smiles as everyone gets up to go dance. "What?" she asks.

"You tell me, why are you pouting?"

"I'm not..."

"You should be having the time of your life, look what you've accomplished."

"I don't like feeling jealous all time. It's something I have to work on," Marilee says.

He feels a tinge of guilt creep up his spine as he looks at her. "Nothing will ever come between us," he says. "Now let's celebrate. You deserve it." They get up to go dance and he spots his targets in the room. He glances for Ruby and she gives him a nod to meet her by the bathrooms. "You know what," Jamie says. "I really need to go to the bathroom first. Those drinks are going right through me."

"Okay, I'll meet you out there," she says.

"I'll hurry." He passes by Ruby and walks to the basement door. She follows as he opens the door. As soon as he closes the door she kisses him. He has to kiss her back if he wants her to think they are a possibility. "Okay," he says backing away. "Focus. The targets are here, but work on Patrick tonight. His wife isn't with him. I'll be sending Tyler away for a week so he won't be here tonight either."

"Oh, a whole week. The things we could get into," she says. She pushes him against the wall and he thinks this is getting out of hand. He grinds his teeth as she tempts him even more. He grabs her hands.

"Get the job done first," he says with all the strength he has.

"Fine," she pouts. "But let me at least do one thing for you." She suddenly falls to her knees.

"That's not necessary," he says. "Fuck!" he says leaning against the wall. For a moment he thinks of giving in. "No!" he growls, pushing her off of him. "Look," he says lowering his voice, "You are great and I appreciate everything, but this won't happen yet. Get the job done." He leaves her and returns to Marilee with guilt pressing on his gut.

~

Marilee watches as her friends dance under the stars wondering where Jamie is and hoping he is okay. She decides to go and find him, but Dylan stops her.

"Hey," he says. "Come and dance with us until Jamie gets back. He is probably working. No rest for the King." Dylan hands her a shot of Fireball and she agrees.

"Okay, why not?"

About fifteen minutes later Jamie comes to join them. "Hey, where were you?"

"Sorry, he says. "I had to go upstairs and use our bathroom." He holds his stomach.

"Are you okay?"

"Yeah, I'll be fine. Are you having fun?"

"A blast," Marilee says. "I'll understand if you need to go upstairs."

"I'll make it," he says noticing the shots on the table. "These yours?"

"Well, all of ours, but if your stomach is hurting you probably shouldn't."

"This stuff will burn it right out of me," he says shooting them all down. "Let's dance." He notices Ruby pulling Patrick upstairs and he tries to forget about what he has done, but it doesn't work so he drinks until he can't think anymore.

7

Jamie wakes the next morning to a knock at the door. He turns over to see Marilee still sleeping. Sighing softly, not wanting to get out of bed, he gets up to answer before it wakes Celia up. Vanessa smiles as he opens the door.

"Hey," she says. "Did I wake you?"

"Nah," he says. "What's up?"

"I was going to go for a walk and was wondering if you'd like to catch up. Since you passed me off to your friend last night."

"I didn't—"

"It's okay," she says. "But I would like to talk, if we could."

"Yeah, of course. I'll meet you outside on the porch."

"Great," she says.

A few minutes later they are walking down the trail that leads into the woods. "So how are you, really?" he asks. She shrugs her shoulders.

"It's been hard," she says. "But since I've come home it's been better. Mom and Dad helped me a lot."

"How long have you been back?"

"About three months."

"And you're just now dropping by?" he says, pulling her to stop her from walking.

"I know," she says, giving him a nudge. "I'm sorry, but I had to get settled and start my practice. It was a busy time, for both of us."

"You heard?"

"Yeah, you had a lot going on. I didn't want to show up and—"

"And what?"

“Nothing,” she says. “This reminds me of when your dad used to take us camping.” She looks around at the view.

“You remember that?” Jamie says with a laugh.

“Well, if you could call that camping. How is he anyway?”

“Good,” he says. “He had to stay in Tennessee with Missy.”

“I’m glad he’s happy.”

“Vanessa, do you want to talk about that day?” He stops her from walking again and lightly turns her head to look him in the eye. “What happened?”

She sighs and starts walking again until they reach a nearby bench. She sits and stares out at the water. “It’s so beautiful here.”

He sits down next to her. “Yeah...it is.” He waits for her to start talking.

“It was early morning and Marcel had a meeting with the other faction leaders of France. I decided to go with him. I was waiting in a back room for him to finish. We were going on a trip because I had news to share with him.” She begins to tear up. I heard the shots and I ran to see. I hid, but I could still see. I saw you shooting everyone.” She breaks into tears and he comforts her by putting his arms around her. “I knew it wasn’t you when I saw your eyes. Marcel saw me hiding. I wanted to run to him so badly, but he told me to stay put. Then you, or the other you pointed the gun to Marcel’s head and pulled the trigger. Then, he heard me scream and shot me in the stomach. I tried to call you, but I blacked out from the pain. I woke up in the hospital and they told me Marcel was dead of course, I already knew that.”

“I am so sorry, Vanessa, but I killed that bastard.”

"I heard," she says, wiping her eyes. "Thank you."

"No problem," he says. "Vanessa, if you don't mind me asking, what was the news you were going to share with him that day?" Tears come pouring even faster and she holds her stomach. She bends over from crying. "It's okay," he says, rubbing her back. "You don't have to tell me." He straightens back up and wipes her eyes.

"We were going to have a baby, Jamie," she says. He holds on to her tighter as she cries again trying to fight through the anger so he can be supportive. His jaw tightens as he remembers the day he killed the asshole. He lets her cry a bit more, but realizes that she needs to stop thinking about it.

"Hey," he says. "You know what you need?"

"What?" she says as she wipes her red face with her sleeve.

"Breakfast, come on." They walk back towards the lodge.

"The kitchen staff won't be there for a bit, but I make a mean omelet."

Jamie starts to make the omelet as Vanessa chops up the vegetables. "So when did you learn to cook?" Vanessa asks.

"What?" Jamie gasps. "I've always known how to cook."

"You burned mac-n-cheese Jamie," she says.

"The mac-n-cheese burned because you didn't put enough water in it," he replies.

"It was your job to put the water in, not mine." She throws a tomato at him.

"Oh no it wasn't," he argues.

"Yes, it was!" She takes an egg from the carton and throws it at him. It breaks on his chest.

"You did not just do that!" He laughs and chases her around the island throwing everything he can think of at her. After throwing just about everything in the kitchen at each other they fall to the floor laughing. When they look at each other and smile he wipes some food off of her nose. "You are going to be fine," he says.

"I know," she says. "Thanks, Jamie. I needed that."

He looks around and sighs. "Crap, we better get this place cleaned up before Marilee sees it. You won't be thanking me then. She will come apart."

After cleaning, they finally sit down for some breakfast. "You were right," she says. "You rock on the omelet thing."

"Told you."

"What is all of this?" Dylan says walking through the door. "Did we make enough for everyone?"

"Not quite," Jamie says. "But the staff will be here shortly."

"Great," Dylan says. "I am starving."

"Well, I'm going to let the two of you get caught up now," Jamie says. "Word to the wise, Dylan, keep her away from the kitchen."

"Ha, ha," Vanessa says. "Thanks for the talk."

"No problem." Glad he could help Vanessa feel a little better, he heads upstairs to check on Marilee and Celia.

"Hey," Marilee says as he walks through the door. "Feeling better?"

"Yes, very much, thank you." He kisses Celia on the forehead as she sits in her highchair eating breakfast.

"Coffee?" Marilee asks and when she smiles at him it feels like someone has punched him in the gut. He suddenly goes pale thinking about how he could have screwed everything up last night. Everything he has could all be taken away if she found out. “Are you sure you’re okay? You just got really pale.” She places her hand on his forehead.

“Yeah,” he says, kissing her cheek. “I think if I take a shower I will feel better.”

“Well, Sonya is going to finish feeding Celia. I have to go meet the staff. If you need anything let me know.”

“Thanks,” he says as she gives him a peck on the lips. “I should be okay, though.” He quickly goes and sulks as he takes shower. He tries to forget what happened with him and Ruby. Why does she affect him so much? He loves Marilee and he wants to marry her. He just can’t be alone with Ruby anymore. It is way too dangerous. He doesn’t want to risk losing Marilee, but if Ruby suspects he is playing her, she could turn everyone against him. His throne is on the line so he has to protect it, but at what cost? He has to meet her to see about Patrick so he will meet somewhere public.

~

Marilee gives Celia a kiss goodbye and runs downstairs to meet the staff. Everything is going great. The breakfast buffet is doing great and to her surprise the Family seems to be enjoying themselves. As soon as she is confident the restaurant is doing fine, she goes to check on the front desk. Bryce is stationed there. “Daddy!” she says greeting him with a hug. “What are you doing here?”

“I got someone to look after the boys so I could come and help with checkout. There will be a lot to do at noon.”

“I know and thank you so much,” she says. “But y’all were sick. You should go back home and rest. Jamie hasn’t been feeling well either.”

“Well, more reason for me to stay. I hope he isn’t coming down with the flu.”

"You and me both."

"Has Celia had her flu shot?"

"No, I guess we all better get one. I'll go call the doctor now, if you're sure you can handle this?"

"Go," Bryce says. "I got this sweetheart."

"Thanks, Dad," she says, kissing his cheek. "You're the best. Call me if you need me. We actually have a doctor staying here." She goes to call Jamie to get Vanessa's number but sees her coming down the stairs. "Vanessa!"

"Oh, hey," Vanessa says with her lips in a hard line. Marilee can tell she doesn't want to talk to her.

"I'm sorry for my behavior last night. I was a bit jealous of you and I should have handled it better."

Vanessa sighs. "No," she says with a sincere smile. "I didn't think about that. Let me assure you that Jamie and I are like brother and sister.

"I know, thanks. Do you think you could do me a favor?"

"Of course," Vanessa says.

"Celia hasn't had her flu shot yet."

"Oh my," Vanessa says, folding her arms across her chest.

"I know, I'm lagging behind. None of us has had one. I don't know where Jamie has run off to, but if you could give Celia and me one I would really appreciate it."

"I actually don't have any of my things here, but I can run to town to pick them up."

"Do you need us to come there?"

"No, no. Don't be silly. There is no need in getting Celia out. It won't take me long."

~

As Vanessa drives towards her office, she realizes how many times she has been in Marilee's situation. Woman after woman would bang on

Marcel's door to try to be with him. They tried and tried to push the two of them away from each other. She really doesn't blame Marilee for putting up her guard. She pulls into the small parking lot of her office, but before going in she walks to the nearby coffee shop to get her and Marilee a coffee; a gesture of no hard feelings.

~

Jamie sits and waits for Ruby, his stomach in knots again. Glancing from the back of the room to the front as she walks in, he worries someone will see them together. "The job is done," she says as she sits down in front of him.

"Really?" he asks.

"Did you have any doubts?" she says with a smirk. "All I had to do was blackmail them and they all caved."

"Thank you," he says. He takes out his phone to text Dylan the news. "I guess I will see you later then."

"Wait," she says, grabbing his wrist. "Are you forgetting something?"

"When I hear from—

"We had a deal, Jamie!"

"Quiet," Jamie says, sternly enough to make her jump. He sighs. Anxious someone will hear them fighting, he grabs her hand and takes her to the bathroom.

"Why?" he asks, a bit annoyed with her persistence on the matter. "Why me?"

"Maybe I like you," she says.

"You have a funny way of showing it. You know this could mess up everything, my whole life." She looks away for a moment and then back to him.

"I know what people think of me, Jamie, I'm not stupid."

"Ruby," He takes a breath, not knowing what to say.

"No, it's okay and I know I will never get the chance to be Queen or even high up the ladder. Men in this Family have been taking advantage of me since I was eighteen years old. I decided I had enough, so I started doing things my way. Love isn't an option for me anymore. I don't have the luxury of a happily ever after, but when I'm with you I've never wanted anyone more. If it was just for one night, I'd be the happiest woman alive. I got my opportunity and I'm taking it." Jamie is speechless for a moment. He can't deny the attraction to her, but he can't lose everything he holds dear. "It's just sex," she says, trying to convince him to feel better about it. She moves in closer to him. "You can forget about me as soon as our deal is done, or not." She pins him against the wall. "Would it really be so bad?" Her hands unbutton his shirt. "Nobody will ever know, Jamie, I promise." She whispers in his ear and nibbles on it a bit.

"Argg!" Jamie growls. "Why do you make me feel so—?

"How, Jamie, how do I make you feel?" Say it!"

He glares at her, trying to make sense of it all. He strokes his hair and sighs. "Rub—

Before he can turn her down yet again, she kisses him. Before he can push her off of him, the door flies open. His eyes widen as Vanessa looks at them with repulsion.

"Oh my God!" Vanessa shouts. She turns and runs. Jamie runs after her, but she gets in her car and steps on the gas. He thinks only a moment and then steps in front of the car. She slams on the breaks, but it doesn't stop her from hitting him. Knocking him to the ground, she gasps. "Shit!" she says, jumping out of the car. "Jamie, are you okay?"

"Ouch," he says. "I got you to stop, though."

"You are such a dick!" she says, kicking him as he lies on the ground in pain.

"Help me up," he says. "I'm hurt." He holds his leg in pain. She helps him up and takes him to her office. When they get inside she throws his arm off of her.

"Sit down," she says with hostility toward him. "We need to make sure you didn't break anything. Take off your pants," she snarls. "That shouldn't be an issue for you."

He sighs. "Nothing happened," he says.

She laughs. "Not for the lack of trying."

"Look, there are circumstances."

"It's none of my business. It's just...from what I heard about you and Marilee, it sounded like what Marcel and I had. I guess I was wrong. Marcel would never—

"Not even to save his Family, to save everything he worked so hard to get, or to save his title as King?"

"What are you talking about?" she says, feeling his leg for injuries. Taking a breath he tries to explain everything that has happened.

"It will all be over as soon as the papers are signed," Jamie says.

"You know this will never be over," Vanessa says. "Trust me, someone will always want what you have and if they can't have it they will try to keep you from getting it. So you better find a better way of dealing with it besides sleeping with people."

"I know, you're right. I just couldn't think of anything else. I was desperate."

"What I walked in on didn't look forced."

"I was about to stop her, okay," he says. "I'm glad you walked in when you did. It won't happen again. I love Marilee and I don't want to lose her over this."

"Well, she won't hear it from me, I promise. If you promise me that you won't entertain that woman again. You can't see it, but all she wants is to be Queen."

"I promise," he says. "I'm done with Ruby."

"Good," she says with a leer. "Now, I'm done with you. No broken bones."

"Thank you. I'll see you back at the lodge." He knows she is still disappointed with him, but he leaves hoping she keeps her promise to not tell Marilee.

8

"Dad," Marilee says, tapping her fingers on the counter. "It's getting late, you can go."

"I know," he says with a laugh. "Just finishing up some last minute reservations. How was the flu shot?"

"Just lovely," she says. "I'm just glad we got it taken care of, thanks to Vanessa. Speaking of..." Marilee says as Vanessa walks up to them.

"Hey, it wasn't a problem to book another night was it?" Vanessa asks.

"No problem at all," Bryce says.

"Thank you so much," she says. "Marilee, do you want to have a girl's night tonight? You can see if the others want to come as well."

"Sure," Marilee says, not sure why Vanessa would want to take her out.

"Great," Vanessa says. "Meet me here around seven." She walks off and Marilee notices the way she walks. She walks so elegant and graceful. Her presence is demanding and the heads of onlookers turn as she glides up the stairs as if a queen was leaving her royal ball.

Marilee unconsciously sighs as she peers down at her own mediocre clothing and her worn down nail polish. Her dad notices and his lip curls upward. "Maybe she can help you with your wardrobe," Bryce says with a snicker.

"Shut up," she says with a roll of her eyes. "Go home, Dad, love you."

"Love you too," he says with a grin. "Have fun."

Marilee walks off trying to glide like Vanessa did but quickly decides to stop trying. She passes by the bar to see Jamie and the girls sitting by the fire. "What's going on?" she asks, walking up to their table, worried.

"The agreement signing was today," he says.

"Oh, that was today?" She places her hand over his. "No wonder you've been sick." She sits down next to him after Charlotte gives her chair up.

"We'll know something any minute so we are keeping him company," Charlotte says.

"Thank you, guys, but I told you I am fine," Jamie says.

"Well, the strangest thing happened to me just now," Marilee says, after a moment of awkward silence.

"What?" Jamie says, curious and happy she has changed the subject.

"Vanessa just asked to have a girl's night," she says, noticing Jamie looking a bit pale again. "But I don't have to if you—"

"No," Jamie says. "You go. It has been forever since you've gone out."

"Are you guys in then?"

"Of course," Charlotte says. "Let's find out what the verdict is first—

Jamie's phone buzzes. He takes a swig of his drink and then turns it over to look. He takes a sigh. "They all signed."

"Yes!" Charlotte says as she bangs on the table. "I told you not to worry." She stands up and walks over to him with a big smile. "Nobody could ever be as good of a king as you will be." She kisses him on the cheek. "Let's go have us a girl's night."

"Congratulations, Jamie," Arianna says, following Charlotte's lead.

"She's right," Betty says. The corner of Jamie's mouth curves up and he snickers.

"Thanks," he says.

"I'll meet y'all in a bit," Marilee says as they walk away. She looks back to Jamie with a smile. "I can stay if you want."

"Nah," he says. "The guys will be back soon anyway. I'm sure they will want to celebrate."

"Okay, I'll be back down before we leave." She kisses him on the cheek. "My King." She bows, making him beam.

"Get out of here," he says. He shakes his head as she begins to leave, smiling. He thinks of how lucky he is to have her and how he almost screwed everything up. He quickly feels that guilt creep up in his stomach again. As Marilee starts to walk away, Vanessa comes in with the girls.

"Vanessa," Marilee gasps, almost amazed at her appearance. "You look awesome."

"I stopped the girls on my way down. I thought we could have some drinks before we head off."

"Sounds good," Jamie says. "Bartender, six rounds of Fireballs, please." They all gather around the table.

"Okay," Vanessa says. With a slight clearing of her throat she picks up a fireball and hands it to Marilee. "A toast to the new King of the US Factions. Congratulations, Jamie." She holds her glass up. "To the king!"

"To the King!" The crowd in the bar shouts holding up their glasses. Jamie smiles, but looks back to Marilee. She smiles and takes her shot. "To the king," she says.

"Okay, girls," Vanessa says. "Go get ready. I have a big night planned."

Marilee smiles. "You're going to be a great king," she says, giving him a quick kiss. His teeth clinch together as she kisses him and she loves it.

His jawline drives her crazy as she rubs it with the tips of her fingers.

~

"So," Vanessa says. "Anything I need to know?"

"Nothing happened," he says.

"And yet you're still king." She grins. He gives her a leer. "Well, I'm happy for you. You really will make one hell of a king."

"Well, thanks."

"And I'm going to do you a favor," she says as she takes another fireball.

"What's that?"

"I'm going to show your soon-to-be wife how to be a queen."

"What do you mean?"

"Jamie, she needs to know what she is in for. This whole thing with Ruby was nothing." She notices the vein in Jamie's temple and she sighs. "I wish I had someone to tell me what I was in for when I married Marcel. It almost tore us apart. Trust me." She grabs his hand. "You will thank me later. Especially, if you can't handle advances from just one woman. She needs to have a presence that will let every woman know that she would kill for you." Jamie laughs.

"Good luck with that," he says, trying not to spit out his drink. "Marilee is just about the kindest person that I know."

"Well, we will just have to change that."

"And I can handle advances," Jamie says.

"Okay," she says in a goofy voice that makes him laugh again. "It sure looked like it." He rolls his eyes. "It's time to put your big boy pants on now, Jamie. Every woman is going to have their claws out. They will try to blackmail you, Marilee, and your friends."

"You are over-reacting," Jamie says.

"You'll see," she says placing her glass down and standing up to leave. "Just be ready."

"Hey," he says as she starts to walk off. "Take the limo. It's already waiting."

"Thanks, and Jamie, behave while I'm gone."

"Yes, ma'am," he says. "By the way, you do look amazing tonight."

"See, those are the comments that get you into trouble, but thank you." After the girls come in for their final goodbye, he picks up his phone to call Dylan. Ruby comes in dragging her suitcase. He sighs placing his phone back down on the table.

"Hey," she says.

"Hey, you leaving?"

"Yeah, I think it's about time I bowed out." Jamie simpers. "Congratulations, I heard they all signed."

"Thanks to you," he says. "About our deal, I just–

"Don't worry about it," she says. "I knew it was a long shot. Can't blame a girl for trying, right?"

"Well, thanks, for going through with it."

"Jamie, I would have done it either way. Nobody would make a better king than you."

"Thanks, Ruby."

Smiling her smile she puts a strand of hair behind her ear. "Well, I better get going."

"Oh and can you stop trying to kill Marilee?"

She laughs. "You know he was just trying to scare her."

"Well, what about the one with the knife? That was a bit more than a scare."

"Wait, what are you talking about? What man with a knife?"

Jamie jumps up and grabs hold of her. "Tell me you had her attacked more than once."

"No, I told him to scare her, the night we had drinks, that's all. I promise."

"I believe you," he says, grabbing her tighter, "but I need your help again."

"Sure, what do you need me to do?"

"I guess someone else is trying to kill Marilee. I need you to ask around. See if anyone knows anything."

"Of course," she says, noticing his grip on her.

He quickly releases her and strokes his hair back. "Just let me know if you hear anything." She nods and walks out the door. After he regains his composure, he slumps back into his chair to have another drink, thankful she is finally gone. As he begins to pour himself another, he senses someone else in the room. The corner of his lip turns up and he turns around. His eyes widen at her, the love of his life, as she walks in. Marilee stands there in jeans and a black top with sparkles on it. Not at all as fancy as Vanessa, but somehow twice as beautiful. She blushes at the way he looks at her. "You look amazing," he says.

"Thank you," she says. "But I know it's nothing like Van—

"Hey, don't for a second think you aren't just as beautiful in jeans. I like you just as you are. Don't try to be someone else." He grabs her and pulls her close. "Are you sure you want to go out?" He whispers in her ear. "We can just stay here if you want."

"Well, I think Vanessa would kill us both for that," Marilee says pushing him away.

"Okay, okay," Jamie laughs. "Have fun." He pulls her back to him and gives her a kiss. "I love you."

She sees his eyes sparkle in the glow of the fireplace and her knees get weak. He catches her as she wobbles. "I'm glad you still have knee troubles around me," he says as the corner of his mouth turns upwards the way that she likes.

"Shut-up," she says as her cheeks redden. "I love you too."

Betty, Charlotte, and Arianna interrupt them at the doorway. "Come on Marilee," Betty says, looking at her phone. "Vanessa says if we don't get out there in two seconds—"

"Okay," Jamie says. "I'll walk y'all out." Putting his arm around Marilee, he walks her to the door. "Charlotte, can I have a word?"

"Sure," Charlotte says.

He gives Marilee a kiss on the cheek. "Be safe." After she is out of hearing reach, he turns to Charlotte.

"What's up?" she asks.

He sighs. "Someone else is trying to kill her. Ruby told me that she only had the one guy scare her and she was never intending on killing her. So the guy with the knife was someone else."

Charlotte rolls her eyes. "And you believe her?"

"Yes, I do." He gives her an annoyed look as she folds her arms over her chest. "Just keep an eye on her tonight, please. Don't tell her though. I want her to enjoy herself."

"Whatever," Charlotte says. "I'll keep an eye on her. I always do."

"I know," he says. "Thank you." She turns to walk away. "Hey, is something wrong?"

"It's just, do I need to know something?"

"What do you mean?" he asks.

"About you and Ruby...the way she looks at you—"

"Nothing is going on with me and Ruby, I promise." He bites his jaw. "She just left and I told her to leave Marilee alone, that is all."

"Okay, but you are attracted to her. I can tell—

"Charlotte, you have nothing to worry about. I love Marilee. I wouldn't mess that up." She narrows her eyes at him. "Okay, she did come on to me again, but I told her no. Please don't tell Marilee. I put a stop to it."

"Okay," Charlotte says with a sigh. "Just stay away from her."

"I will." He sighs. "Thank you. Now go have fun."

He watches as the limo drives away and walks back inside to finish the drink he poured.

~

"So where are we headed?" Marilee asks.

"You'll see," Vanessa says. "I want to talk first. So, apparently someone else is targeting you."

"What? What do you mean?" Marilee says.

"How did you know?" Charlotte asks, her eyes bulging.

"I read his lips when you were talking." Vanessa rolls her eyes as Charlotte glares at her. "I know he didn't want Marilee to know too, but it is in her best interest to know these things."

Marilee looks to Charlotte. "Why wouldn't he tell me?"

"He wanted you to have fun tonight and he was going to tell you after," Charlotte says.

"This is what you have to look forward to," Vanessa says. "There is always going to be someone who wants you dead."

"Don't scare her!" Arianna shouts.

"I'm not trying to scare her," Vanessa says in a calm tone. "I just want her to face the reality. I once had three of my closest friends try to kill me and I still showed up to have brunch with them the next day."

"I don't get your point," Marilee says.

"Not to show that I needed them," she laughs. "To say, fuck you, you missed."

"Okay," Marilee says, giving her friends an unnerving expression.

"Tonight I want to show you how to become a queen. You are extremely lucky to already have loyal friends. I was not so lucky."

"So what are we to expect first," Arianna says.

"First lesson is to look like a queen. You need to own the room and don't show any weaknesses. I believe Arianna and Charlotte already possess this quality."

Betty notices Marilee's face and she can tell she feels bad. "Marilee, that isn't a bad thing. You are a nice person. Don't let her make you feel bad about that." Betty gives Vanessa a glance.

"I'm not the bad guy here," Vanessa says with an edge to her voice. "I just don't want her dead."

"She isn't wrong, Betty," Charlotte says. "We could all use some advice."

"Just learning to have fun and still be aware of your surroundings is the best advice I can give. This world can be tough, so you have to learn to enjoy yourself or it will destroy you." The limo pulls up to the Michaelson Hotel.

"Why are we at the Michaelson?" Marilee asks.

"This is the go-to place for the Family, but we aren't going there yet. We are going there." Vanessa points to the shop next door.

"Why are we going to a dress shop?" Betty asks.

"First lesson, to look like a queen." Vanessa smirks.

"Can we just go dancing?" Marilee says with her nose scrunched up.

"No, trust me. This won't take long."

9

Staring at the fireplace, Jamie thinks about how he can change things within the Family. He hopes to get rid of the rivalry within the factions, but this life is so cut-throat he doesn't know how to go about it yet. While he is sulking, the guys come back from the signing. "There he is!" Dylan shouts, making Jamie jump. "My king." They all bow before him.

"Ha, ha," Jamie says.

"Time to celebrate your coronation, my lord," Will says.

"I'm not even your king, Will," Jamie says with a laugh.

"Just go with it, Jamie," Devin says. "It's tradition."

"Oh, so all of you have to bow before me?" He sneers at Devin.

"Shut up," Devin says. "Where's the King's thrown?" A group of men come in carrying a gold chair and Devin pushes him down in it while Will puts a crown on his head. They lift him off the ground and cheer. "To the Michaelson!"

~

As the girls walk into the Michaelson the crowd falls silent. Marilee's heart starts to pound. "And that is how you silence a room, ladies," Vanessa says. As they walk through the crowd of people watching their every move, the girls aren't as confident as Vanessa seems to be. "Follow me." She whispers something in a waiter's ear and he leads them to one of the balconies overlooking the stage.

"What are we doing here?" Charlotte asks as they sit down and overlook the Michaelson ballroom. She rewinds her memory back at the first time she was here with Dylan. She smiles at the thought as she glances at the chandelier.

"You'll see," Vanessa says as the lights dim.

"Ladies and gentlemen," a man announces over the speakers. "The Michaelson Hotel is proud to present a ceremony that hasn't been performed for nearly fifty years. A tradition that has been passed down through generations. Ladies and gentlemen we are here tonight to have the honor of witnessing the coronation of our new king, James Garrison!" Marilee whips her head around to Vanessa. "What is this?" she asks.

"It is tradition, but I have never seen it done. I don't think anyone has for a long time. I thought you guys would like to watch."

"So what about showing us—

"Shush," Vanessa says. "It's starting." The crowd starts to cheer as they bring Jamie on his thrown. The light is shining only on him as they set his thrown on stage.

"Ladies and gentlemen...masks on." The announcer says. Everyone reaches down and puts on masquerade masks over their faces. The waiter comes and hands Vanessa a bag. She pulls out some masks that match their dresses.

"Here you go ladies," she says. "It's time for the fun to begin." The waiter is kind enough to put their masks on for them.

"What are the masks for?" Marilee asks.

"Just for fun," the waiter says. "It is a special occasion so the hotel manager wanted to go all out." Marilee notices his hand and realizes that the waiter has on one of the Garrison rings.

"Thank you," she says after he ties on her mask.

A man in a hooded robe comes out on stage and the spot light come on. Dylan, Will, and Devin are in the background. “Good evening,” the man says taking off his hood to reveal himself.

“Dad?” Jamie says with a smile. Scott is also wearing a mask. He gives Jamie a wink.

“It is an honor to be able to perform not only this coronation, but two.” Dylan’s eyes widen as Scott points to him. “Can we get another thrown up here, please?” They bring another thrown up and push Dylan down in it. “And if I could add two more to this coronation I would, but unfortunately I do not have the authority. I would, however, like to acknowledge and congratulate two outstanding young men. Mr. Devin Macleary, who will be taking over Ireland and everyone knows what that makes him.” Scott bows and everyone laughs. “And Mr. Will Wellington, who will be heading up the London faction. I am extremely proud of all of you and I am sure they will do amazing things.” He claps his hands together in excitement. “So let’s get started. Will both of my boys come and kneel before me, please.” Dylan and Jamie come and kneel before their father. “James Garrison, do you, King of New Orleans, willingly pass down your crown to your brother, Dylan Garrison? Do you trust that he will protect it and guide it to a brighter future and do you trust him with all your heart, soul, and mind?” Jamie looks to Dylan and smiles.

“I do,” he says. Scott removes the crown from Jamie’s head and places it on Dylan’s.

“Dylan Garrison, do you swear that you will keep the New Orleans faction safe, prosperous, and strong with all of your heart, mind, and soul? Do you promise to be there for your Family in their time of need and protect them from all harm with all the power you now possess?”

"I do," Dylan says with his heart pounding. He has waited so long for this moment. He is finally King of New Orleans.

"Ladies and gentlemen," Scott says. "I give you...the new King of New Orleans." The crowd stands and applauds while Charlotte cries with joy and pride.

"Congrats, brother," Jamie says as they are still kneeling before their father.

"Your next," Dylan smiles and stands to go sit back down on his thrown. Before he does his father gives him a quick embrace.

"Now," Scott says. "It is time I passed my crown on. Though I only had it for a short time, it was an honor. I will still stay on as head of finances, because let's face it, nobody could do a better job than me." The crowd laughs and Jamie rolls his eyes. "Sorry, okay, James Garrison, I hereby pass on my crown as High King to you. Do you swear to protect all the factions equally, seek justice for every Family member, show mercy when it is needed, and seek vengeance when it is required? Do you swear to love this Family and commit yourself to it with all your heart, soul, and mind?"

"I do," Jamie replies.

"Then I, Scott Garrison, declare you, James Garrison, the New High King of the US faction." As the crowd applauds, Jamie stands and notices Marilee. He gives her a wink and as Scott embraces him he whispers something in his ear. "That is a great idea," Scott says. "One more thing," he announces to the crowd. "Before we get this celebration started. It wouldn't be right to introduce the kings without their queens to be. So ladies, if you would come stand beside your kings, please." Arianna, Charlotte, and Marilee giggle and stand.

"Come on, Betty," Marilee says.

"No, you guys go on," Vanessa says. "I need to talk to Betty."

Marilee gives her a hesitant look, but Betty waves her away. They get to the stage and Marilee freezes. "What is the matter?" Charlotte says.

"I can't." Marilee says feeling the pressure of everyone judging her.

"Yes, you can," Charlotte says. If you don't, it will embarrass him!"

"I just can't go out there in front of all those people, I'm sorry."

"Marilee Jackson," Arianna says with her hands on her hip. "Tonight is Jamie's night. It isn't about you!" She turns and walks on stage beside Devin.

"Sorry, but she's right, Marilee," Charlotte says with sympathy in her eyes. She holds out her hand for Marilee. "Come on, we will do this together."

"Okay, you're right," she says, grabbing Charlotte's hand. "Let's do this." They go out on stage and it isn't as bad as she thought. The lights are so blinding she can't see the crowd anyway.

"Thank you," Jamie says as she reaches him.

"You're welcome," she says as he kisses her cheek.

"You look breathtaking."

"Thanks," she says, blushing.

"Let the celebration begin!" Scott says and the lights come back on with just a faded glow so you can see where you are going.

~

"So where is your love tonight," Vanessa asks Betty.

"He is with our Dad and brothers," she says noticing Vanessa's confused expression. "No, they adopted me, it's not weird."

"I'm just messing with you," Vanessa says. "I already knew." Charley and Bryce pop their heads in.

"Surprise," Charley says.

"What are you doing here?" Betty says, jumping up to hug them.

"I called them," Vanessa says. "I didn't think they would want to miss this."

"We are glad you did," Bryce says. "I'm going to congratulate them. Charley you want to come."

"Yeah, we will be right back," Charley says, giving Betty a kiss on her cheek. After a moment Vanessa sighs.

"You know she is going to need you more than ever."

"What do you mean?" Betty says.

"This world will eat her alive if you girls aren't there for her," she says, detecting a group of women approaching Jamie and Marilee. "We got to move."

"Why?" Betty says as Vanessa jerks her up from her seat.

"Lesson is about to start."

~

"Excuse me," a woman says to Marilee. She holds her hand out to introduce herself. "Hi, Marilee, my name is Haley."

"Hello," Marilee says as Charlotte and Arianna come to stand beside her.

"I head up the Leading Ladies of Louisiana. You and Charlotte should come and have lunch with us one day. Our organization is for the most elite ladies in Louisiana. We would love for you to join us."

"Oh, thank you," Marilee says.

"We'll check our schedule and get back to you," Charlotte interrupts. "We need to get back to our friends now."

"Sure thing," Haley says. "Here is my number." She hands Marilee a card. "Hope to hear from you two soon."

When Haley leaves they are all swarmed by women trying to get a word with Jamie, Dylan, and Devin. Vanessa reaches them and gives Marilee a raised eyebrow. "You want to leave?" Jamie asks.

"No, this is your night," Marilee says. She looks at the women and then back to Jamie and decides to kiss him. The women giggle, but leave and give them some privacy. Jamie starts to laugh. "Well, that's one way to go about it." Marilee looks at Vanessa and gives her a wink.

"Sir," a security guard says, tapping on Jamie's arm. He leans in to whisper. "Ms. Ruby is here to see you in room 321." Jamie nods to the man and turns back to Marilee. "Can you get me a drink? I have to go take care of something, but it will only take a second."

"Is everything okay?"

"Yeah, go have fun."

Jamie takes the elevator to the third floor and finds room 321. He takes a breath before he knocks. He always gets nervous when they meet. The door opens and he enters quickly to scan the room until he is satisfied. "You still don't trust me?" she says with her hands folded across her chest.

"Actually," he says. "That was for your protection, not mine."

"Oh," she says as his smile makes her blush. "Thank you."

"So what did you find?" he asks.

"Right," she says snapping herself out of her daydream. "Here are some women who could be responsible." She hands him some photos and he laughs.

"What?" she asks.

"These women are downstairs right now. What makes you think they are responsible?"

"Haley Watson, Rita Hastings, and Michelle Sanchez are the top Leading Ladies of Louisiana."

"So?" Jamie says.

"They are all single and not one is a member of the Family."

"What about another faction?"

"Nope."

"How are they even here then?" Jamie asks.

"Dates, I assume," Ruby says.

"This doesn't mean—

"Remember Big Mike's wife, Ellen?"

"Yeah, she died of cancer last year," Jamie says.

"Michelle Sanchez was her nurse. Now the doctors I interviewed said that Ellen took a turn for the worst overnight. They couldn't explain it, but the autopsy report said that her cancer spread rapidly overnight."

"Well, there you go," Jamie says, handing her the pictures back.

"But guess who did the autopsy?" she says. Jamie raises an eyebrow with interest. "None other than Diego Sanchez, Michelle's son."

"Okay, that does sound a bit suspicious."

"And remember Carla Singer, Bobby Townsend's fiancé?"

"Car wreck, three years ago?" Jamie says.

"Yes, but that morning she had brunch with Haley at their spa in Baton Rouge."

"But it doesn't make sense," Jamie says. "They didn't make a move on anyone in the Family. Why kill them?"

"Not sure, but I'll keep digging," Ruby says.

"Thank you," Jamie says. "Good work."

"If you need anything else, just let me know. I'll bring these by the lodge later tomorrow. You don't want anyone to see you with them."

"No, I don't want anyone to see you there. I'll swing by your apartment tomorrow and pick them up."

"Oh, okay," she says, flabbergasted that Jamie would even consider coming to her apartment.

"I'll see you then," Jamie says as he kisses her cheek. He don't know why he did it and he curses himself inside as soon as he walks out the door.

"Hey," he says, placing his arm around Marilee.

"Hey," she says and hands him his drink. "Is everything okay?"

"Yeah, just a security issue. Some people are here that shouldn't be."

"Who?"

"Oh, just your new friends from the Leading Ladies of Louisiana."

"What harm can they do?" She laughs.

"You'd be surprised," Jamie says, raising a finger to get the guards attention.

"Yes, sir," he says bending down to hear Jamie.

"Those women," Jamie points to Haley and her friends. "They don't belong here. Escort them out, please."

"Yes, sir, right away."

"Jamie, was that necessary?" Marilee says, feeling sorry for the ladies.

"Yes, this is a member only event."

"How did they get in then?"

"I'll find out later, let's just have a good time right now."

Marilee shrugs her shoulders. "Okay, first I need to go to the little girl's room."

He snaps his fingers and a man comes up to them within seconds. "My bride-to-be needs to use the little girl's room." Jamie snickers at the way he said it. "Can you escort her, please?" The man gives him a nod and Marilee gives him a sigh. "Just go with it."

Marilee leaves and the man follows. A waiter comes over and hands Jamie a drink. "This is for Lady Marilee."

"From who?" Jamie raises his eyebrow.

"I'm not sure," the waiter says, "but I can find out, sir."

Jamie nods as he walks away. Marilee comes back and sees the drink. "Oh, thanks," she says, grabbing the drink from him. She starts to drink, but Jamie stops her.

"I would wait on that," he says, grabbing it out of her hands. The waiter comes back and whispers in his ear. Jamie sighs. "Thanks," he says. "You can take this back and pour it out, but bring us a couple more made fresh. Make sure you watch them make it."

"There has to be a better way to tell if someone is poisoning you than wasting a perfectly good drink," Marilee says. "Maybe you can get some kind of test strip before you take a sip or something."

"That is actually a brilliant idea," Jamie says, looking at the waiter and they both smile.

"Yes, sir," the waiter says, leaving quickly. As Jamie looks through the window, he sees Haley staring at them. She gives him a wink and gets into her car.

"What are you looking at?" Marilee says, stretching her neck to see.

"Nothing, don't worry about," Jamie says as their drinks arrive. "Let's enjoy this evening."

10

Marilee wakes up to breakfast in bed, a newspaper, and Jamie staring at her. “Morning beautiful,” he says.

“Good morning,” she replies, wiping her eyes. “What is all of this?”

“Read the paper,” he says with a grin. She looks down and starts to read and after a moment her eyes widen. Her head whips back up toward Jamie.

“We have our first review!”

“Keep reading.” She tilts her head back down.

“Oh my God!” she shouts almost knocking over her breakfast. “They love it!”

“I told you they would,” he says kissing her cheek. “Now eat your breakfast. I’m going to go and get Celia’s breakfast ready.”

“You’re the best,” she says as she takes a bite of her jelly toast. He gives her a wink and leaves to go get his other girl.

~

As Marilee brings her breakfast tray back to the kitchen, she sees Jamie trying to feed Celia. She laughs. “You know she is pretty good at doing that on her own.”

“I know,” he says. “I just want to.” He takes the spoon and pretends it’s an airplane. The noises make Celia laugh. “I love to hear her laugh. What are you doing today?”

“I have interviews today for new managers,” she says.

“What brought this on?” he asks.

"Well, I don't think it is too safe for me to be prancing about all the time. It's too predictable. If they want to attack me, I guess I need to make them work for it."

"I'm glad you are finally thinking about your safety, but I thought you loved the work?"

"I do and I'm still going to work in the kitchen. As long as I get to cook a bit, I'm good. I just wish I knew the person I hire could be trusted."

"If you want I can look into it and send you some good candidates."

"That would be great," Marilee says. "Just please make sure they have never had a crush on you before."

Jamie snickers. "I'll make a note of that."

"Are you good with Celia for a while? Sonya said she would be back around nine."

"Of course, we are good, aren't we my angel?" Jamie says in a squeaky voice making Celia giggle.

"Okay," Marilee says with a smile. She loves it when he plays with Celia. "Then I will see you both later." She kisses them both bye and heads out the door. Jamie finishes feeding Celia and then gets her dressed. He plays with her until well past nine o'clock. His phone rings and he realizes it is ten o'clock.

"Hello," he answers, assuming it is Sonya.

"Jamie, this is Kyle, Mr. O'Neal's secretary."

"Who?" Jamie says, not recognizing the name.

"Sonya's dad's assistant."

"Oh, how can I help you?"

"Sonya has been in a car accident. It happened about an hour ago."

"Oh no," Jamie says, standing up from playing with Celia. "Is she alright?"

"They don't know the severity of it yet, but it doesn't sound good."

"What hospital is she in?"

"New Orleans East, Mr. O'Neal would have called—

"No, of course. Tell him anything he needs, just ask."

"Yes, sir," Kyle says.

He hangs up and picks Celia up. "Come on, sweetie. Let's see if Aunt Betty wants to play with you for a bit. Betty rushes in a few minutes later and Jamie rushes out the door thanking her.

He runs into the office where Marilee is giving an interview. "Sonya was in a car accident. I'm going to the hospital."

"Oh, God!" she says, jumping up. "Sorry, we will have to reschedule. I'll give you a call soon. Thanks." They both run out the door and head to hospital, hoping Sonya is okay.

~

Running in the ER they see Mr. and Mrs. O'Neal talking to the doctor. They start to cry and Jamie reaches Mrs. O'Neal just in time before she falls to the floor with grief. Marilee runs to Mr. O'Neal and comforts him as he sobs on her shoulder. Her and Jamie exchange heart-broken expressions. They both know that Sonya didn't make it. She was the same age as Marilee.

~

A few hours they are back in their apartment. "What happened?" Betty asks. "She didn't make it," Jamie says, still a bit in shock that she is gone.

"Oh, no," Betty says, with her hand covering her mouth.

"I can't believe it," Marilee finally says after being speechless on the way back home. "I should have never let her go by herself."

"Don't go blaming yourself," Jamie says, bringing her in for a hug. "It was an accident."

"I know, but I can't help to think, if I hadn't gave her that coupon to that Spa in Baton Rouge she would have been here with Celia."

"Spa?" Jamie says. "In Baton Rouge?"

"Yeah, that Haley woman gave it to me last night at the coronation."

"Was it in your name?" Jamie says, grinding his teeth in anger.

"Yes, why?"

"No reason," Jamie says, trying not to show his anger. He doesn't want to let her know that she was more than likely the real target. She would never forgive herself.

"Look, do me a favor and stay here for the rest of the day. Betty, can you keep her company while I'm gone."

"Of course," Betty says.

"Thanks, I'll bring back some Chinese food, okay."

"Okay," Marilee says. "Be careful."

~

As Jamie walks into the Chinese restaurant, they give him a nod so he continues around the counter and into the back. He climbs a set of stairs and knocks on the door. A Chinese man, who is known for finding people, answers the door. "Mr. Wang," Jamie says with a bow. "May I have a moment of your time?" The old man walks away leaving Jamie in the doorway. "Mr. Wang, I need your help."

"What could I possibly do for you?" he laughs. "A man with your power and money does not need me. Now leave—

"Please, Mr. Wang," Jamie steps inside without being invited. He is willing to take the risk of disrespecting him. "Someone is trying to kill my fiancé and it is someone outside the Family and outside of any other crime organizations."

Mr. Wang sighs. "What would you need from me?"

"Information on three women who run a spa in Baton Rouge."

"Intel?" Mr. Wang raises his eyebrow. "I believe you and your men are well equipped for this sort of thing. I don't have time for this—

"Please, Mr. Wang," Jamie says. "These women know all of my men." Jamie notices the old man's face and realizes he is not getting through to him. "Look, I know you and my grandfather didn't care for one another and if it helps I didn't care for the bastard either, but I need to be one hundred percent sure these women are guilty before I attack them."

"Your grandfather would have only needed twenty percent."

"I am not my grandfather, sir," Jamie says.

"I see that now," the old man stands and walks to Jamie. "Bring me what you have and I will get what you need."

"Thank you, sir," Jamie says with a smile and a bow. I will be back with what I have in about thirty minutes. He leaves the apartment and puts in his food order.

"It will be about thirty minutes or so, Mr. Garrison," the cashier says. "It is a pretty big order."

"That is just fine," Jamie says. "I'll pick it up shortly."

He walks a few blocks down the street to some apartments. He takes the penthouse elevator and pushes the buzzer. "It's Jamie," he says with a knot in his stomach. The elevator door opens and he walks in to the apartment. It's quiet and smells of vanilla. "Hello," he shouts. "Ruby?"

"Just a minute," she says. "I'm just getting out of the shower." He rolls his eyes with frustration.

"Damnit," he whispers.

"What?" she asks.

"Nothing, just tell me where the information is and I'll be on my way."

"Don't be silly," she says. "I'm almost done. Grab a drink at the bar."

"Okay," he says, but curses himself. He pours a drink so that maybe the burn will help him focus on the task at hand.

"Make me one too," she says.

"Sure, what do you want?"

"Whatever you are having."

He pours them both whiskey and waits while searching for the information. The sooner he gets it, the sooner he can leave. As he searches a nearby desk, Ruby walks in the room.

"It's not in there," she says, holding up an envelope. Jamie spits out a little whiskey when he sees her turn the corner with a skimpy night gown on.

"What the hell, Ruby?" he says, wiping the whiskey from his chin.

"What?" she says with a giggle. "This is what I always wear at home."

"Whatever," he says placing his glass down on the table. "Give me the envelope and I'll go."

"I'll go put something else on," she says, knowing she has upset him.

"No," he stops her. "It's fine. We have a bigger problem anyway."

"What?" she says as she grabs her robe off the couch and covers herself.

"Our nanny was killed today in a car wreck."

"Oh my God, Jamie, I am so sorry," she says, placing her hand over her face in shame for coming on to him again."

"On her way back from a spa in Baton Rouge." Ruby's eyes widen as she sees the connection. "Yeah, she was using a gift card in Marilee's name."

"They meant to kill Marilee," she says. "I bet she is freaking out."

"No, I didn't tell her," Jamie says. "She would never forgive herself. I got someone looking into those women you told me about. I just need the information you got last night."

"Okay," she says coming toward him. She can't help trying again. Even with everything that has happened, she can't help the way she feels around him. "Here it is." She puts the envelope in his hand and runs her hands up his chest. Her touch sends chills up his spine. He bites his lip and grabs her hand to push it away, but before he can she kisses him. He pushes her away a little too hard and she falls down on the couch. "Ruby, I'm sorry."

"Just go," she says. She starts to cry and Jamie sighs with guilt.

"I didn't mean to push you so hard." He sits down beside her on the couch and grabs her hand. "I just can't. I love Marilee and I don't want to risk losing her for—"

"Me?" Her head turns away from him with the thought of her being nothing to him.

"It's not that I don't feel something for you, Ruby."

"Then what, Jamie," she says as she looks at him. "Why did you even come here?"

"For this," he says, holding up the envelope.

"I could have mailed those or gave them to someone. You didn't have to come here. So, why?"

"I don't have time for this, Ruby." He sighs and turns. "We can't see each other anymore. Stay away from me."

"Don't be mad at me because you want me, James Garrison!" she shouts. He stops and turns to her again, grabbing her by the throat and pushing her against the wall. She smiles at him, realizing that she might get what she wants after all.

"Damn you, Ruby!" he says and kisses her. She grabs his hair and kisses him harder. He finally stops himself and pushes her away again. "Ahhh!" He paces back and forth with his thoughts.

"What is stopping you?" she says.

"Just shut-up!" he says. "This is all because of you. I would never do this if you weren't throwing yourself at me! Leave me alone! I don't want to see you again, do you hear me?" She doesn't answer him. "Do you understand? If you try this again, I will kill you." She flinches at his threat.

"Understood," she says with a shaky voice. He turns and walks out the door, hitting himself for kissing her again.

"Stupid," he says as the monster inside him begs him to go back inside. He hurries back to Mr. Wang before he changes his mind.

When he returns home, Marilee is interviewing again and Betty is watching Celia. "How was she?" he asks.

"Good, as always," Betty says. "Marilee got a little anxious, though."

"Yeah, I noticed. Do y'all want some Chinese food? There is plenty to go around."

"Of course," Charley says. "Thanks."

"We actually needed to speak with you alone anyway," Betty says.

"Oh? About what?" he asks as he makes him a plate of noodles.

"We have been thinking a lot about it and we want to move here to help out," Betty says.

Jamie sighs as he sits down at the kitchen island. "Betty, I appreciate that, a lot, but what about school?" He takes a big bite of noodles and waits for her answer.

"I can go here," she says. "And Charley...well, he already dropped out."

"What?" Jamie says, choking on his food. "Why?"

"College didn't suite me. Don't tell Dad."

"Look, y'all need us here," Betty says. "You just lost your nanny, the lodge is getting pretty busy, and you just became king. I think our time will be used better helping out our family."

"But—

"No, but," Betty says. "I wasn't asking for permission. I just wanted to run it by you to see if we could stay here."

"Of course you can, but—

"That's all," Betty says. "I'll tell Marilee later."

"Okay," Jamie says with a laugh. "I guess that's settled."

"Thank you guys and it will be nice to have you two here. We've missed y'all."

"Good," Betty says as they all sit and eat. "Besides, wouldn't you rather us watch Celia than some stranger you can't trust."

"Good point. I'd lead with that when you tell Marilee and Bryce that you dropped out of school."

~

Marilee finally comes in around six o'clock. Jamie can tell she is tired. "Hey, he says. "You okay?"

"Yeah, just tired. She sits beside him and Celia on the couch and Celia grabs at her face. "Hey, sweetie," she says, kissing her on the cheek. "Sorry it took me so long."

"It's okay," Jamie says. "I figured you needed the distraction. Any luck?"

"No," she says. "I just don't think anyone can do this job. Nobody had the experience I want."

"Well, let me call around."

"Sure, do you mind if I take a bath?"

"Go ahead," Jamie says kissing her, "we'll be right here."

"Thanks." As she goes to take a bath, there is a knock at the door.

"I got it," Jamie says. "You go ahead." He puts Celia in her playpen and opens the door to see everyone out in the hallway. He laughs. "Hi, what's up?" he says as he gestures for them to come in.

"Just wanted to say we were sorry about Sonya," Dylan says. "And we brought food."

"Thanks," Jamie says, but we still have some food left over from earlier."

"Cool," Charley says. "That was some good Chinese food." Jamie shakes his head.

"Okay, then, just set everything up in the kitchen. I'll go and let Marilee know y'all are here. Would y'all mind keeping an eye on Celia for a few minutes?"

"No problem," Betty says.

As he walks in and sees Marilee soaking in the tub, he immediately feels the guilt build up. He can't understand why he would do something so horrible to her. He tries to clear his mind. "Hey," he says, making her jump. "Sorry." He laughs. "The guys are here and they brought some food, though we still had plenty left. We should have enough for the next day or two."

"Oh, okay, I'll get out then."

"Or..." he says with a playful grin. She laughs as he takes off his clothes and jumps in the tub with her.

~

"It's about time," Charlotte says as Jamie and Marilee finally make an appearance. "The food is cold now."

"Sorry, guys," Marilee says. "Thanks for coming."

"No problem," Arianna says. "We haven't done this in a while. We brought movies, food, and drinks."

"Awesome," Jamie says.

"We also invited Vanessa," Will says. "I hope that is okay."

"Of course," Marilee says as the door buzzer goes off. "Hey, Vanessa." Marilee gestures for her to come in. Vanessa takes a seat by Will and they all begin to talk and laugh. Jamie is happy but something is nagging at him. His phone rings and he goes to answer it in his office. "Mr. Wang?" Jamie says, shutting the door behind him. "Did you get any information?"

"Yes," Mr. Wang says. "Apparently, they have been keeping tabs on your Family for a while."

"How long is a while?"

"About ten years. About a year after Carla's husband was killed by Frank."

"Oh," Jamie says. "So it's about revenge, again."

"Isn't it always about revenge?" Mr. Wang chuckles.

"When it comes to Frank, yes, but Frank is dead."

"They aren't so sure. Someone spotted him seven months ago, right here in town."

Jamie's eyes widen. "Your silence tells me I am right."

"No," Jamie says. "Frank is dead, trust me."

"I'm not the one who needs convincing," Mr. Wang says.

"Thank you for all your help, Mr. Wang," Jamie says. "How much?"

"I'll be in touch with a favor."

Jamie hangs up the phone and sighs, stroking his hair back in annoyance at Frank's passed behavior catching up with him. Now it is affecting him and the ones that he loves. Marilee walks in and notices his face. "What is it?" she asks, sitting in his lap.

He smiles slightly. "Nothing."

"Jamie, talk to me," she says. He laughs at her comment.

"You want me to talk to you?" She looks at him confused.

"What?" she says.

"Something has been on your mind lately and you won't talk to me either," he says.

"Jamie, it's nothing—

"Do you still want to marry me?" he interrupts her. Throwing her for a loop. She doesn't know what to say in return. She stares into his eyes for a moment. His blue eyes are so intense. She can't deal with this question right now so she sighs and jumps off his lap. She knows he just changed the subject so that he didn't have to talk about what was on his mind. She starts to walk away. "And there you go, walking away again." Jamie snaps.

"My not setting a date for our wedding is not what this is about, Jamie. You're frustrated because something isn't going your way and you're taking it out on me." He takes a breath and lets it go.

"You're right," he says, grabbing her hand. "Come on." He smiles.

"Where are we going?"

"To tell everyone what is going on."

They walk back into the living room and Jamie walks in front of the television. "Hey, Charley says. "Dude that was a good part."

"Sorry," Jamie says, taking the remote and pausing the movie. "But I need to talk to you guys about something. They all sit up from their comfortable positions to listen. "Last night, I found out that the first guy that attacked Marilee wasn't hired by Ruby."

"How do you know?" asks Marilee.

"Because she told me." Jamie scans the room and notices Vanessa giving him a look of betrayal. She rolls her eyes at the fact he told her that he would stay away from her.

"And you believe her?" Marilee says with surprise.

"Yes," Jamie says with certainty.

"What about the second one?"

"She was just trying to scare you."

"Oh, okay," Marilee says with irritation.

"Anyway," Jamie says ignoring her comment. "I had her look into some leads. She brought back some information on the leading ladies of Louisiana."

"Last night?" Marilee says, narrowing her eyes. "That is who you went to meet at the ceremony."

"Yes, and they own the spa that Sonja went to. The card was in Marilee's name."

Marilee tilts her head toward the floor as she figures it out. She sits on the edge of the couch. Betty puts her arm around her for comfort. "Well, I went to Mr. Wang for—

"What?" Dylan asks. "Are you serious?"

"I was going to tell you tomorrow, but Mr. Wang just called and confirmed that they are who we are looking for."

"Okay," Dylan says. "Then let's take care of it."

Jamie nods and looks to Marilee. "Are you okay?"

"No, Jamie, I'm not," she says and walks out of the room.

He sighs and bites his jaw. "Maybe I shouldn't have told her."

"No," Vanessa says, standing up and putting her hand on his shoulder. "You did the right thing." She smacks him in the back of the head for talking to Ruby again and goes to talk with Marilee.

"Ouch." Jamie says.

"You deserved it," Arianna says. He rolls his eyes and sits down to eat on some leftover food.

~

"Hey," Vanessa says, knocking slightly on the door as she comes into the office. "Can I come in?"

"Yeah," Marilee says, wiping her eyes.

"May I?" Vanessa asks, noticing the liquor cabinet.

"Sure," Marilee says. "Have at it?"

Vanessa pours two glasses of Bourbon and brings one to Marilee.

"No thanks," she says. "I don't drink that stuff."

"Maybe you should start." She holds the glass closer to Marilee's lips. "Trust me, it helps." Taking it, the scent hits Marilee's nose and it crinkles. Vanessa gives her a smiles as she takes a sip. "This life is hell," she says.

"I gathered that," Marilee says with a cough from the strength of the Bourbon.

"But yet, here you are."

"So are you," Marilee says.

"Yeah, well, barely. It took a long time to get back to where I was before...Marcel."

"Is that why you moved back?"

"Yes," Vanessa says. "I couldn't stay there after that."

"I can't imagine, I'm sorry."

"You can't dwell on the bad things in this world, Marilee, if you do it will be the death of you. You only need to ask yourself one question before committing yourself to this life forever."

"And what is that?"

"Is he worth it?"

Marilee cracks a smile thinking of him. "Yes," she says. "He is worth a million lifetimes in this world."

"Well, there you go."

"I just don't know if I can measure up?"

"To what?"

Marilee gives her a stare and a sigh. "To you."

"To me?" Vanessa gives her a sincere and confused expression. "Why on earth would you feel like you need to measure up to me?"

"You were the freaking Queen of France!"

"Marilee," Vanessa says, turning to her and grabbing her hand. "We set our own expectations and our own limits. Don't ever let anyone set them for you. Just remember that you know he is worth it when you have doubts. That and the Bourbon will get you through anything."

"Thanks, Vanessa." They sip on their drinks for a moment, but Vanessa has another question that has been haunting her mind.

"Would you die for him?" she asks.

"Yes," Marilee answers.

"I thought so. I just needed to ask. But more importantly, would you kill for him?"

Marilee looks down at her drink. "Yes, I believe I would."

"Good," Vanessa says. She chugs her drink and stands up to leave the room. "Because you just might have to."

11

Marilee ducks as Charlotte's foot passes inches above her head. "You're getting better," Charlotte says.

"Thanks," Marilee says as she leg sweeps Charlotte.

"Very well done," Jamie says walking down the stairs. "Looks like this old basement came in handy after all." He smiles and Charlotte returns the leg sweep while Marilee is distracted. His smile fades for a split moment as he looks to the corner where he was kissing Ruby. He shakes the thought. If Marilee ever found out she would never forgive him, not that he would blame her. It has been two weeks since he has spoken to Ruby, but he still feels the guilt. He laughs as Marilee falls on her back.

"Ouch," she says. "You distracted me."

"Sorry," he says as he grabs her hand to help her to her feet. He pulls her in to his chest and gives her a kiss.

"Any word on the three musketeers?" Charlotte asks.

"Nope, they've left town for good, I guess," he says. "Nobody can find them. They sold the spa. It's like they walked off the earth. Someone had to tip them off."

"You'll figure it out," Charlotte says. "Now go on and let us get back to training."

"Okay," he says. "I'll see y'all at dinner." He gives the corner another glance and continues up the stairs to make himself a drink.

Dylan walks in the manager's office as Jamie is pouring his drink. "So early," he says, shutting the door behind him. "What's wrong?"

"Nothing," Jamie says slumping down on the couch.

"Liar," Dylan says. "I know you way too well. What is it?"

Jamie holds the cold drink up to his temple. "I did something really stupid."

"What's new?" Dylan laughs. Jamie bites his jaw wondering if he should tell him. He sits up and places his drink on the table. "Ah...I really screwed up, man."

"What is it?" Dylan asks getting a bit worried now. He sits down next to Jamie. "What did you do?"

"You remember that little plan we had with Ruby?"

"Yeah," Dylan says, having an idea of where this is leading. "Dude, you said she backed off after they signed."

"She did, but not before..." Jamie can't even finish the sentence.

"No, Jamie, you didn't?" Dylan places his hand on his forehead in disbelief. "I knew I was behind this plan, but that was just to keep you on as King. You were safe—

"I didn't do that!" he says. "We just got real close. She tried to—

"When did this happen?" Dylan interrupts, trying to give Jamie the benefit of the doubt.

"Before the signing," Jamie says.

"Okay, then," Dylan takes a breath. "And that was that? That isn't so bad—

"Well, that would have been that, but I sort of went to her apartment to get the papers on the Ladies of Louisiana."

"What?" Dylan shouts, but quickly lowers his voice. "Why would you even put yourself in that situation, you dumbass."

"Because I wanted her!" Jamie says, putting his hands over his face again in shame.

"Well, guess what," Dylan says. "That is called being human. There are about a dozen women I wouldn't mind having a go with, but do you think I am going to put myself alone with any of them and risk what Charlotte and I have?"

"I know." Jamie sighs. "Nothing happened, not that we didn't go about as far as we could, but I ran out of there. I told her we couldn't see each other anymore and I ran out."

"Ouch, was she angry?" Dylan says, now sympathizing.

"I don't know," Jamie says with sarcasm. "I haven't talked to her since."

"Okay," Dylan says with a breath. "You made a mistake."

"A huge, huge mistake."

"Yes, but it will eventually go away so just deal the best you can for now."

"You don't think I should tell her?" Jamie asks with a furrowed brow.

Dylan shakes his head from side to side. "That is about the stupidest thing you've ever said to me." He can tell that Jamie is on the verge of losing it. "Jamie, listen to me." He grabs Jamie's shoulder. "If you tell her, it will destroy her. That will be the end for you two for sure. If you have ever wanted to protect her from something...this is it. She can never find out. Do you understand?"

"I got it!" Jamie says, irritated. He picks up his drink and chugs it down.

"Come on. You just need to let off some steam." Dylan pats his back and stands up. "Let's go to the gym. It's been a while since you've been in the ring."

~

Jamie gears up to fight at their gym. They bought it last year. After everything settled down, Jamie needed some way to let out his frustrations and they got a very good price on the building. Dylan finishes lacing up Jamie's boxing gloves and moves to the center of the ring. "Okay," Dylan says as he was officiating a fight. "Any takers?" Nobody replies. The crowd looks away and continues with their workouts. "Oh, come on," Dylan says. "Boss-man needs to let off some steam. So who is going to step up?"

"Maybe we shouldn't have established the place for only Family members," Jamie says. After a moment of silence a voice calls from the back of the room.

"I will."

Jamie and Dylan exchange looks. "Oh, shit," Jamie says as Ruby's husband climbs up in the ring.

"So, Mr. Garrison," Tyler says as his friend tapes his hands. "I was wondering if I could have a minute before you kick my ass."

Jamie smirks at his comment. "Sure."

"I was wanting you to look into something for me."

"What is that?" Jamie asks.

"My wife," Tyler says. Jamie glares at him knowing he is trying to bait him. "She's been sleeping with someone else."

"And," Jamie says with annoyance.

"I was hoping that you could find out who."

"I don't think so," Jamie says.

Tyler clears his throat. "Well, I did my own little investigation, but I'm probably way off." Jamie rolls his eyes at Tyler's immaturity.

"Dylan," Jamie shouts. "Get these gloves off. I think I'll let off some steam another day." Jamie turns to Dylan hoping Tyler will just let this go.

"I know it was you," Tyler says. Jamie closes his eyes and hopes he doesn't keep this rant up.

"Breathe," Dylan says. "Just breathe." He notices the vein on Jamie's neck start to pop out.

"So now that you're King, am I supposed to just let you sleep with my wife?"

"Oh, damn," Dylan says as soon as he finishes unlacing Jamie's gloves.

"Dylan?" Jamie says.

"Yeah," Dylan says with a sigh.

"Did he just disrespect the King?"

"I believe he did," Dylan says shaking his head at Tyler as the crowd gathers around.

"Well, the least you could do is be honest with me," Tyler says. Jamie sneers, but his eyes are still blazing with rage. "I mean, after I beat the crap out of her she still couldn't just be honest with me." Jamie's smirk vanishes in a split second. "I told her that the neighbor saw you leaving and she still—

"So you beat her!" Jamie has had enough. He comes at Tyler and punches him on the jaw. As Tyler goes down, he climbs on top of him, beating him. Dylan rushes to reason with Jamie, but realizes that he isn't going to listen. Dylan looks around at the crowd, but nobody else dares to stop him. He keeps beating him until he is nearly unconscious. Jamie's heart is racing and he's out of breath. After one last punch, he wipes off a bit of blood that had spattered on his face with his forearm. "Call Vanessa," he says. Dylan immediately calls Vanessa as Jamie gets in a couple of kicks to Tyler's stomach. He looks to the man in Tyler's corner. "Take him to the back and wait for the doctor."

"Yes, sir," the man says without question. A couple of men come to help.

"Wait," Jamie says, still in a rage. "Bring him to me." They do as they are told. "Stand him up." Jamie looks into Tyler's bloody face and steadies himself, controlling his urge to kill him. He smacks him in the face slightly to get his attention. "Can you hear me?" Tyler is dazed, but he nods a bit. "Good, now if you touch her again," Jamie says, laughing at his own rule about not killing Family members. "You'll be begging for me to kill you. And if you want honesty, I didn't sleep with her. She was working for me, you stupid son-of-a-bitch." Jamie motions to the men. "Get him out of my sight."

"Okay, gym is closed guys," Dylan says. "Sorry. Come back in a couple of hours." The gym starts to clear out and Jamie hops out of the ring and sits on the steps. Dylan comes to sit down beside him. "Hey," he says, stopping a guy headed out the door. "You mind throwing me a water?"

The man throws him a water and says, "Nice fight, King." Jamie gives the man a nod and takes a sip of the water.

"Can I ask you something?" Dylan says, a little hesitant.

"Sure."

"Did you beat him because of your Mom or because you have feelings for Ruby?" Jamie takes another swig of his water, thinking of how he should answer this question.

"Mostly because of my mother, but it is more than that." Jamie says, noticing Dylan rubbing his forehead with frustration. "I don't have romantic feelings for Ruby. It's more protective. I feel the need to protect her."

"But you said yourself that you wanted her," Dylan says.

"I did at the time, but I don't love her in that way. I was just in the moment, you know."

"Okay," Dylan says. "I understand, man. You got close to her."

"But I think I would be pissed no matter who it was. I'm not a total monster...not yet anyway."

"I never thought you were, Jamie, none of us have."

"Like I said, not yet," Jamie says as he looks down at his bloody hands.

Vanessa walks in and gasps. "Oh my God! What happened?" She runs to Jamie to assess his hands. He gives her a smile.

"The man in the back needs you more than I do."

"Then you meet me back there too. I'll check you out next."

"I'm fin— she stops him with a glare. "Okay," he says. "I'll be back in a few."

Dylan shoves him and laughs when she leaves. "You got in trouble."

"Shut up."

"Are you really okay?" Dylan asks.

"Yeah, I'm fine."

"You did good," Dylan says. Jamie gives a slight laugh.

"I almost beat the guy to death, Dylan."

"Yes, but he disrespected you, in front of other Family members no less. If you would've let that slide, I think you would have lost their respect. They at least know not to disrespect you."

"Thanks, Dylan," he says slowly standing up. "I better go get cleaned up or I'm next for an ass kicking."

Jamie washes off the blood and looks in the mirror. Who am I becoming? He knows that Dylan was right. The other men would have seen it as a weakness if he let that slide. "It had to be done," he says, splashing his face with water. Wondering about Ruby, he hurries to meet Vanessa. She is cleaning up bloody bandages when he walks in. "Hey," he says.

"Hey," she replies. "Sit." He does as he is ordered. "So do you want to tell me why you kicked the crap out of Ruby's husband?"

"Not particularly." She grabs his hand and squeezes. "Ouch." She throws his hand back down. "It's not what you think," he says.

"Whatever, Jamie," she says. "It's none of my business."

"He beat her." Jamie sighs in defeat. "He beat her because he thought we were sleeping together." He notices her silence. "Which we are not by the way." Her eyes soften a bit, but she doesn't know what to say. She already knew about the beating because she was called to the apartment the night it happened. Not wanting to tell Jamie, she grabs the other hand to check it out. "Okay, you are good to go." He knows something is wrong with her, but he can't read her very well.

"Vanessa, I promise, nothing is going on with Ruby."

"I believe you, Jamie," she says.

"Thank you."

"No problem. I got to clean up a bit more, but you go on. I'll lock up."

"No need," Jamie says. "The guys will be back in a few. Are you sure you're good?"

"Yes," she assures him. "I will be out of here in a minute."

"Okay, come by tonight for dinner."

"Of course." As he walks out the memories of their childhood come flooding back to her mind. She remembers how hard his mother's death was on him. She spent the days after with him, until Ron took him away. She heard the shots from her house that night. They didn't live far apart from each other. She recalls jumping out of her bed and running through the woods barefoot to make sure Jamie was okay. Flashes pierce her brain of the memory of seeing Jamie leaning up against Scott's car staring blankly at his house ablaze and she can feel the wetness on her cheeks. Dylan's voice brings her back to reality.

"Hey," he says, noticing the streaks of mascara. "Are you okay?"

"Yeah, no, I'm fine," she says. "It's stupid. Jamie told me why he..." She rolls her eyes because more tears start coming out. "This is so stupid, it was so long ago." Dylan hugs her realizing what she is remembering.

"Hey, that day was hard on all of us," he says, remembering when he and his Dad got there. The vision of Jamie clinging to Celia is too much so he shakes it off. "Come on," he says. "Let's go get some coffee." He places his arm around her and walks her out.

"Dylan," she says with a shaky voice.

"Yeah," he says as he tries to wipe the streaks off her cheeks.

"I knew about Ruby."

"What?"

"I knew. I was the doctor that went to the apartment the night he beat her."

"Vanessa, why didn't you say something?"

"I don't know," she says, turning from him, annoyed with her decision. "At first, I thought she got what she deserved. After everything she put

Jamie and Marilee through, I thought, for just a moment that it was Karma. Then, after I thought about it and thinking back to that day I just got sad. After that, I got scared because I didn't tell him to begin with. He is going to be so mad at me."

"Yes, he will," Dylan says. "But he will get over it. He can't stay mad at you and you know it. Now let's go get that coffee. You let me worry about our brother."

12

Jamie makes his way across town. He knows he shouldn't go, but he has to make sure she is okay. He parks the car behind the store and enters through the back door. It is pretty empty and quiet except for the faint sound of music from the speakers above him. She turns the corner scaring them both. "God!" she says. "What the hell, Jamie." She smacks him on the arm, but quickly remembers their last meeting. "What do you want?" He can tell she is still mad at him.

"I heard about," he says lifting her chin displaying Tyler's handy work. "Are you okay?"

"I'm fine," she says, tilting her head away from his hand.

"Well, he's not," Jamie says.

"What did you do?" Her eyes widen.

"Let's just say that he may be on bed rest for a couple of days." Ruby turns to put some patterns on a shelf and smiles, but she doesn't want Jamie to see her.

"Why did you do that?" she asks.

"He got what was coming to him."

"Is that all?"

He sighs in aggravation. "I'm sorry about how we left things."

"Are you?" She turns to walk away, but he pulls her back.

"Yes, I am!" he shouts, making her flinch. He feels guilty the moment he yells because with what she has been through she really doesn't need to be yelled at. "I'm sorry." He reaches for her cheek and she flinches again. He becomes irritated at Tyler again and grinds his teeth to keep from scaring her with his anger. "I just need to know that you're okay," he says.

"I told you that I'm fine," she says, walking to the next room. Jamie follows.

"You don't have to pretend, Ruby."

"What do you want, Jamie?" she says with a giggle. "Do you want me to cry on your shoulder? We both know how that will end."

"Why didn't you call me?" he asks. She stops and turns, narrowing her eyes at him. "I am the king and I need to know when my men are being stupid." She rolls her eyes and walks off again. "Why do you keep walking away from me?" They are now face to face and he regrets it the moment he pulls her close.

"Because," she says. "If I stay mad at you, maybe, just maybe, I won't want you so bad!"

"I'm sorry," he says. "I should have never made you blackmail those men. I think sometimes I'm becoming my grandfather."

"Oh, please," she says as she backs away from him. "You are still telling yourself that every bad thing you do is because you are turning into your grandfather."

"What are you talking about?" he says, stroking his hair.

"You didn't do this because you are becoming like your grandfather, Jamie. You did it because you are a man. Man up and take credit for your actions. You did it because you saw something you wanted and you would do anything you had to get it. You still want it too." She eases closer to him. "That is why you should just leave." He stares at her clinching his jaw, speechless, fighting the demons inside him. "But when you are ready, I won't stop you." He wants to get angry at her comment, but he finds it a bit amusing.

"Is that so?" he says with a grin. He looks away to gather the strength to walk away. As he walks out the door he turns back to her, pushing the door handle down so hard he hears the wood crack. "If he hurts you again...call me."

"Yes, my king," she says with her arms folded over her chest.

"I'll get someone to fix that," he says, gesturing to the handle.

~

Jamie drives around town thinking about his mother. Would she be proud of him? He simpers at the thought. He knows she wouldn't be. He ends up at his old house or the ashes of his old house. Sitting in the car for a moment, he stares at the ashes. He finally decides to get out and walk around. His memories go on overload like someone pressing the rewind button. He walks through the pile that used to be the kitchen and relives some of his fonder memories of him and his mother cooking and laughing. Deciding to go to another place of fond memories, he starts toward the woods. He continues to the stream that runs between Vanessa's old house and his. He remembers it being a whole lot bigger than this. Still, he can picture him, Vanessa, and Dylan playing and going on adventures. They would build a raft, pretending to be Huckleberry Finn. The three would play all day out in these woods. He sits down beside the creek, going through his memories to pick out his favorite one. He hears a twig snap and it snaps him back to reality. He readies his gun. "I guess we all had the same idea," Vanessa says. Jamie sighs and lowers his gun.

"Is this the stream we used to play at?" Dylan asks.

"Yep," Jamie says.

"It looks so small," Vanessa notices.

"Well, it hasn't rained all week. It seems like it used to rain more often."

"What is down there?" Vanessa says pointing to a pile of wood stuck in the mud.

"No way!" Dylan shouts, running to investigate. "Our raft!" He smiles back at them like a kid who just found treasure. "How did the three of us ever fit on it?" Jamie and Vanessa run over to join in the excitement.

"When was the last time we were all here together?" Dylan asks.

"The day before Ron took me to Alabama," Jamie says.

"Oh, yeah," Dylan says. "We were...fifteen?"

"That was a horrible year wasn't it? For all of us." Jamie looks at them both with a half-hearted smile.

"Well," Vanessa says, holding out her hands to both of them. "We are together now and nobody will ever split us up again...promise me."

"We promise," Jamie says as he takes her hand.

"Of course," Dylan says, stepping over the mud to get to them. He grabs her hand as well. "No damn body. Family forever."

They start to head back and Vanessa wonders aloud. "Why haven't you guys ever rebuilt this place? You could build a massive house on this land."

"It was too painful to ever come back, but you know, I think I'm ready. I think we should build the biggest house in New Orleans."

"For just the three of you?" Dylan laughs.

"No, for all of us."

Dylan and Vanessa laughs. "Are you sure about that?"

"Why not?" he says. "We are practically all living together now anyway."

"But Marilee loves the lodge," Dylan says.

"She'll come around. It will take a while to build anyway." He notices Vanessa biting her lip, unsure.

"What do you say Vanessa?" Dylan asks. "You know you belong here with us."

"Don't make us beg like we used to," Jamie says. They all titter as they remember. Dylan and Jamie get on their knees.

"No, no, don't sing, please," she says. They don't listen and start to sing the song they used to sing to her.

"My girl, my girl, talking 'bout my girl, my girl, oohooo."

"Okay, okay," she says. They take her to the ground and laugh until they can't breathe. "I missed you guys. I love you both."

"We love you too," Jamie says. "So you're in, then."

"Yeah, but run it by Marilee and Charlotte first, please. I already feel like they don't like me much."

"Well, let's get back for dinner and let's keep this to ourselves for a while. Until I get back from Georgia at least."

13

"About packed?" Marilee asks, placing Celia on the bed so she can play.

"I better not miss her first steps," Jamie says.

"Don't worry," Marilee kisses him. "You're only going to be gone for the weekend."

"This part of the job really sucks," he says. "Leaving you two." He picks Celia up and flies her around the room like an airplane and his phone buzzes. "That would be Dylan and Vanessa."

"I'm glad they are keeping you company. Y'all just be careful."

"Always," he says. He kisses them and as he walks down the stairs, everyone is waiting for him.

"I thought we'd all see you off," Marilee says as she walks up behind him. "This is your first job as the King. She leans in close to him and whispers in his ear, "Go change things." He smiles, but his stomach is in knots.

"Please have someone with you at all times," Jamie says. "Will, you guys are staying until I get back, right?"

"Of course," Will says. "I will keep her safe."

As he heads out the door he looks to Dylan and Vanessa. "Are y'all ready for this?"

~

"Ready for training?" Charlotte asks.

"Yep," Marilee says. "Let me go get Celia settled with Betty and I'll meet you down there."

~

"So," Charlotte asks as they get ready to begin Marilee's training. "Are you ever going to set a date?"

"Charlotte," Marilee says with annoyance.

"Well," Charlotte replies. "We know you love him, you want to be with him forever, and he's the father of your child. What is the hold up?"

She puts her hand on her hips. "Well, when is your date?"

"That is different," Charlotte says. Marilee raises her eyebrows. "It's not like I don't want to set a date. I just haven't set it yet."

"Oh my God!" Arianna says as she comes down the stairs. "I have a beyond brilliant idea. Why don't we all get married together?" Marilee's eyes widen along with Charlotte's, but for different reasons. Charlotte is excited and Marilee is scared as hell.

"That is an awesome idea!" Charlotte says. "What do you think, Marilee?"

"Ah...I don't know," Marilee says. "But Arianna, wouldn't Devin want to have the wedding in Ireland or at least London?"

"There is nothing that says we have to make a spectacle out of this," Arianna says. "I say we go to Vegas."

"I love that idea," Charlotte says. "I really didn't want to plan a wedding. Marilee?"

"I don't know," she says, noticing the disapproval in their expression. "Fine, I'll think about it." Charlotte and Arianna squeal. "But don't tell the guys yet."

"Sure thing," Arianna says and Marilee knows all they heard her say was yes. "Why not ditch training today and go get some coffee."

"Sounds good, but I need to take care of some things here first."

~

Jamie, Dylan, and Vanessa land in Georgia and the car takes them straight to the meeting.

They pull up to a large warehouse with high fencing. Guards block the entrance and one comes to check them for clearance. Jamie gives Vanessa and Dylan a cautious glance as the gates open. He hates this part of the job. He knew it would come up eventually. They step out of the car and walk inside. It looks like a normal warehouse until they get further toward the back. They all three try to play it cool as they see the thousands of bags of drugs put in boxes and thrown on a truck. "Shit just got real, boys," Vanessa whispers.

Just remember how Dad said to handle it," Dylan says.

"This is wrong on so many levels, "Jamie says. Taking a breath. "Let's get this done."

They continue further back to the offices for the meeting. A man greets them as they enter a room just big enough for them and two other men. "Mr. Garrison," an older man says and stands up and holds out his hand. "It's nice to finely meet the new king."

"Likewise, Mr. Baker," Jamie says. "I've heard great things about your business strategies."

"Well, thank you," Mr. Baker says.

"But I also noticed that production costs and labor have doubled this year."

"How did you know that?" Mr. Baker asks, looking toward his associate. He squirms in his chair. "I haven't even sent out a quarterly yet."

Vanessa hands him some papers from her purse. "You mean these reports." Jamie leers. "I hacked the system and got them last night so that I would be prepared. I don't like coming to a meeting without doing my homework."

"I see," Mr. Baker says. "Your grandfather trained you well, I see." Jamie's leer vanishes.

"And what would my grandfather do next, Mr. Baker?" Jamie says, his eyes blazing with irritation.

"He would probably fire me, sir," he says with a shaky voice.

"No, no, no, Mr. Baker," Jamie says with a chuckle. "My grandfather would kill you." Baker's eyes widen with fear as he waits. He looks back and forth between the three of them. "But I'm not my grandfather and I'm not going to do either." Mr. Baker let's out a breath, relieved he isn't going to die today.

"Thank you, sir," he says.

"But you have to get these costs under control. Everyone has a bad quarter every once in a while, but this is your first and only warning, so might I make a suggestion?" Baker and his associate laugh but quickly stops, realizing his situation. "Something funny, Mr. Baker?"

"No, no—

"Yes, what is it?"

"I mean no disrespect, sir, but what—

"What do I know about drug distribution?" Jamie says, scratching his forehead. He gives Dylan and Vanessa a crooked smile. "How old do you think I am, Mr. Baker?"

He looks to his associate and shrugs his shoulders. "I don't know...twenty-two?"

"Actually," Jamie says. "I'm twenty-three and New Orleans is the most successful faction in the US and I want that for Georgia as well. I'm proud to be the youngest king ever to run the US factions. I am five years younger than my great, great grandfather was when he started running things. You are right though, I know nothing about drug distribution. There is one thing I know how to do and I do it quite well and that is how to kill."

Vanessa hands the man a card. "I've already called. He will be here tomorrow. Make sure he feels welcome. He has done wonders for our weapons distribution costs. Give him whatever he asks for. As for you, Mr. Baker..." He notices the man swallow hard as he comes closer to him. "You will need a new title."

"Excuse me, sir?"

"You will be the new head of distribution. You will lead all operations here in Georgia, that is, if you wish to accept."

"Ah, yes, sir, thank you, sir," Mr. Baker replies.

"But everything falls on you. There will be a hefty raise. Hire whomever you like to take your place here, but make sure you can trust them with your life because that is what is at stake." He nods with a smile. "Good, then if all goes as planned, you will never have to see me again." They start to walk out the door. "Tyler will send me a report," Jamie says. As they exit the warehouse Jamie sighs. "I'm glad I don't have to worry about that anymore."

"We still have other States with dealings, Jamie," Dylan says.

"Which one are you closing down first?" Vanessa asks.

"Let's make some friends first and then we'll make enemies." As they get into the car Dylan gets out his phone. "Who are you calling?"

"Dad wanted to know how things went."

"Tell him, thanks for the confidence in us," Jamie says as he gets his phone out as well. "Hey," he says as Marilee answers.

"Hey, how is everything?" she says.

"Great, busy. How about you?" she says.

"One meeting down and two more to go."

"Well, be safe, Jamie, please."

"You too. How's Celia?"

"Good," Marilee says with a laugh. "Not walking yet."

"Okay," he says with a chuckle. "Good to know. I'll call y'all later." He hangs up and knots form in his stomach again.

After their day of meetings, Jamie falls down on the bed at the Landry Hotel. "I'm so tired."

"This suite is huge," Vanessa shouts. "You know, we could have made due with standard rooms."

"Why?" Jamie says. "This is nicer, besides, you have your own room and it's the biggest I might add." She rolls her eyes at him. "We need to stick together."

"I know," she says, sticking her tongue out at him. He always feels like a kid again when she is around. Dylan runs to her, picks her up, and throws her on the bed. They both tickle her until she begs them to stop. "Who's hungry?" he asks.

"Starving," Vanessa says.

"Room service or the Restaurant downstairs?" Dylan asks.

"I have a better idea," Vanessa says, holding up some pizza brochures. "Movie and pizza, just like the old days."

"Awesome," Jamie says. "Y'all go ahead, I'm going to take a shower after I call the girls. He takes out his phone as he walks toward the bathroom. "Shit!"

"What?" Dylan asks, picking up his phone as well. "Shit!"

"What is it?" Vanessa asks.

"We got like fifty messages from Will," Jamie says as he dials.

14

Marilee sips her coffee, thinking of Jamie. "Marilee!" Charlotte shouts to snap her out of her thoughts.

"Yeah," she says. "What?"

"The spa...do you want to go to the spa at The Michaelson later?"

"Sure, but do you think it's safe?"

"Yeah, it's The Michaelson," Arianna says.

After some lattes, Arianna talks them into going shopping. "It's just this one shop and Jamie's friend owns it. We will be perfectly safe."

"I would still feel better if we called Will," Marilee says. "Jamie will freak if we go alone. You know how he is."

Arianna sighs. "I know," she says. "I love him, but–

"I know, but he is just trying to keep us safe," Marilee says.

"Yeah, a bit over-protective," Charlotte says. "I'll call Will."

They meet Will at the shop and he waits as they buy out the store. "Sorry, Will," Marilee says. "I know you probably have better things to do than to babysit me."

"Not at all, Love," Will says. "I'm just glad you called instead of going off by yourself. Jamie would've killed me."

"We would have been just fine on our own," Arianna says, coming out of the dressing room.

"I know, my dear sister, but let's just say we are doing it for Jamie."

"Fine," she says. "Well, do you think he would mind us going to the spa at The Michaelson later on then?"

"It should be okay," Will says. "I'll do a quick sweep of the area first, but it should be okay. The girls at the spa know you and Charlotte."

"Great," Arianna says.

After hours of shopping, they need to recharge. "Are y'all getting hungry?" Marilee asks.

"I thought you'd never ask," Dylan says. "Where to?"

~

As they walk into the Michaelson Hotel, all eyes are on them. "Just keep moving," Charlotte says, noticing Marilee hesitant. They walk straight back to the spa where a lady greets them.

"Arianna, Charlotte so nice to see you again." a petite woman with her hair in a bun hugs them.

"Hey, Bridgette," Charlotte says, returning the gesture. "Can we get three rooms, please?"

"Of course," Bridgette says. "Right this way."

"Guys," Marilee whispers as they walk down the hall. "I've never been to a spa before. What do I do?"

"They will tell you what to do," Arianna says, going in to the first room.

"Don't worry," Charlotte says. "You'll be fine." Charlotte enters the next available room and Bridgette motions for Marilee to come to the third.

"Mrs. Garrison," she says. Marilee follows her into the room and looks around. She smells roses and lavender and hears soothing music. "What would you like today?

"Ah..." Marilee says. "I have no idea." She doesn't correct the woman when she calls her Mrs.

Garrison. She is getting used to it anyway. "This is my first time. What do you recommend?"

"Don't worry," she says. "I'll give you the best. Go ahead and take your clothes off behind the screen and I will run you one of our special baths."

"Oh, okay." Marilee does as she is told, but doesn't like the idea. She notices a bathrobe hanging on the screen. "Oh, thank God," she says.

"Okay," the woman says. "Mrs. Garrison, your bath is ready. I'll be back to check on you in a little while, enjoy."

While Marilee sinks into the bathtub, she relaxes instantly. "Oh, I could get used to this." Her mind wanders off to different things. Celia eating breakfast this morning, Jamie being goofy with her, and other things. After a few minutes, she hears a commotion in the next room and then gunfire. She jumps up, startled, but someone pushes her back down under the water. She splashes around, trying to get free, but the person is too strong. She is finally able to get above water, after scratching their arm. The man growls when she draws blood. She takes a breath before he grabs her by the throat and slams her under the water again. Trying to calm down, she thinks about her training, but she just can't use any of it in this situation. Suddenly, she remembers the knife that Charlotte gave her and told her to wear it at all times, no matter where she was. She tries to reach down to her ankle, but she can't. She twists her leg behind her butt, which isn't very comfortable, but with her small frame, easily done. Finally, she can feel the strap. Pulling the knife from its sheath, she cuts the man's arm and he releases her. She gasps for air as the man screams and comes at her again. She quickly stands up, ready to cut him again. He hesitates, staring at her naked body for a split second, giving Arianna the moment she needs. She bursts through the door and shoots the man in the head. Charlotte runs in a moment later naked, bloody, and out of breath. They smile when they see Marilee holding the bloody knife.

"Welcome to the Family," Arianna says. Marilee takes a breath, soaking in what just occurred. "We better call Will."

~

"What the hell, Will?" Jamie shouts over the phone.

"They went to the Michaelson, I thought they would be safe!" Will says. "I secured the front and back entrances, Jamie what else should I have done!" They all gather around knowing poor Will is getting chewed out by Jamie.

"I told you to protect her!"

"Jamie!" Dylan scolds him. "Enough."

Jamie pulls at his hair. "I'm just mad at myself, Will. It's not your fault, can I talk to her, please?" Will hands the phone to Marilee.

"Hey," she says and Jamie takes a breath after hearing her voice.

"Are you okay?"

"Yes," she says, knowing he is beyond pissed at her.

"I thought I told you to stay put," he says. She sighs at his comment and gives the audience a glance. They turn and pretend not to be listening, but she knows that Jamie's voice is loud enough to hear, even from the phone.

"No, you told me to be safe and to have someone with me at all times and I did."

"Marilee," he says with a huff. "You have to think."

"Excuse me, she says, a bit hurt at his tone and remark.

"How am I supposed to travel to these meetings if I can't trust you to do the simple task of staying put?"

"Don't treat me like a child, Jamie!"

"Then stop doing stupid shit!" He immediately regrets his words. Biting his jaw he tries to apologize. "Marilee...I'm sorry."

"She's gone," Will says, watching Marilee go back to the office. She slams the door and pours herself a drink.

Jamie throws his phone on the bed. "Son of a bitch!"

Dylan is on the phone with Charlotte. "How is she?"

"Pissed, very pissed."

"We have to cut this trip short," Jamie says. Dylan widens his eyes.

"No!" he says. "Jamie, you can't. There is too much riding on this."

"Well, obviously we can't leave them alone!"

"Enough!" Vanessa yells. "Jamie take a minute and breathe. It's only one more day. Marilee is probably too upset to go anywhere else, especially how you just treated her. Dylan, ask Charlotte to stay with her all day tomorrow." She smiles at Jamie. "Now, problem solved, so go take your shower."

"Did you hear that?" Dylan says to Charlotte.

"Yep, got it," she says. Jamie rolls his eyes and leaves the room, still aggravated. "I'm liking this sister of yours more and more."

~

Jamie tries calling Marilee between his meetings, but she hasn't returned any of his calls or texts since they talked last night. "Marilee, I'm sorry...I was angry..." he sighs. "I love you."

Looking out the window he thinks of the possibility that she may not forgive him. "She'll let you off the hook," Vanessa says. "She's just trying to prove her point."

"What point?"

"That you can't treat her like shit, you jackass." Jamie smirks at her comment. "Just use that Garrison charm on her when you get home and all will be back to normal. Now let's get this last one over with so we can get you back to her."

~

Marilee hears her phone buzz for the hundredth time today. She smiles at the fact that he is trying to apologize. She has already forgiven him, but she wants to let him suffer a bit more. Though he already should have been on his way home. She starts to worry for a moment and dials his number, but quickly hangs up. "I'll wait a few more minutes," she says resisting the urge to hear his voice. A few minutes of pacing the floor, her phone rings. She quickly picks it up. "Jamie," she says, but the other end of the line is silent. She closes her eyes as she smells a familiar scent. She looks toward the doorway. "I'm sorry," he says. Her face fills Jamie with hope. Running into his arms, she is thankful that he is safe. He silently thanks God that she has forgiven him. "Where is Celia?"

"She is with Betty and Charley."

"I want to see her, but first," he says, picking her up. She giggles. "I'm really sorry."

"I know," she strokes his cheek and he whisks her to the bedroom as if it were the first time.

~

So, I wanted to run something by you," Jamie says, slowly getting dressed.

"Shoot," she says, following his lead with getting dressed.

"Well, I went to my old house the other day."

"You did?" she asks.

"Yeah, and I was thinking of clearing the land and rebuilding."

"Really?"

"Yeah, how would you feel about having a place out there?"

She gives him a confused expression, biting her lip. "What about the lodge?" she asks.

"His eyes narrow. "Well, your dad's down the road, Charley and Betty can move in here to help run this place, and the land is only a few minutes away."

"Wait," she says, shaking her head. "Charley and Betty?"

"Oops," Jamie says, biting his lip. "I wasn't supposed to say anything about that."

Marilee likes the idea of having a place a bit more private, but she is also attached to the lodge. "Wouldn't you love Celia to play in her own backyard, the one that I used to play in?"

"Guilt much?" she says. "I would love a bit more privacy."

"Don't worry," he says. "You will have all the privacy you want. We will all have our own wing of the house. It's going to be massive."

"We?"

"Yeah," he says, hesitant to finish. "Dylan, Charlotte, Vanessa."

"Vanessa?" Her forehead crinkles.

"Come on," Jamie says, sensing her reluctance. "She's practically my sister. I don't want to put her out on the streets."

"Well, what about Charley and Betty? They are family too."

"I already talked to them. They want to stay at the lodge to help out. I already told him that it was okay with me if it was okay with you. They can have this apartment."

She is silent for a moment and he playfully nudges her. "So,"

"I'll think about it," she says, not wanting to disappoint him, but she doesn't know how she feels about having everyone in the same house. She likes Vanessa, but she really doesn't know her well enough to live with her.

15

After speaking with Charlotte and Dylan, Marilee gives in about letting Vanessa live with them. Once the decision is made, Jamie wastes no time getting started with the build.

"Wow," Marilee says as she walks into the massive construction zone they have created in a matter of weeks. "Do you think it will be finished by Celia's birthday?"

"I will make sure of it," Jamie says as his phone rings. "Crap," he says. "I'm running late for a meeting. Can you tell the contractor which floors you want?"

"Sure," she says.

"Great," he says, kissing her cheek. "I'll send a car back for you."

"No need," Vanessa says, walking carefully over the equipment laying in the floor. "I'll give her a lift."

"Awesome," Jamie says. "I'll see you girls later."

Marilee smiles at Vanessa. "So, I just need to tell the contractor what kind of floors I want and then we can go."

"No rush," Vanessa says with a shrug. "What floors are you choosing?"

"Hardwood, I guess. I like what we picked out for the lodge."

"Have you ever considered marble flooring?" Vanessa asks.

"Not even once," Marilee says.

"Come here, let me show you." She pulls her into the kitchen where a product book lies on an incomplete countertop. She flips through the pages to find the marble flooring. “See, look.”

“It seems way too fancy,” Marilee scrunches her nose.

“Well, yeah,” Vanessa says with a laugh. “That’s the point.”

“I want this place to feel like a home, not some fancy hotel,” Marilee says.

“Fine,” Vanessa says, feeling let down. She closes the book and Marilee sighs. She sees the disappointment on Vanessa’s face and she knows this is going to be her home too. She should be able to pick something out to make it feel like home to her as well.

“How about we compromise?” Marilee says. Vanessa’s eyes light up.

“What did you have in mind?”

“How about marble in the kitchen, bathrooms, and dining room?”

“Sounds marvelous,” Vanessa says, clapping her hands together.

“But I want hardwood floors in the living room and the bedrooms. You can do whatever you want with your wing of the house.”

“Deal,” Vanessa says. “Let’s go grab some coffee after we are done here.”

~

Sitting in the coffee shop that is beside Vanessa’s office, Marilee automatically brings up her job. “Do you get a lot of business?”

Vanessa chuckles. “I get plenty. I’m more of an on call type of doctor. When someone calls, I come running.”

“Oh, so you’re like “the Family” doctor,” Marilee says with a hint of a laugh.

“Yeah,” Vanessa says. “I guess you could put it that way.”

"Does it ever get to you?" Marilee asks. "All the blood and stuff."

"Nah," Vanessa shrugs her shoulder. "I've never been the squeamish type. Some things do bother me though."

"Like what?"

"Men in this world of ours can be a bit rough."

"What do you mean?" Marilee says, hoping nobody has hurt her. "Has someone hurt you?"

"No, nothing like that, but I got a call a couple of weeks ago. When I got there, it was horrible. The man beat his wife. He thought she was cheating on him. There was so much blood. I could hardly recognize her."

"Oh, God," Marilee says, grabbing her hand. "You knew her?"

"Yeah, well we weren't close or anything, but I knew of her. The man opened the door for me, pointed to the bedroom, and made himself a drink." She wrinkles her nose with disgust. "It was like another day to him."

"Isn't that something Jamie should know about?"

"He does."

"Oh," Marilee says, releasing her hand and straightening her posture. "Well, what did he do?"

"Let's just say, he took care of it."

Marilee rolls her eyes from the lack of details. "Okay."

"He beat the shit out of the guy." Vanessa sighs. "Look, I know you get annoyed when we don't tell you certain things, but," Vanessa picks at her fingernail polish that is starting to flake. "It's not that we don't want you to know. It's just that dealing with this drama is exhausting. That is how we deal with it, we keep it buried deep down. That and the bourbon helps."

Marilee softens her expression to try and understand where they are coming from. "I can get that, but won't that just make you explode, eventually."

"Exactly," Vanessa says. Marilee narrows her eyes, not understanding the comment. "We need that rage to be bottled up. Especially Jamie. To do what he has to do...what we have to do. We need all the rage we can get." Marilee sits quietly and finishes her coffee for a moment to process the conversation. It finally comes into her mind, the girl Vanessa was talking about.

"The girl, who was the girl?"

"What?" Vanessa eyes widen, hoping she can come up with anything, but the truth.

"The girl that was beaten by her husband, what was her name?" Marilee bites the corner of her mouth waiting for her to answer.

"Oh," Vanessa hesitates, but decides to tell her anyway. "Her name was Ruby."

Marilee takes a little breath and closes her eyes, trying not to overreact. "It was Jamie, he was the one who she was cheating with." She feels a knot form in her stomach, but before she can start to cry Vanessa takes her hand.

"No, no," she says. "He thought she was cheating with him, but trust me, he was not. I promise you—

"I know, of course," Marilee says with a smile to assure Vanessa.

"Jamie is going to kill me," Vanessa says, sinking down in her chair to pout.

"I won't say anything," Marilee says. "I promise. As long as you buy me one of those muffins over there." Vanessa smiles and gives her a wink.

~

"So, did you get the floors figured out?" Jamie asks.

"Yeah," Marilee says a she sifts through her dinner.

"What's the matter?" he asks noticing her sulking.

"Oh, nothing." She laughs off her thoughts on her earlier discussion with Vanessa. "You'll be happy to know that Vanessa and I came up with a compromise on the floors. She wanted marble and I wanted hardwood so we got both."

"Cool," he says. "I'm glad y'all are getting along."

"Yeah, we went to have coffee at that place beside her office." Noticing Jamie's eyes widen, she stops before taking a bite of her food. "What?"

"Nothing," Jamie says, shaking off the thought of Vanessa betraying him. "What did y'all discuss?"

"Nothing much," she lies. "Just her job."

"Oh, okay," he says, smiling at Celia eating her mashed potatoes.

"Anything interesting happen today?" She decides to change the subject.

"Not really." His brow creases as he takes a sip of his drink, wondering why she is so interested.

"What was the meeting about?"

"What? Do you really want to know?"

"Yes," she says. "Actually, I do."

"Okay, let's see. I met with the manager of the Michaelson to make sure the new security team is trained properly."

"Isn't that Dylan's territory now?"

"Yes, but I wanted to handle it."

"Don't you think that might make him feel like..." she hesitates.

"Like what?"

"Like you don't trust him."

"That's ridiculous," he says, but it strikes the back of his mind that she may be right.

"I don't know, how would you feel if your Dad came back and made decisions that you were supposed to make?"

"Did he say something?" Jamie asks.

"No, no." Marilee quickly puts that idea out of his head. "I was just thinking that you have been taking on a lot of problems that you shouldn't have to worry about now."

"Fair point," he says. "I'll talk to Dylan."

"Have you heard anything else on the Ladies of Louisiana?"

"Nope, not a word. I'm beginning to think someone took care of them for us."

"You think they had something to do with the Michaelson?"

"Maybe," Jamie says, with a doubtful shake to his head. "But I would think I would have some information by now." He sighs and Marilee can tell he is stressed.

"Hey, how about a boat ride?"

He laughs. "Now?"

"Sure, why not? We won't be able to do this before too long."

"Sure we will, just not this late at night." He smiles and wipes his mouth. "I'll start cleaning up." He gives her a wink.

"I'll call Betty."

~

"God," Marilee says as they float down the bayou.

"What is it?" Jamie asks, kissing her neck.

"You still give me shivers all over."

"I know what you mean," he says with a laugh and slides his finger down her belly.

She grabs his hand and places it on her cheek. "Promise me something."

"Anything," he says.

"Never hurt me or Celia," she says.

"You know I would nev–

"Just promise to never hurt or leave us, okay." Her eyes meet his and he is a bit concerned that she may know something.

"Where is this coming from?" He straightens himself showing his concern.

"Nowhere, just promise."

"I promise," he says, stroking her face. "Now can you make that same promise?"

"Of course. I promise."

Jamie stands up and throws out the anchor. "Now that we have that all sorted out." He give her a wink and the world slips away.

~

"Jamie!" Marilee shouts as the morning light hits her in the face. "Wake up!"

"What?" he says.

"We fell asleep. She grabs his phone that is buzzing on the floor beside them. "Your phone is going crazy. Dylan's text says you are late for a meeting."

"Oh shit!" Jamie jumps up to get dressed. He grabs his phone and dials Dylan. "Hey, man. I'm on my way."

"Everyone is here waiting, Jamie," Dylan says, grinding his teeth.

"Sorry," Jamie says. "You can handle things on your own today, right?"

"Um, sure," Dylan says. "Is everything okay?"

"Yeah. I'll see you later today then."

"Very well done," Marilee says.

"Now we can take our time." He looks around and breathes in a deep breath. "It is so beautiful out here. A lot of people don't appreciate the beauty of the bayou."

"Probably because of the snakes, alligators, and mosquitos," Marilee laughs.

"Well if you are prepared," he says, taking down the mosquito netting they put up the night before. "It can be very romantic."

"I agree."

16

"I'm cooking tonight at the restaurant so make sure everyone knows to be there at seven." Marilee says as she fixes her hair in the mirror.

"Sounds awesome," Jamie says. "Can't wait to eat anything you put together." He kisses her on the cheek. "I'm going to hop in the shower and then I have a short meeting downstairs.

"Okay, I'm going to have a workout. See you in a bit. Betty is coming over to watch Celia."

"We really should get her to move in here." Jamie says with a laugh.

"Actually, Dad will be here to get her in a few minutes. He took the day off and is taking her to the zoo. Charley is working the front desk today."

"Cool. Well, I'll be sure to tell her goodbye before I leave then. Have a good workout."

~

Marilee finishes her workout and starts back upstairs to take a shower. On her way up the stairs a man stops her. "Marilee?" he says.

"Yes," she answers, hesitantly.

"I've been wanting to introduce myself to you for a while."

"Oh..." Marilee says.

"I'm Tyler, Ruby's husband." Marilee takes a step back. "Ah," he laughs. "I see you have heard of me."

"Yes, I have so if you will excuse me." She turns to go upstairs, but he grabs her arm.

"Look, I just got back from Georgia and I'm tired. I just needed you to know that I am not the bad guy here. I just want to know the truth."

"Mr. Brown—

"Please, call me Tyler."

She sighs. "Tyler, I assure you that Jamie is faithful to me and always will be. Maybe you should trust your wife the same."

Tyler laughs. "You are so sweet. They were right about you."

"What?" Marilee narrows her eyes at him.

"Never mind," he says, arrogantly. "It was a real pleasure to meet you, Marilee." He grabs her hand. She cringes as he kisses her knuckles. "Until we meet again." She watches him walk out of the lodge, a bit taken by his visit, but she tries to let it go and continue with her day. As she gets her clothes ready she notices a card lying on the bed. Thinking it is from Jamie, she smiles. She opens the card and falls on the bed with shock.

"Marilee?" Jamie asks, walking through the door. She jumps up as he walks in, dropping the pictures on the floor. She backs away from him. Noticing the intense look on her face he follows her stare toward the floor. "What's the matter?" he asks as he leans down to see the pictures of him and Ruby. Looking up, he sees the pain in her eyes. "Where did you get these?" he asks. She is silent as he stands up and looks down at her. "Where did you get these?" His voice makes her flinch. She tilts her head to the side, shaking her head.

"That is all you have to say?" she says as tears run down her face.

"This..." He waves one of the pictures around, "...is nothing."

"There is a whole lot of nothing on the floor, Jamie," she says.

"Ah," he shouts. "This is crazy, how did you get..." He pulls his hair out of frustration. "Marilee," he says, trying to think of a way to explain things to her. "I need a drink." He goes into his office and pours two drinks. Marilee sighs and picks up the pictures off the floor and follow him into his office. She throws them down on the table. I deserve an explanation." She says, giving him the benefit of the doubt, even though she feels like she has been stabbed a million times. He hands her a glass.

"Yes, you do," he says. "But first drink, you'll need it." He takes a sip with her and he readies himself for her reaction. "I did not sleep with her." She gives him a blank stare. "Do you believe me?" She turns to the evidence on the table and sighs because despite of all the evidence sitting right in front of her, she does believe him.

"Yes, I believe you," she says rolling her eyes. "But that doesn't change the fact that you kissed her, a lot."

"Sit down," he says, softly. "I'll explain." He fills her in on the whole plan about getting the signatures he needed for being king.

"So she wanted you in exchange for the signatures? And you said yes?"

"I wasn't going to go through with it. I just needed those signatures. I needed to play her for a little while until I got them."

"And you got the signatures."

"But she didn't get me, I promise." He grabs her hands. She nods and bites her lip, letting all of it sink in. She glances at the pictures again.

"Okay, let me ask you one more thing," she says, trying not to let this get the better of her. "Was the signatures the only reason you wanted to play her?"

"Of course," he says.

She picks up a single picture and throws it in his face. "Then why is that one dated after the signing?" He closes his eyes knowing he has screwed up. He can only look up at her speechless as he notices an expression he has never seen on her before, loathing.

"I'm sorry," he says. She walks away and the sound of the bedroom door makes him jump. He stands up and throws his glass against the wall and picks up the phone. "Dylan, meeting downstairs, now. Tell Charlotte to come upstairs, Marilee found out about Ruby."

"Shit!" Dylan says. "On our way."

He cleans up the broken glass and throws it in the trash as they both walk in the front door. He meets them in the hallway.

"Dumbass," Charlotte mumbles as she passes by him and toward the bedroom.

"I guess she knows too?" Jamie says. Dylan shrugs his shoulders. "Let's go downstairs."

~

Charlotte looks at the pictures disgusted. "I can't believe he would do this." She throws them down. "What was he thinking? I'm so going to kick his ass."

"I would rather you kick hers," Marilee shouts from the shower.

"Done." Charlotte stands up to leave.

"I was kidding," Marilee says, seeing her through the shower door. "Sit down."

"Fine," Charlotte says, sitting back down. "So what are you going to do?"

"What do you mean?" Marilee says, wrapping a towel around herself.

"Are you going to leave?" she asks, scared to know the answer.

Marilee laughs. "Don't be ridiculous," she says, confusing Charlotte. "Remember the story Vanessa told us about her friends trying to kill her a dozen times, but she always came back just to say they missed."

"Yes," Charlotte says, still a bit confused.

"Well, why should I give that bitch the satisfaction of thinking she could shake our relationship?"

"Wow," Charlotte says as Marilee comes out of the bathroom. "That's very mature of you."

"Vanessa is right, they'll keep coming unless I show them that nothing they can do will scare me off."

"Okay, does this mean Vegas is still on?"

"I never said yes to that." Marilee smiles.

"You never said no either." Charlotte winks.

"Are you going to tell Jamie that you are okay? He is probably destroying the city by now."

"Let him wallow a bit," Marilee says with a smile. "I'll tell him later."

~

I want to find out who sent these pictures now!" Jamie shouts as he throws things around the room while Dylan is on the phone.

"Yes," Dylan says holding up his finger to Jamie to tell him to stop. "Thank you. Call if you hear anything." He hangs up the phone. "Jamie, calm down. You are going to scare the guests." Jamie collapses on the couch as Charley comes in.

"What is going on?" he asks.

"Sorry," Dylan says. "Jamie is having one of his melt downs."

"Hey," Jamie asks, jumping off the couch. "You were working the front desk this morning, did someone drop off a card for Marilee?"

"Yeah, it was sitting on the counter so I took it to the apartment and set in on her bed. Why? What is going on?"

Jamie wants to punch Charley for putting the pictures in her hands, but he feels he may be the one getting punched in a second. "Jamie had to do something stupid to ensure the signatures to be king and now it is coming back to haunt him." Dylan says.

"What did you do?" Charley asks.

Jamie stands still while Dylan explains. He waits for the punch but it never comes. Charley just glares at him with the same look of disgust that Marilee gave him, bites his jaw, and walks out slamming the door behind him. "Damn," Dylan says. "I really thought he would punch you."

"I need to go let off some steam," Jamie says.

"How pissed was Marilee?" Dylan asks.

"A bit, but she was more disgusted and hurt. She never looked at me that way before."

"Well, let's get to work then, it will help you destress."

"What do you got?"

"There has been some activity at the marina. Boats have been coming and going, but we haven't made a move yet."

"Well, let's move now," Jamie says.

"It could be nothing. They keep a tight schedule so they should be pulling up to the marina in about fifteen minutes." They walk out of the office and Jamie spots Marilee coming down the stairs. She looks away from his stare and he wonders if she will be here when he returns.

~

As Dylan and Jamie pull up to the marina their target arrives. Dylan waits for his moment to tell his men to move. "They definitely look suspicious," Jamie says. Dylan notices one of them pass the other an envelope.

"Move," Dylan says over the phone. Dylan and Jamie run out to meet their men. Grabbing the men as if they were cops on a sting operation, they tie their hands and walk them to the boats and look under the tarps. Jamie sighs as they uncover all kinds of weapons. He looks toward the young men that exchanged the envelope.

"Let's take a ride, boys."

Dylan looks over one of the guns and looks back to Jamie. "Ethan," Dylan says.

"Damnit, Ethan," Jamie says. "What are you doing? Tell someone to go and get him and meet us at the warehouse." He pushes the men to the car. "Let's go, boys."

When they get to the warehouse, Jamie gets his phone out. "Who are you calling?" Dylan asks.

"Vanessa," Jamie says with an evil grin. "Yeah, give me about fifteen and work your way to the warehouse off Barclay Street."

"Why did you call Vanessa?" Dylan asks, confused why they would need a doctor when they should be killing these men instead.

"Do these two runners look familiar to you?"

"Um," Dylan looks hard at the two young men. "No, why?"

"Well not only are they the ones who were escorting the Ladies of Louisiana to our ceremony at the Michaelson, they are also Family. They are Jon Labette's boys."

"Oh, hell," Dylan says.

"Go ahead and give a courtesy call." Dylan sighs, but does as he is told. Jamie closes the big warehouse doors and then closes his eyes to let the monster inside come out a bit.

17

"Maybe I should have told him I'm okay," Marilee says, turning to Charlotte for guidance after seeing Jamie leave. "They are about to do something stupid, aren't they?"

"I have no doubt in my mind," Charlotte says as she sends a text to Dylan. "Do you want me to tell him to tell Jamie that all is forgiven, just to be on the safe side?"

"Yes, please."

"Done," Charlotte says. "Let's go get some lunch."

"Good idea."

"Hey, Charley," Marilee shouts as she passes the front counter. "We are going to get some food, you want something?"

"Yeah, hey, come here." Marilee walks over to the counter. "Are you okay?"

"Yeah, why?" she asks.

"Marilee, I know about the photos."

"Oh, no, I'm fine," she says.

"Okay, I'm confused. How could–

"We'll talk about it later," she says, interrupting his rant.

"Fine," he says. "Drama, drama, drama."

~

Jamie closes in on his target for answers. "Why? He says to Ethan. "Are we not paying you enough? Why would you stab us in the back like this? Who else are you selling to?"

"Jamie, I don't know what you're talking about," Ethan says. "I really don't know why they have these guns. They must have stolen them."

"Oh, I see," Jamie says. "Is that true fellas? Did you steal my weapons?" Neither answer so Jamie walks away. Dylan's phone goes off and he reads both text from Charlotte. He smiles and almost tells Jamie, but then, sees the old look in his eyes. It may be what he needs to get this taken care of so he decides to wait. "Did you call John?" Jamie whispers to Dylan.

"He said do what you have to do, just send them home after." Jamie shakes his head and pulls out his gun.

"Who is going to tell me the truth?" he says. He points his gun and shoots Ethan in the leg. As Ethan falls to the ground, Jamie kicks him in the face. "Now, who are you selling to?"

"I swear, Mr. Garrison, I'm not selling– Jamie kicks him again.

"I know you're lying, Ethan," he says. "Those boats are in your name. You are insulting me by playing this game!" He walks over to the young men. "What about the two of you?" he says, pointing the gun at them. They only look away. Jamie grabs the youngest by the shoulder and pushes him to his knees. The oldest flinches. Punching the younger one until he is unconscious, he can tell the older one is about to crack. He pulls his gun out and points to the younger one's head.

"No, the older one shouts. "I'll tell you. Please, don't kill him."

"Very good," Jamie says, shooting the older one in the shoulder. He screams in pain and falls to the ground.

"I said I would tell you," he says.

"I know. That is why you are still alive. That was for letting me beat your brother for so long. Now who are these weapons going to?"

"A man in Baton Rouge," the older boy says.

"Name!" Jamie says.

"Saunders, Jason Saunders."

"You idiot!" Ethan shouts toward the boy for talking. Jamie walks over to Ethan. "You are in way over your head, boy."

"You may be right," Jamie says. "But I think I'll manage." Biting his jaw, sweat beads on Jamie's forehead. His finger grows heavier on the trigger of his gun. He thinks about the look on Marilee's face again, that look of revulsion. He closes his eyes as the gun fires. "I guess we need a new arms dealer," he says, opening his eyes and motioning to his men to clean up the mess. Vanessa walks through the doors, giving Jamie a glance. He turns away from her so she proceeds to the job at hand and evaluate the boys. "When she is done with them, take them home to their father. You good with them?" he asks Vanessa. She gives him a nod to leave. "Let's go Dylan," Jamie says, hurrying out the doors.

"Do we feel better?" Dylan asks.

"A bit," Jamie says, combing his fingers through his hair.

"Maybe this will help," Dylan says, showing the earlier text from Charlotte. Jamie takes a long breath.

"When did you get that?" Jamie asks.

"Um," Dylan says, biting his lip.

"That in there," Jamie points to the warehouse, "could have been avoided, Dylan."

"Which is why I didn't tell you? That in there needed to be done."

"Well, you get to find the replacement, then."

"Worth it," Dylan says. "Let's get you back to Marilee."

~

When he gets back to the lodge and she isn't there, he gets worried. He dials her number. "Where are you?"

"We went for some Chinese food. Do you want us to bring you something back?"

"Ah, yeah, that would be great," he says. "We'll talk when you get back."

As he hangs up, he bites his jaw. "What now?" Dylan asks.

"Nothing, they're bringing back Chinese food."

"Great," Dylan says. "What's bothering you then?"

"I don't know, she doesn't seem mad at all now."

"Now you want her to be mad at you? You are straddling the line of sanity right now, you know."

~

As Marilee and Charlotte wait for their Chinese food, she sees Tyler walk in. Charlotte notices her eyes widen. "Do you know him?" she asks.

"Marilee," Tyler says. "What are you doing here?"

"Just getting Jamie some food. He love this place."

"Probably because it is right by my house," Tyler says with a hint laughter. Marilee rolls her eyes at the comment, but remembers when Jamie brought them Chinese food the other day.

"Charlotte," a man says from the back of the kitchen.

"Hi, Li," she says with a smile. He comes to give her a hug. "Li, this is Marilee."

"So nice to meet you," he says. "Wow, you are a vision." Marilee blushes. "Charlotte, my uncle would like a word, if that is okay with you?"

"Oh, sure," Charlotte says. "Are you going to be okay?" she asks Marilee as she glares at Tyler.

"I think I can manage," Marilee says, making Tyler laugh. As Charlotte leaves she tells Li to keep an eye on them. "Looks like he had other reasons to be here."

"Maybe," Tyler says. "Did you get the pictures?"

"I thought those came from you. Why?"

"I just wanted you to know what I have known for a while."

"They were just kissing," she says.

"Come on," Tyler says. "You mean you forgave him after that." Marilee looks down at the floor as Tyler laughs. "You are so cute and innocent. I love it." He leans in to whisper in her ear. She flinches a little. "If you ever want a little payback, I'm game." He takes his finger and slides it down her arm and tears begin to fill her eyes. Doubts fill her mind again about Jamie and Ruby. Li notices.

"Brown!" Li shouts. "Your order." Li shoves the order into Tyler's hands. "You can go now."

"Okay, okay," Tyler holds his hand up. "But that invitation stands, princess."

"Are you okay?" Li asks as he grabs Marilee by the shoulder. She wipes her eyes.

"Yeah," she says, embarrassed. "I'm fine. He's just some jerk. Thank you for getting him to leave."

"No problem," he says. Knowing she is taken by Jamie he quickly releases her and coughs. "Right, sorry for lingering there."

Marilee laughs and blushes again. "You're fine."

"So, I'm going to see about that order."

"What was that about?" Charlotte asks coming in on the awkwardness.

"Nothing."

"I think Li took a shine to you," Charlotte says. "Don't worry, your secret is safe with me."

"Shut-up," Marilee says, but is definitely flattered.

~

As they walk back through the doors of the lodge, Jamie is sitting on the couch. He stands up when he sees her come through the door.

"You want to set this up in the office? Charlotte asks as Dylan comes to help them with the food.

"Sure," he says.

"We'll be in there in a minute," Marilee says. Jamie meets her half-way. "Hey," she says.

"Hey," he replies.

"Charley!" Charlotte calls out to him as he watches them with concern. "Come get some food."

"I'm coming." Charley grinds his teeth, but follows Charlotte into the office.

"We can go eat and then talk if you want," Marilee says, trying to avoid the conversation. The thought of Ruby with her lips on his makes her tense up. He strokes her cheek and she grabs his hand. She melts at his touch and smiles, trying not to fall apart.

"You didn't leave," he says.

"I promised I wouldn't," she says. "But you promised you would never hurt me and you did."

"I know," he says, placing their heads together. "I'm so sorry. He looks her in the eyes with more passion than she has ever seen. She wants to hold him so she knows they are okay.

"Don't do it again."

“Never again, I promise.” He picks her up and kisses her. The guests start clapping as he carries her upstairs.

“I guess everything is back to normal,” Dylan says.

“Am I not the only one just a little bit pissed at him?” Charley asks.

“No, of course not, but considering why he did it—

“I don’t care why he did it!”

“You should,” Dylan says. “You benefit from this life just as much as any of us and all you have to do is stand behind a counter and smile.”

“Dylan!” Charlotte shouts, slapping him on the arm.

Charley laughs. “It’s okay, Charlotte. He’s right.” He wipe his mouth with his napkin and stands up. He throws it down on the table, glaring at Dylan. “Maybe it isn’t a good idea for Betty and me to move here.”

“No, Charley,” Charlotte says, pulling at Dylan’s arm.

“Charley,” Dylan sighs. “I didn’t mean—

“I would love to stay, but I have to go stand behind a counter and smile for a few more hours.”

He leaves and Charlotte bites her jaw as she looks to Dylan. “I’m sorry, but he’s always looking down on what we do. You don’t see him running away from the perks of it, do you?”

“It was still mean,” she says.

“I’ll apologize tomorrow.”

“Thank you,” she says. “Oh, I forgot,” she says, pulling out the envelope from earlier. “Li told me to give this to Jamie. It’s from Mr. Wang.” Dylan opens it.

“Oh, shit,” he says.

“What is it?” Charlotte asks.

"Nothing, I'll be back," Dylan says and runs out. She knows if Dylan wanted her to know he would tell her, but it still hurts when he doesn't confide in her. She starts to pack the food up to take upstairs. She knows that is where he is headed anyway and she wants to know what is going on, whether he wants her to know or not.

~

Dylan bangs on Jamie and Marilee's front door. "Jamie!" He texts him too, just to hurry him. His banging doesn't quit until Jamie opens the door.

"What the hell?" Jamie says as he opens the door.

"Sorry," Dylan says, pushing his way through. "I need a word in your office."

"Alright, give me a minute." Dylan paces frantically until Jamie returns. "What is wrong with you?" Dylan hands him the envelope. Jamie glares at Frank's face in the picture.

"Mr. Wang sent it back with Charlotte today," Dylan says. "As far as I know this is the only copy, but what if–

"Marilee?" Jamie says as he sees the door open.

"What's going on?" she asks.

"Nothing, just dealing with the past coming back to bite us in the ass again."

"What past?" she asks.

"Don't worry about it," Jamie says.

"Marilee?" Charlotte says, peeking her head around the corner. "Guys, I brought the food up here. Marilee, can you help me warm it up?"

Pressing her lips in a hard line, she sighs. "Fine." She follows Charlotte to the kitchen. Jamie shuts the office door.

"If these pictures get out," Dylan says.

"I know," Jamie says with a growl. "Let me think."

"Why does it matter anyway?"

"If the factions think that there is the slightest chance Frank is alive, they could void the agreement, Jamie! The one you worked so hard to get signed. And when they find out he died by your hand, and they will, how many of those leaders do you think will resign in your favor?"

Jamie stares at the picture for a moment. "Why are you still ruining my life?"

"We need to call a meeting," Dylan says.

"Okay, set it up," Jamie says, falling down in his chair. "Why must things stay so fucked up?" Dylan pours them both a drink.

"That's the life," Dylan says. "Should I call in Will and Devin?"

"Definitely," Jamie says. "We'll need all the support we can get."

~

While Jamie and Dylan are in the office, Celia, Betty, and Bryce come back from the zoo. "Hey," Marilee says as she scoops Celia up in her arms. "Did you have fun? Thank you so much for taking her to the zoo, guys."

"No problem," Betty says. "I had fun, but I think Dad may have worn himself out."

"Hey, I'm not as young as I used to be," Bryce says as he gives Marilee a kiss on the cheek. "We had a great time, but I am off to bed. Sorry, sweetie, I know you planned a big dinner for everyone."

"Don't worry about it, you go rest. Thanks, Dad," Marilee says.

When Bryce leaves, they catch Betty up on everything that has happened. "I think the dinner will have to wait for another night," Marilee says. We still have plenty of Chinese food anyways."

"Do you want me to take Celia tonight?" Betty asks. "She will be out as soon as her head hits the pillow."

"No, that's okay," Marilee says. "But if you guys want to stay the night—"

"Say no more," Betty says. "I'll go and talk to Charley."

"Thanks again, Betty," Marilee says.

"No problem," Betty says. "See y'all later."

18

Marilee knows Jamie is keeping something from her, she just doesn't know what. After Jamie falls asleep, she sneaks back to his office. She checks all the desk drawers and finds nothing suspicious. Not that she really knows what she is looking for. Noticing a tiny top drawer, she pulls. It's locked. "Ah, ha," she whispers. Now searching for keys, she goes through the drawers again but comes up empty. "Damnit," she says. Tip-toeing into the bedroom, she grabs Jamie's keys on the bed-side table. She flinches when he turns over, breathing a sigh of relief when he drifts back to sleep. As quietly as she can, she returns to the office. After a few tries, she finds the right key and smiles. "Now, let's see what was so important." As she opens the drawer, she gasps. Seeing Franks face hits her in the gut, but the date when the picture was taken is what really takes her breath away. "What the hell? This was taken when we came here."

"Shit! Marilee!" Jamie says in the doorway.

"Is Frank alive?" she asks, with hope in her eyes.

"No," he says with a sigh. He grabs the pictures from her, throwing them back in the desk.

"But the date–

"Is faked," he says, thinking up a lie quicker than he thought he was capable of. "This is why I didn't tell you, Marilee. I didn't want to get your hopes up."

"Are you positive?"

"I am one-hundred percent positive that Frank Garrison is dead." He kisses her forehead. "I'm sorry you had to see that, but I did have the drawer locked for a reason. Now go and try to get some sleep." He follows her back to bed. "I really am sorry you had to see those pictures."

"It's not your fault that I'm nosey." He laughs and kisses her, thankful that she didn't find out his secret. They snuggle up with each other and fall back to sleep. Jamie's sleep was a restless one. Wondering if he should tell her, he ends up having nightmares about her leaving him.

~

"Any news?" Jamie asks as he sits to eat breakfast with Dylan at Celia's.

"It's been a couple of weeks since we got the envelope, if something is going to happen it would be now. Will, Devin, and Arianna should be here today."

Jamie leans in closer to Dylan. "Marilee found the envelope."

"What? When?"

"The day we got it." Jamie says, knowing he is in for a good lecture.

"What? And you are telling me this now...after two weeks?" Dylan says, trying hard not to yell across the table at him.

"I told her it was a hoax and she believed me, so all is good."

"So you lied to her," Dylan says with a sigh. "Again."

"Well, what was I supposed to do?" Jamie says, grinding his teeth. "It was late. I woke up to her snooping, no, breaking in to my locked desk drawer. I had to think fast."

"Come clean, Jamie and face the consequences. We have both got to start being honest with the girls. Why do you think they think they need to sneak around and do things without telling us? If we aren't honest with them, they aren't going to be honest with us."

"What is done is done!" Jamie says, stoking his hair with annoyance. "Anyway, I thought it may work with the factions too."

Dylan laughs. "Do you actually think they are going to fall for that?"

"It's worth a try," Jamie says. "If we can get someone to say the photos were fake—

"No!" Dylan says.

Jamie arches his eyebrow at him. "Wasn't it you who told me to come up with something else because when the factions find out they wouldn't resign the agreement?"

"Yes, I'm sorry," Dylan says with a sigh.

"What is wrong?" Jamie says, leaning in again to whisper. "Why are you so on edge?"

"Charlotte and I had a fight," Dylan says.

"Oh, you two never fight."

"I know because I usually tell her everything, but here lately she knows I've been keeping stuff from her."

"Sorry," Jamie says.

"I told her everything, Jamie."

Jamie glares at Dylan, trying to contain his anger. He takes a deep breath and bites his jaw. "Why would you do that?"

"Because she deserved to know and Marilee does too," Dylan says. "It's time to tell the truth."

"But the factions—

"I talked to William last night," Dylan says.

"And?" Jamie takes a hard swallow.

"He said that he thinks we should tell the truth."

"Really?" Jamie says with a laugh.

"It doesn't matter if they don't sign anymore anyway." Dylan smirks and takes a sip of his coffee.

Giving a side-ways glance at his surroundings, he gives a little snicker of confusion. "What are you talking about?"

"Guess who our new boss is?"

"Who?"

"Devin." Dylan notices Jamie's surprise. "Jamie, did you hear me?"

"Yeah...you could have led with that," Jamie says, straightening himself after being frozen in shock for a moment.

"Sorry, but how great is that."

"How?" Jamie asks, still a bit confused as to how Devin of all people is heading up the Ireland faction.

"Well, most of the Ireland faction leaders was killed off by that psyco Nigel. The obvious choice was Devin's father, but he declined. The next choice, Devin. He made the announcement last night. If you'd read your email every once in a while..." Jamie fiddles with his coffee cup for a moment. "Oh my God," Dylan says with a laugh. "You are jealous of Devin."

Jamie chuckles. "That is just stupid. I'm just worried about Arianna."

Dylan straightens up in his chair as he sees Marilee coming. "Well, you only need to worry about one woman right now and here she comes. Tell her now." Dylan stands up when she reaches the table. "Hey, Marilee, take my seat," he says. "I'm headed back upstairs anyway."

"Okay, thanks," she says noticing Jamie's face looks a bit rigid. "What's wrong?"

"Let's take a ride." Jamie sighs.

~

On his way upstairs Dylan notices Charley at the front desk. He sighs, dreading the apology. "Hey, Charley," he says.

"What?" Charley says, not even giving him a glance. Charley rolls his eyes at his immaturity, but he was eighteen not too long ago too so he gives him a pass. They haven't talked since Dylan made the comment.

"Look, what I said a few weeks back, I'm sorry. I just don't like when you talk down about our life. I know it's not an ideal life, but we have to secure it at all costs."

Charley sighs and throws his pen down, finally looking up at Dylan. "It's the at all costs thing that bothers me."

"And I get that, I do, but you have to understand—"

"Understand what?" Charley says as he comes around the desk to get closer to Dylan. "Should I understand that he can hurt my sister any time he wants?" He lowers his voice, but brings his face as close to Dylan's as he possibly can without causing a scene. "And then make an excuse up about how it was for The Family, it had to be done, or it couldn't be helped. I'm sorry, but I just can't do that."

"You are like a brother to me, Charley, and I know you think there is a different life out there for your family." He puts his hand on Charley's shoulder to help him grasp his next statement. "This is it, Charley. There is not another life. I'm sorry, but you, Marilee, Betty, your brothers, and Bryce will never be safe. If you think hard about it, you know I'm right, so just start being good with. Pick a role within the Family. The sooner you pick, the sooner you can get used to your life here." Charley bites his jaw. He knows that Dylan is right, but he also knows it will take a lot of time to get used to turning his head when they do something dreadful and if he has to do something dreadful, will he be able to?

Dylan pats Charley's face and starts to walk off. "You suck at apologies, you know." Charley says.

"I know," Dylan says. "Why do you think it took me two weeks?"

~

"Okay," Marilee says as they get on the boat. "You can't get me on a boat every time you think I'm going to run away. Just tell me what is going on."

"Okay, sit down," Jamie says. "I lied to you again."

"About?" she says as she sits cautiously. He tries to grab her hand, but she pulls it away. "Not until you tell me." His stomach gets tied up in a knot and he thinks of lying again, but thinks better of it.

"The envelope..."

"Oh my God!" Her eyes light up with hope. "Is Frank alive?"

"No," he says, watching her hope disappear. "I mean, he was, but..." He pulls his hair because he don't even know how to begin.

"Jamie, you aren't making any sense, just tell me."

"Remember Nigel and how he looked exactly like me?"

"Yeah."

"Well, Frank, the Frank you knew wasn't—

Her eyes widen as she figures out what he isn't telling her. "No," she says, shaking her head back and forth. "That's not true. Why would you—

"Marilee, I'm sorry, but that wasn't the real Frank. It was some man who was already dying. They paid him to pretend—

"What exactly? To pretend to love me and Celia until he died!" Tears begin to stream down her face.

"I didn't say he, whoever he was, didn't love the two of you."

She tries to hide how hurt she is, but it has struck a nerve inside her. "So where is the real Frank?"

"He's dead. I killed him."

She chuckles as she bites her lip. "Of course you did." She wipes the tears from her eyes. "How long ago?" He doesn't answer her because this could be the end of it. She may be okay with everything. But if he answers, he knows that she will be mad about how long he lied to her; after he promised he never would. "How long have you been lying, Jamie!" she yells.

"A while," he says. He looks at her and he can tell she isn't satisfied with his answer. "When we first arrived here." Tears fall from her eyes again, but they are silent tears. "I wish I didn't have to tell you, but—

"Then why? Why now?" she says.

"The factions were going to find out and I knew that you would eventually—

Tears stop flowing as she looks at him. The expression on her face is very apparent to him. She is even more pissed than she was when she knew he kissed Ruby. "So the only reason you are telling me now is because you had to?"

"No, I didn't...I was just trying to look out for you."

"No, Jamie," she says, standing. "You were just looking out for yourself. How can I marry you when all you do is lie to me?" His head jolts up to look at her.

"What are you saying?" He stands up to put his arm around her.

"No!" she says, backing away. "I can't, I can't keep doing this. You keep hurting me and I'm not strong enough for this!"

"Marilee, I'm sorry, let's go back inside and have a drink. We can calm down—

"No, how can I marry you..." She thinks about Frank, the old Frank she once knew. She is reminded that this is something he would do and it hits her hard. "You are just like him, Frank, a monster. How can I marry a monster?" He looks down ashamed, but mostly hurt and shocked at her words. She steps off the boat and runs back to the lodge. He falls to his knees to let what she just said sink in.

"She thinks I'm a monster," he says as his eyes become glossy. "She isn't coming back this time." With a blank stare, he sits until his friends find him.

"There you are," Arianna says. She puts her arm around him and he jumps out of his thoughts. "Are you okay?"

"What happened?" Charlotte asks. "Marilee came storming in the lodge crying. She ran out a few minutes later with her suitcase. She left, Jamie." He looks back to the ground and shakes his head. "She's gone," he says. "She called me a monster."

"Why didn't you go after her?" Dylan asks, a bit confused. He thought Jamie would do whatever it took to keep her from leaving.

"She said she couldn't marry a monster," Jamie says with gritted teeth.

Charlotte sighs. "She didn't mean it, Jamie."

"No," Jamie says with a glare. "She meant it."

"She'll be back, Jamie," Dylan says. "I know it."

"Not this time. She's gone."

~

Jamie waits all day, but Marilee doesn't come home. Sitting on the floor of Celia's room, he flicks through some photos of them all together. He had everything and he blew it. Throwing the photos down he goes to his office to have a drink. One drink turns into five and when he finishes the bottle the pain is still there. He calls for his driver to drive him into town. He doesn't want to deal with everyone judging him at the bar downstairs. He wants to be alone so he goes to the Michaelson. He keeps drinking until he is a bit numb. The room is spinning, but as long as he doesn't think about her he doesn't care. "Mr. Garrison?" the bartender asks. "Would you like me to call your driver?"

"No, Roger," Jamie says, pushing himself off the barstool and throwing his money on the counter. "I think I will stay here tonight." He stumbles to the elevator, but makes it to his room. Before he gets the key in the door he hears someone call out his name.

"Jamie?" Ruby calls. "What are you doing here?" She asks. When she gets a closer look she genuinely becomes concerned. "Are you drunk?" she says, noticing he can barely stand.

"Well, Mrs. Brown, your timing is impeccable.

"Yeah, why is that?" she asks as he comes closer.

"I need to let off some steam." He opens his door, trying to steady himself. "Are you game?"

She hesitates, but smiles. "Always, Mr. Garrison," she says, walking in the room. He follows in behind her and closes the door.

19

Feeling a bit of guilt for calling him a monster, she looks back for a split second. That is the one thing Jamie has always been scared of becoming. That is why she said it, to hurt him, but now she wishes she could take it back. That's probably why he never came after her. She throw her suitcase on the bed and heads for the door to go and comfort him. The thought of Frank enters her mind and anger feels her heart again. How could he lie...again? Does he not know how much it hurts her when he lies? She packs some clothes in her suitcase, just enough to scare him, and she tells Betty to meet her at her Dad's. As soon as she exits the lodge, she knows she will be back, but she has to do something drastic to make him start being honest with her. Charlotte tries to stop her, but she runs past her. If she stops now she may not be able to leave.

~

She sits at the table with her family as they eat dinner. "So," Bryce says. "What's new?" She hesitates to tell her father what is going on, but she tells them all. Why lie? She is tired of everyone lying.

"Oh," Bryce says, after her story. "Well..."

"That is all you can say," Marilee says.

"What do you want me to say?" he says. "I'm on your side. I think he should stop lying to you, but..."

"But what?" Marilee sighs.

"I don't want it to sound like I'm on his side, but being a man, I can sympathize. You know he didn't tell you those things for a reason. He wanted to spare your feelings. You would have been devastated if you knew back then that it was all a lie."

"I was still devastated, but I get your point. It probably would've hurt more back then, I guess. I just can't help think what else he is lying about. How can I marry him if I can't trust him to tell me the truth?"

"You have two choices," Bryce says. "You can be good with the lying, knowing that he does it for your own good? Or you can trust him enough not to lie to you in the future? That is something you need to decide. But we all know waiting around here is only postponing it. You will go back to him in the end."

She rolls her eyes at her dad. "Thanks."

"It's true," Charley says. "You know you will be back so how are you going to play it? Though I am a little happy knowing he is suffering, the monster thing was a bit much."

"That was a bit cold," Betty says.

"Hello, whose side are y'all on?"

"Always yours, sweetheart," Bryce says. "But that is Jamie's worst fear. You might have caused some damage."

She thinks for a moment. "Crap," she says. "You don't think he'd do anything crazy do you?"

"Like what?" Betty says. "Burn down the city?" She notices the uneasiness in Marilee's eyes. "I'm kidding. I wouldn't worry. I'll call Charlotte to make sure."

"Tell her I'll be back in the morning," Marilee says. "But don't tell Jamie."

~

They all get to the lodge early. Marilee takes Celia to her room and waits for Jamie to return. The bed is still made so he never came home last night. The apartment feels empty and she is getting worried.

Calling his phone, she jumps as she hears the buzzing on the table. "What did I do?" she says, pacing in Celia's room. As the silence of the apartment sends chills down her spine, thoughts of worst-case-scenarios enter her mind. Pulling her hair in frustration, she almost falls to her knees, but hears the front door open. She gasps. "Jamie," she says.

As Jamie walks through the front door, he smells a familiar perfume that makes his stomach fall to the floor. He looks up as Marilee runs down the hallway. With a lump forming, his speech is taken from him. She runs into his arms and her touch breaks him out of his frozen state. With his eyes closed, he grips her tight taking in everything that is her. Her smell, her touch, and the way she feels in his arms and then it hits him how stupid he was. "I thought you left me for good," he says, trying to make last night seem okay in his head.

"I'm sorry, I just needed to think. I didn't mean it. I never want to be away from you again."

Jamie can't think straight as he pushes her back to look at her. "I thought you left. You said you would never leave."

"You hurt me, you lied."

"I know," he says. "I'm sorry, but..." she looks into his eyes and she can see something...hurt, shock, something she can't decipher. "Never mind, your back."

"And I will never leave again," she says. "So how about the end of the month?"

"For what?" he says, still amazed that she is back.

"To get married."

He gasps. "What? But...how...what?" he stutters. She gives him a kiss to snap him back to the conversation. He grabs her face and smiles. After her kiss, he can think again.

"Are you sure you want to marry a monster?" he says.

"I didn't mean that, Jamie," she says. "I'm so sorry."

"That hurt more than you know," he says, finally getting his stature back.

"I know, I know," she says. "Forgive me and I'll forgive you."

"Don't ever leave me again and we have a deal."

"I won't," she says, "never, ever," she says. He kisses her again to make sure she is real.

"Celia?" he says with excitement.

"She is in her room." Marilee smiles as he runs back to go see her. "I'll make some coffee. She looks around glad she decided to come home. Shaking her head, she can't believe she almost messed this whole thing up. She texts everyone that she is back so that they don't worry and then goes back to stand in the doorway of Celia's room. She watches silently for a moment as Jamie plays with Celia. "Do you want to go get some breakfast downstairs?"

"Sure," he says, kissing Celia on the forehead. "You two go ahead, I need to take care of something."

"Okay," she says, bending down to pick Celia up. She notices that he is avoiding eye contact with her. "Is everything okay?"

"Yeah," he says with a smile to reassure her. "Everything is great."

"I really am sorry," she says as she strokes his cheek.

"I am too," he says with a sigh.

~

Everyone is waiting downstairs as Marilee and Celia walk in the restaurant. "You had us worried sick!" Charlotte says, giving Marilee a hug.

"I just had to think a bit and then I realized how silly I was being."

"Did you really call Jamie a monster?" Arianna says, raising her eyebrow.

Marilee sighs at Arianna for bringing it up. "I didn't mean it; I was upset."

"Well," Devin says to change the subject. "You are back now. So let's have some food."

"And we never got to celebrate Devin' new promotion!" Dylan says.

"What promotion?" Marilee asks as she gets Celia situated in the high-chair.

"He is now in charge of all the factions...world-wide," Arianna says as giddy as a little girl.

"Congratulations, Devin," Marilee says. Jamie joins them at the table.

"Yeah, congratulations, boss man," Jamie says with a smirk. Devin grabs a biscuit from a tray as the waiter walks by and throws it at Jamie. "That's wasting food." Jamie says.

"After breakfast, we need to have a meeting," Devin says as the waitress brings them their mimosas.

"Well, to Devin," Jamie says, raising his glass. "And I never thought I would say this, but I'm glad you married Marilee." Laughter spreads across the table.

"Here, here," says Arianna. "But I am also glad you divorced her." Everyone laughs as Charley and Betty finally join them.

"It's about time, guys," Jamie says as they take their seat.

"What are we celebrating?" Betty asks.

"The fact that Devin is the new boss man," Jamie says.

Charley laughs as they all take a sip of their drinks.

"So," Charley says pointing to Devin. "He gets to tell you..." he says as he points to Jamie, "...what to do?"

"Yes, Charley," Jamie says with an eye roll. "That is how it works."

"That's awesome," Charley says as he takes his drink from the waiter.

"I couldn't agree with you more, Charley," Devin says as he clinks his glass to Charley's.

"Well, I'm glad we are all one big happy family then," Jamie says.

Jamie's head turns to the entrance of the restaurant as Vanessa walks in. He waves her over. "Can I join you guys?" she says.

"Of course," Dylan says pulling up an extra chair and kissing her on the cheek. The waitress immediately brings her a mimosa. "To Family," she says. As they toast Jamie smiles for a split second knowing the moment couldn't be more perfect...until he remembers what he has done. He glances at Marilee, but when she looks back at him he turns away. Her smile fades and she wonders how bad she must have hurt him when she left. A pain creeps up in her stomach. Wanting to cry, she takes another drink and holds in the pain.

After breakfast, the guys go to their meeting in the manager's office. "So, Jamie, I hear you need a new arms dealer." Devin jumps right to business.

"Yes," Jamie says with a sigh ready for a lecture. "It couldn't be helped."

"I know," Devin sneers. "But I may have someone who can take his place." Devin hands him a card. "He's a bit skittish, but loyal. Please don't scare him off." Jamie gives him a nod. "Now, have the two of you decided who your advisors will be?" Jamie and Dylan give each other shrugs.

"Shit," Dylan says. "I didn't even think about it."

"Neither did I," Jamie says. Can't we just be each other's advisors?"

"I was thinking that too, but with one change," Devin says.

"What is that?" Jamie says, folding his arms over his chest.

"Well, you two can advise each other because that is what you do, but I would like to bring in a third advisor."

"I don't know," Dylan says. "It sounds like they'd just be in the way. Plus, we handle things pretty good alone."

"I'd have to disagree," Devin says. Jamie bites his tongue and Devin notices.

"Sorry, Jamie." Devin laughs. "What I meant is, though you two make a great team, you're both kings and you can't be together all the time. I think we need a third person to half their time with each of you."

"Okay, so who did you have in mind?" Jamie asks with a hint of frustration in his tone.

"Well, I know it may be a little peculiar, but I was thinking of someone that could keep you two in line when needed."

Will laughs at his remark. "Who the hell could do that?" Jamie and Dylan turn to him with a glare.

"Should we bring up all of your unfortunate...how should I put it, Will?" Jamie puts his finger to his chin to think. "Oh, yes, misunderstandings."

"No, no," Will says, getting a giggle out of them. "So, Devin, who is this person you speak of?"

"Well," Devin says as he walks to the door and opens it. Starring as Vanessa walks in, they are silent for a moment.

"Seriously," Jamie says, rubbing his forehead.

"Hey," Vanessa says, insulted.

"Sorry," Jamie says, quickly standing to pat her on the shoulder. "But this goes against tradition."

"You forget," Devin says. "I have the power to change any tradition." He gives Jamie a wink. "Of course it is your decision who you appoint, but she was Marcel's unofficial advisor for years and my dad highly recommends her."

"Come on guys," Vanessa says. "What do I need to do, cut my hair?"

"No!" Will shouts. "Let's not do anything drastic." He walks over to Vanessa and takes her hand. "And might I add that if these dumbasses say no, I would gladly take you as my advisor." Vanessa blushes and pulls her hand away.

"Okay, down boy," Jamie says as he looks to Dylan for an agreement. "Vanessa, we would be honored for you to be our advisor."

"Of course," Dylan says as they all come in for a hug.

"This Family hugs a lot, don't they?" Devin says.

"I know right," Will says as he joins in.

Charley walks in and rolls his eyes. "Sorry, I'll come back later." Jamie grabs him and pulls him inside their huddle. "Not necessary," Charley says.

"Yes, it is," Dylan says. "You're Family."

"Yes, and eighteen so we need to figure out what to do with you," Jamie says. Charley gives him a glare. "Only if you think you are ready." Jamie adds. Devin gives them both a strange look and Jamie quickly changes the subject and breaks away from the huddle. "So what is it that you wanted, Charley?"

"Oh, Dad wanted the reservation list for this weekend. He said you had some high priority guests."

"I almost forgot," Jamie says, opening the desk drawer. "Here it is."

"Thanks," Charley says and walks out feeling everyone's eyes on him.

"Thanks, Charley," Jamie says as his eyes go to Devin.

"Okay," Devin says. "Jamie, you know he has to do something."

"I know, but I want him to come to a decision on his own and not feel forced," he says staring blankly at the wall. "Like I was."

"Got it," Devin says with a smile. "But maybe you could show him a bit while he's deciding. Show him all the...perks."

"Like what?" Jamie says with a hint of laughter.

Devin rolls his eyes and leans on the desk with his arms folded. "He is eighteen, Jamie. What does he like?"

"Betty," Dylan says with a snort.

"Well then, make Betty happy, make Charley happy."

"That would be where I come in I suppose," Vanessa says. "And I have a brilliant idea, that is, if you boys can move along without me." As Vanessa leaves the room they both glare at Devin.

"Are you sure about this?" Dylan asks.

"Most definitely." Devin grins.

20

Marilee waits patiently back at the apartment for Jamie's meeting to be over. Hours go by and she starts to think he may not want to see her. Tears begin to fall and she quickly wipes them away as she drinks her coffee. Lunch time comes so she fixes Celia some lunch still pondering the thought of Jamie's standoffish behavior. A knock sounds at the door as she sits Celia in her high-chair. "Coming," she says, hurrying to get to the door. When she opens it she freezes for a moment and then gasps. She stares in disbelief as she looks at the familiar face in the doorway. "Sasha!" Marilee says. "What...how...?" She grabs Sasha by the hand and pulls her inside the apartment, hugging her. "How did you get here?" Sasha smiles and looks back toward the doorway. Jamie walks in with a strut and gives her a wink.

"I thought we could use her," he says.

"Oh my God!" she cries and runs to into his arms. As she runs to Jamie, Sasha runs to Celia.

"Oh, I missed you so much my little Celia," Sasha says picking her up and twirling her around.

Marilee pulls Jamie's head down for her to whisper in his ear. "I didn't think you wanted to see me."

"Why on earth would you think that?" he says.

"Well, it's been like five hours since–

"I'm sorry," he says. "I've just been a bit busy."

"I see that," Marilee says with a smile and gives him another hug. "Wait, what about Betty? She had her heart set on helping out."

"I think she is going to be okay with it," Jamie says.

"You already told her didn't you?" She narrows her eyes.

"Come on," Jamie says with a chuckle. "I want to show you something."

"But Sasha just got here," Marilee says, turning back to Sasha and Celia.

"Well, we will all go then," he says grabbing Celia's diaper bag and points toward the door. "Ladies." Marilee arches her eyebrow, but starts toward the door.

"Where are we going?" she asks.

"You'll see."

Marilee is beyond happy that he isn't mad at her and excited to have Sasha back. They spent a lot of time in Ireland together. She was like an aunt to her and Sasha always loved Celia. It is like she has got a part of herself back that she thought was lost. It does bring the pain back to the surface about Frank being a fake, but at least Sasha was always real with her and Celia. "Have you seen Devin yet?"

"Not yet Miss Mac...I'm sorry," she says quickly. "What shall I call you now?"

"Just call me Marilee."

"It will be Garrison before long," Jamie says.

"Well, I will call you Miss Garrison then," Sasha says.

Marilee smiles as she notices where Jamie is taking them. They pull up to a big iron gate with a guard standing out front. He pushes a button and the gate opens. Marilee's jaw drops as she views the massive estate. "Jamie, how?"

"I hired someone to work around the clock. I know people," he says with a smirk.

"It's beautiful," she says, turning back to him. "You are amazing."

The driver pulls up to the large porch that wraps all the way around the house. She notices the big white columns first. They are huge. Then as they step out of the car she notices the elaborate friezes. It looks like an old plantation house, but new. "I love how it looks old...not old, but historical." Jamie grabs her hand to walk her up the steps. "Oh, look at the balconies." She grabs his arm with excitement. "I would think this was a restored plantation if I didn't know better."

"Wait until you see the inside," Jamie says as he opens the giant, mahogany front door. Marilee touches it to feel the wood and traces the Garrison crest that is carved in it. She walks into an open living room that again takes her back in time. Huge columns divide an elegant dining room and a massive living room. Jamie watches as she admires everything. "Do you like it?" Jamie says biting his lip.

She rolls her eyes at him. "I guess it will do," she says. "Of course I like it! Are you kidding me? It's a dream come true. Where is Celia's room?"

"Follow me," he says as he grabs Celia from Sasha. "Come on, Sasha, I'll show you your suite as well."

"I have a suite? Sir, you didn't have to give me a suite."

"I had to up one on the castle," Jamie says. "Plus, you need your own private area to get away once in a while." They continue to climb the stairs and Marilee runs her hand up the banister with an astounded expression. She turns upward to look at the elegant chandeliers and shakes her head. "I may have went a bit overboard," Jamie says noticing the familiar look.

"Not at all," she says. They reach the top of the stairs and Jamie hesitates.

"This way, I think," he says, making them laugh. "One way is Charlotte and Dylan's wing, one is Vanessa's, and the other is ours. As they walk down the hallway he remembers. "This is it." He turns and they walk in the doorway of Celia's room. "I was going to decorate, but I felt that you may want to take that."

"Wow," Marilee says. "This is perfect."

"You haven't seen the best part yet," Jamie says, walking over to the bathroom. "Come on." They follow him to the large bathroom and opens two double doors to reveal walk-in closet.

"Oh my," Marilee says. "She is going to love this when she is older."

"Yes, but that isn't what I wanted you to see." Jamie opens one of the drawers and pushes a button. The back of the wall slides open revealing another hallway.

"Oh my God," Marilee and Sasha say together.

"I learned something from Ron after all," Jamie says. "Would you like to see your suite Sasha?" She arches her eyebrow as he motions for her to go inside. "No, your room isn't inside." He laughs. "This is just another entrance, just in case." They walk down a hallway to another door. Marilee notices two more doors.

"What do those doors go to?" she asks.

"That one goes to stairs that lead down underground and to the woods. The other goes to our room. And this one..." Jamie says opening the door. "Goes to your room, Sasha." He smiles as her eyes light up. She continues to look around with the same excitement Marilee had.

"Mr. Garrison, you really shouldn't have went to so much trouble."

"Of course I should have. You are Family now and please call me Jamie."

"Thank you, Mr. Gar...I mean, Jamie."

"Now, if you could take Celia for a moment, I'd love to show Marilee our room."

"No problem," Sasha says, taking Celia from his arms. He takes Marilee and pulls her down the hallway.

"This is crazy," she says.

"You should see the basement," Jamie says.

"You didn't," she says, remembering how Jamie described Ron's old basement.

"Oh, I did," he says with a laugh.

"I can't believe you brought Sasha here. That was so—" He pushes her up against the wall.

"It's the least I could do," he says. "After everything."

"No, this is my fault. I should have been more understanding and I'm sorry for everything I said. I didn't mean it, Jamie, I promise. You have to know that. I'd never think that about you."

He sighs and brushes her cheek. "I know that now," he says. "But I did think you were gone for good."

"I was angry," she says. "Let's just put it all behind us, okay."

"Okay," he says. "But promise me you won't ever leave again."

"I promise."

"Good, because next time I will find you and bring you back."

She laughs, but wonders if he would. He opens the door and reveals their closet. The bathroom is huge and luxurious just as she would have thought. "Oh, Jamie," she says entering their room.

"It will look better once all the furniture is here."

"It is perfect," she says turning around to kiss him. As their lips touch she moves her hands down, but he stops her.

"What are you doing?" he says with a grin.

"They won't hear us," she says. He sighs as she touches him. He never thought she would touch him again. He buries the thoughts of the night before and takes her as she wishes. In the back of his mind he knows that this isn't going to end well.

~

"So when can we move in?" Marilee asks as the waiter brings them their food.

"Whenever you want," Jamie says. "It still needs furniture and decorating. That is going to be a lot of work."

"We can hire someone can't we?" she asks.

Jamie gets a knot in his stomach at the thought. "We could, but can't you do it?" he asks, hoping she complies with his request.

"That is a lot. I don't think I will have the time. I have a lot to do here. You usually don't have a problem with hiring people. What's up?"

He sighs, trying to hide the sick feeling in his stomach. "It's just that I would have to hire..."

"What?" Marilee says with her nose scrunched upward. "Why? There are other decorators."

"Well, she is the only one in the Family who decorates. We try to only hire Family. It is the way it has always been. We have a lot of friends, I'll see if I can find someone else." Marilee tries to hide her jealousy, but after she has seen photos of them kissing she can't help it. All the hurt he caused her comes back. She tries to rationalize it by thinking about her hurting him yesterday. It works enough for her to entertain the idea of Ruby decorating their house.

"As long as I don't have to see her I don't see the harm."

"Well, you may have to come in contact sooner or later," Jamie says. "It is your house." Jamie tries to convince her to hate the idea. "We can figure out something else."

"You know...it will be fine," she says. "I can get Vanessa to deal with her."

"Well, okay," Jamie says. "If you are sure." Jamie's head is spinning. He can't see Ruby again after..." He thinks quickly and decides that he will do just what Marilee said. Let Vanessa take care of it.

~

It has been about a week since Marilee has visited the house and she is getting a bit excited about taking this next step. Though she will miss living at the lodge, Celia is going to love her new room and the backyard. She is excited to have an actual home "I can't believe you won't be living at the lodge anymore," Betty says as she helps Marilee with the dishes at the restaurant, "and I can't believe your dishwasher quit on you."

"I'll still be here a lot," Marilee says. "And I know right. I hate when they just up and quit at the last second." She hands Betty a dish. "I can't believe you are going to be a doctor."

"I know, it's crazy." As they are giggling, someone comes through the swinging doors of the kitchen. Marilee's eyes widen when she looks up. Betty notices and turns to see a very good looking man Asian man with his jet black hair falling over one eye. She freezes, waiting for Marilee to introduce them.

"Li?" Marilee finally acknowledges him. "What are you doing here?"

He walks a bit closer to them, placing his hands in his pant pockets as he leans on the counter. "I had some business with Jamie so I thought I would come and say hi."

"Hi," she says, blushing. "This is my sister Betty. Betty this is Li, from the Chinese restaurant. Betty remembers Charlotte telling her about him.

"Oh," she says with a smile and holds out her hand. "That Li." Marilee widens her eyes at her as she shakes Li's hand. "Nice to meet you."

"It's nice to meet you too, Betty," Li says, blushing as well. He takes a look around the kitchen. "This is impressive."

"Would you like something?"

"Maybe some other time. I'm late for a meeting with my uncle. I just wanted to pop in to say hi. I'll see you another time perhaps. He nods his head toward Betty. Until next time."

"Okay, see you later," Marilee says. Betty waits for him to leave and turns to Marilee.

"Wow," she says.

"What?" Marilee asks, clearing her throat.

"Oh, come on," Betty says. "You mean to tell me that you didn't think he was totally hot?"

"I don't know," Marilee says with a shrug. "I guess he is okay."

"Alright, then," Betty says. "Denial it is."

"Who is in denial?" Jamie walks through the door making them both jump.

"Nobody," Marilee says greeting him with a kiss. "Where are you off to so late?" she asks, noticing his attire.

"I have some meetings to go to so I will be home late. Charley is going too."

"Really?" Marilee asks, looking toward Betty.

"Yeah, he might as well try to entertain the idea of being part of the Family," Betty says.

"Fine," Marilee says. "But please keep him safe."

"Of course," Jamie says. "Oh, did you get a chance to look at those patterns?"

"Yeah, I put them on the bedside table," Marilee says.

"Great, I'll drop them off on the way. See you later." She gives him a smile and he gives her a quick peck on the cheek. "See ya Betty." He turns back to give Betty a peck on the cheek as well. She gives him a quick smile and a nod and resumes cleaning the dishes.

"Okay, be safe," Marilee says as he walks out the door. Betty glances at the door and then to Marilee.

"Umm, what was that about?" she asks.

"Nothing," Marilee says, rinsing the soapy dishes Betty has placed in the sink. "We are getting the house decorated."

"Why?" she asks, handing Marilee another pot.

"I don't have the time to do my own decorating," Marilee says, motioning to the mess in the kitchen.

"Good point," Betty says with a laugh. "Who did you hire to do it?"

Marilee rolls her eyes not wanting to tell Betty because she knows it will lead to a lecture. Plus, she really hates even saying her name out loud, but she doesn't get a chance to say anything. Betty sighs knowing Marilee's silence means they hired Ruby and she throws another pot down in Marilee's side of the sink. "Really?" Betty says. "After Jamie and her kissed? What is wrong with you?"

"Look, Jamie hasn't even had contact with her that much. He has been getting Vanessa to do it all. She is the only decorator in the Family and they have to hire Family. Besides, she is probably almost done by now anyway."

"Fine, but when something goes down I'm going to remind you that you put yourself in the situation."

"What situation?" Marilee laughs.

"Jamie is still a man, Marilee," she says, giving her a stare. "I know he loves you, but let me paint you a picture." She places her soapy hands in the air and waves them around. "Jamie goes to her work to drop off the patterns, but she is nowhere to be found, suddenly, he yells out to her. She yells back to him to come upstairs. Jamie thinks it is weird, but goes up anyway and finds her naked."

"That wouldn't—

"Wait," Betty says, placing her finger up to Marilee's face. "I'm not done. He tells her no because he loves you, but she takes her naked body and places it up against him. He says no again and shoves her away." Betty gasps for effect. "But Ruby is relentless and comes toward him again. He scans her naked body as she steps toward him; because, after all, he is still a man. He backs away, but eventually he backs up against the wall. He tells her that nobody will ever take him away from you and she laughs. Her naked body presses up against him and he swallows hard. The pressure is building up inside him. Soon it is too much for him to take as she—

"Okay, Betty," Marilee says. "I get it. What have you been watching on the television?" she laughs. "There is no way that happens in real life."

"You never know," Betty says.

"Let's just go Miss Storyteller." Marilee giggles again, but the story did make her a bit nervous. She rinses the last pot and places it the drying basket. I'll put these away tomorrow morning. Go aggravate Charlotte or something."

"Okay," Betty says, giving Marilee a hug. "Just don't let Ruby drag this out to long. She may want to keep this gig up forever."

"I won't. See you tomorrow." Betty leaves and Marilee goes to lock everything up. On her way to shut off the lights she gets an eerie feeling. She stops for a second, but decides to trust her instincts and she runs out the door as fast as she can. She calls security and has them check it out. She heads back upstairs and quickly locks the door behind her."

21

"Alright, guys, are y'all ready to show Charley a good time?"

"Hell yeah," Dylan says.

"I thought we were going to a meeting," Charley says as he gives the guys a curious look. They laugh.

"We just had to tell the girls that," Devin says. "They wouldn't have liked where we are going."

"And that is?" Charley says.

Jamie rubs his hands together in excitement. "Fight night."

"What exactly is fight night?" Charley asks, not liking the name of it.

"Another tradition," Devin says. "Don't worry, it isn't as bad as it sounds. It used to be, but now they have rules. Now it is just two men in a cage letting off steam."

"I've been waiting for this for a while," Jamie says.

"Here we are boys," the driver says as they pull up to the warehouse.

"This place is packed!" Charley says as they all step out of the limousine and smile.

"They all came to see the King fight." Dylan says, patting Jamie on the back.

Charley arches his brow and looks to Jamie. "You're fighting?

"Got to let some steam off somehow," he says, giving him a wink. "Have you ever seen the Ultimate Fighting Championship?"

"Well, yeah," Charley says.

"It is the same thing," Jamie says. "But it is only for the Families. They don't like outsiders so put this on." Jamie hands him a ring with a 'G' on it. "It is yours...if you want it." Charley looks at it and runs his fingers over it. As he turns it over he notices his initials carved on the inside. He slides it on his finger and it seems to fit perfectly. They nod to the guy at the door and they walk inside the warehouse. Walking through the fog of smoke and smell of liquor, they see a cage in the middle of the huge warehouse. Chairs are packed with people waiting for the fights to start. Everyone stares as they work their way to the stairs that will take them to the second landing. Charley has never seen anything like this. He turns to Jamie.

"Only you could turn a warehouse into an arena," he says. Jamie gives him a snicker.

"You guys go on and get the seats. I need to go speak to some people," Jamie says. The announcer starts his speech over the intercom and everyone cheers. The guys get drinks and takes their seats. The women's fights are first.

"Yes," Will says. "The women's' round." He shakes Charley's shoulders as he gets amped up and this is the first time that Charley has felt like one of the guys. After the first fight is over Jamie comes to join them. He orders more drinks as the next fighter is announced. They all freeze when they see her come in the ring. "What the hell?" Will says. "Is that Vanessa?" He turns to Jamie and Dylan. "Did you guys know about this?"

"No," Jamie says, standing up to get a better view. Vanessa turns up to get a look at where they are sitting. She notices them standing up to get a better view so she gives them a wink.

"I'm sorry guys," Will says. "But I'm in love with your sister."

"I just hope she is good," Dylan says. The fight begins and they start to get worried.

"Come on," Jamie says. "This is Vanessa. You know she is good." They squirm every time she gets hit and Jamie starts to come down to the cage. He sees her put her hand up to him so he stays. She regains her focus and starts to win. She has the same anger as Jamie and she shows no mercy on her opponent. When the announcer stops the fight and raises her hand, a feeling of joy comes over her that she hasn't felt in a long time. She takes a glimpse up at the boys cheering at her victory and the corner of her mouth turns upward. She knows in an instant she is finally where she belongs. She is back with her Family. She steps out of the ring and walks to the second landing where the guys are. Will is the first one to greet her. "Awesome fight!" he says.

"Thanks," she says as he gives her a hug.

"Why didn't you tell us?" Jamie says, pushing Will out of the way to get to her.

"Because you two would have tried to talk me out of it," she says.

Dylan takes her towel and wipes the blood from her lip. "Well, yeah," he says, raising an eyebrow.

"It will heal," she says, grabbing her towel back. "Don't make a fuss. Just buy me a drink." He smiles and waves his hand to the waiter.

"Round of Bourbon!" Dylan says.

"So," Vanessa says as she sits down beside Charley. "They finally got you out and about?"

"Yep," Charley says, taking a sip of his beer. "That was a good fight."

"Thank you," she says. "Sometimes you just have to let off some steam...you know?"

"Sounds good to me," Charley says with a crooked smile.

"Well, go for it, then," Vanessa says making Jamie's head turn as if someone screamed his name. "I think they–

"Vanessa, not tonight," Jamie says. "It's his first time here. Let's just show him a good time."

Turning back to Charley, she gives him a wink. "Maybe next time."

"So we can party until Jamie's fight then," Will says as he clinks glasses with everyone. "Awesome." He chugs his drink in two seconds and calls the waiter back. "Keep them coming please, good fellow."

"Sandra!" Vanessa yells. A small, half naked, petite girl comes over and Charley spits a bit of his beer out. "I'd like to buy a dance for someone."

"Sure thing," Sandra says. "Who?"

Vanessa puts her hand on Charley's shoulder. "For this cutie right here."

"Oh no," Charley says. "I'm good." Sandra pulls Charley to his feet as he resists a bit.

"Oh, come on," Sandra says. "I won't bite...too much." She giggles as she pulls him by the hand. He gives a worried look toward Jamie, but all Jamie can do is laugh and shrug his shoulders.

"Betty is going to kill us all."

"He needs to lighten up just a bit," Vanessa says.

"Well, this is a start," Devin says. "We just need to help him feel like part of the group and with all that pinned up anger, Vanessa had a good idea about fighting him."

"Yes, but Marilee would kill me if I brought him back battered and bruised the first night we take him out," Jamie says.

"Good point," Devin says with a laugh. "All we can do is show him a good time, get him drunk, and make him feel important."

"Hey, Sarah," Vanessa says. Another half-naked girl comes over and she hands her some cash. "When Sandra is done with that one. Show him a good time."

"You got it," Sarah says.

"Vanessa!" Jamie shouts. "Betty is our friend."

"I know," she shouts back. "It's just a dance. Besides, Betty will thank me when he gets home." Jamie rolls his eyes and drinks his Bourbon and the rest continue to party.

Charley works his way back to the group, feeling guilty as hell. They smile when they see him coming. He rolls his eyes at their immature teasing and giggles as he sits back down next to Vanessa. "That was so not cool," he says. She smiles and kisses him on the cheek.

"You are just too adorable," she says. He smiles and blushes as Jamie hands him another beer.

"Charley, you sure you don't want something stronger," Will asks.

"Nah, I'm good," he says. "Thanks."

"Hey, Jamie," Dylan says as the announcer starts to announce the next fight. "It's almost time for you to fight."

"Right," Jamie chugs his drink down. "I'll see y'all in a bit." His Adrenaline is pumping as he gets ready. He really needs this. All this penned up rage is getting to him. Not knowing who he is about to fight, he continues to warm up in the locker room. When he hears his name called, he shivers; and not a scared shiver, but an excited and thrilling shiver. Making his way to the cage, his eyes are full of fury. Even Dylan spots it and smiles. As Jamie steps into the ring, a bearded Irishman stares at him. Trying to intimidate Jamie, he flexes his muscles and growls. Jamie gives the man a nod and his lip curls upward. Confused, the Irishman looks to the crowd.

Of course the man knows he is fighting a king, but rules state that no matter status it is to be a fair fight and nobody is to take a fall. Considering the size difference, the Irishman is sure this will be a quick fight. Jamie closes his eyes for a moment and breathes in deeply, letting the rage take control of him. As the bell rings to start the fight, Jamie opens himself up so the man can get in a few good punches.

"What the hell is he doing?" Dylan says, jumping up with worry.

"Getting pissed," Vanessa says with a smile. After Jamie gets punched a few more times Dylan yells down to him.

"Enough, Jamie!" he says. "Take him out!" Jamie smiles with blood coming from his lip, shaking off the punches.

Looking up at the Irishman, he shrugs his shoulders. "Well, that was a bit of fun." His stance changes and he unleashes all the anger that has been festering inside. He is giving the poor Irishman a good beating as the bell sounds to end the fight, but Jamie doesn't stop.

Vanessa looks toward Dylan and knows what is going through Jamie's head. "You better go pull him off, Dylan," she says. Dylan rushes to the cage. He is the only one that can stop him when he is fighting like this. As he gets to the cage, he grabs Jamie and pulls him off yelling in his ear. Jamie calms down when he hears Dylan's voice. "Brother, it's me...it's me...calm down." Patting him on the chest, he pulls him out of the cage.

Charley stares down at Jamie as if he were a madman. "Don't judge," Vanessa says, noticing his nose curling upward.

"I wasn't," Charley says, taking another swig of beer.

"Yes," Vanessa corrects him. "You are always judging." He doesn't correct her this time. "That is alright," she says. "It just hasn't hit you yet."

"What?"

Vanessa looks over and notices that Devin is listening to their conversation. "You know," she says, waving at the waiter for two more beers. "Most people don't choose this life. They are either born into it or forced."

"I know, but it just seems like sometimes they like it a bit too much."

Vanessa can't help but laugh. "You think he likes that?" She points to Jamie wiping the blood off of himself. "He needs that to keep him sane. We all have to let some demons out every once in a while or they rip our soul to bits."

"But you are a doctor. At least you help people."

"Well," she says with a snicker as she sips her drink. "Girls in the Family have to, well most, have to give back to the Family somehow. I chose to be a doctor because I figured with as many people as we hurt, though all were bad, maybe I can save just as many."

"That is what I'm talking about," Charley says, sliding a bit closer to her. "You still care about the world."

She rolls her eyes. "You don't think that they do? Those two down there," she points as they start their way up the landing. "Those two care more about this God forsaken world than they should." She gets even closer to him and talks a bit lower. "You know he has plans to change this world for the better. He can't tell you his plans until he is sure this is what you want. He has a method to his madness. You just have to trust him. We do the best we can in this world, Charley. We make the best of a bad situation...until we don't have to anymore."

"You say you didn't have a choice in being a part of this world, but I do. Y'all want me to choose this world, but would you have chosen it if the choice was given?"

"You've already chosen, Charley," Vanessa says. "You just don't want to admit it. I think this Family could use someone like you. The more that care, the more we can do. Think about it." She stands up, swaying a bit and leans on Charley to get her balance. "Wow," she giggles. "I think it's about time for me to go home. Can someone please give me a lift?"

"Yes, please," Will says. She smiles. "I was hoping you'd speak up."

Charley thinks on what Vanessa has said to him as Devin comes and sits next to him. "So are you enjoying yourself tonight?"

"Yeah, thanks," Charley says with a sigh. "I need your help, Devin."

"With what?"

"Where do you see me? I know nothing about any of this. Where would I even fit?" Charley looks down at his feet, feeling ignorant of their world. Devin smiles and places his hand on Charley's shoulder.

"I felt the exact same way, my friend, we all did. The first step is learning about all the in's and out's. We won't make you dive right in. You can shadow for a while and see what interests you." Charley nods and finishes his beer as Jamie and Dylan come back to sit down.

"Where did Vanessa go?"

"Will took her home," Devin says.

"Well, that was inevitable," Jamie says.

“Are we ready to go?” Dylan says, looking toward Charley.

When they are all in agreement they head back to the lodge a bit on the tipsy side.

22

Marilee's eyes slightly open as the morning light from the window hits her face. Turning over in the bed she snuggles up to Jamie, noticing the bruising on his cheek. With a slight sigh, she wonders what kind of trouble he got into last night. Biting her lip, she decides to let him sleep for a while. As she walks to the bathroom, his phone starts to buzz. She quickly picks it up so it doesn't wake him. Her eyebrow arches at the message. It reads, "Where are you?" It is from Ruby. "I miss you."

"What the hell?" Marilee says, waking Jamie. He looks at her holding his phone and he sighs. Grabbing it from her, he rolls his eyes.

"Reading my messages now?" he says with annoyance in his voice.

"No," she replies. "Your phone was going off, jerk. I was trying to stop it so it didn't wake you." Hurt, she stomps out of the room. Sasha and Celia are already up eating breakfast. Jamie reads the message and curses himself.

"Good morning," Marilee says, kissing Celia.

"Good morning," Sasha says. "I made pancakes."

"Awesome, thanks, Sasha."

"Is everything okay, ma'am," Sasha asks as Jamie walks in and kisses Celia.

"Yes, Sasha," Marilee says. She watches Jamie as he pours his coffee. "Rough night?"

"Nah," Jamie replies. Marilee rolls her eyes at his lack of information and he gives her a smirk. Even though he won't mention what the message was about, Marilee knows that it didn't mean anything and she should trust him. She cracks a smile as he kisses her cheek. “Let’s eat.”

“What are you doing today?” Marilee asks before sticking an obscene amount of pancakes in her mouth.

“Showing Charley the ropes,” he says. He laughs as he watches her eyes widen, but she can’t say anything with the amount of food that is in her mouth. “He chose it...last night. He got his ring and everything. Don’t worry, he is just shadowing me and we will keep him safe.”

Marilee swallows and takes a sip of her coffee. Shaking her head in agreement. “Okay.” She picks at her food and wishes Charley had just stayed in school. Though it wouldn’t matter if he had because she has doomed the whole family to this life forever.

Charley walks to the front desk of the lodge and greets his dad. Bryce smiles and looks down at Charley’s hand. “Well, I guess you have chosen your future.”

“We both knew it would happen, whether I chose it or not,” Charley says.

“Oh, don’t give me that,” Bryce says. “You could be in school right now.”

“I was flunking out, Dad,” Charley says. “I tried the school thing and it didn’t fit. Sorry to disappoint.”

“Son, you could never disappoint me,” Bryce says, grabbing Charley’s shoulder. “Just be safe.”

“I’ll be with Jamie,” Charley says.

Bryce laughs. “Right.”

“And me,” Vanessa says as she walks up to the counter.

“Well, at least there is that,” Bryce says.

"Don't worry, Bryce," Vanessa says. "I will make sure he is brought back in one piece."

"Thank you, Vanessa." Jamie comes down the stairs, dressed in his black suite. He notices the unwelcoming expression from Bryce.

"Don't worry," he says. "Only introductions today, no danger involved." He takes a glimpse of Charley's attire and bites his lip. "We will need to stop and buy a few things."

"Ah, man," Charley says.

"You will need to look the part," Jamie says.

"Like you own the town," Vanessa says.

"She's right," Devin says, hitting Charley on the back. He turns to see Will, Arianna, and Dylan standing behind him. "Don't worry, you will get used to it." He turns back to Jamie and leans in to whisper to him. "About the problem with Frank's pictures, it is taken care of."

"Thanks," Jamie says, giving him a quick hug.

"We must head back today," Devin says. Arianna comes and gives him a hug and then fuses with his tie.

"Do be careful, Jamie," she says.

"Always," he replies. "Y'all will be back for the housewarming party, right?"

"Wouldn't miss it," Devin says. "We just said goodbye to Marilee and Celia."

"Great. Will, keep these two straight," Jamie says.

"Always," he says giving them all hugs.

After Marilee checks in with the new restaurant manager, she goes upstairs to talk to Betty. "Hey," Betty says, opening the door. She runs back toward her bag and starts stuffing things in it.

"What's wrong?" Marilee asks.

"Oh, nothing. I'm just in a hurry. My first day of class is today."

"I thought you weren't starting until the fall?"

"Well, apparently, Vanessa pulled some strings. I was going to tell you, but I just found out and I've been so rushed."

"No, don't be silly. I just thought I'd get to spend a little time with you before you started, that's all."

"I'm sorry—

"Don't be sorry. Go live your dream, girl."

"Thanks," Betty says. "I got a long way to go, but these summer courses will help."

"Well, good luck and we'll talk when you get back." As she walks down the hallway she runs into Charlotte. "Hey, Charlotte, do you want to go workout?"

"I wish I could, but I have to go with Betty to make sure everything at the school is secure. You are more than welcome to come along."

"No, thanks," Marilee says with disappointment. "I really need to let off some steam."

"Why? What happened?"

"Nothing, don't worry about it. I know Betty is in a hurry. We can talk later."

"Okay, are you sure?" Charlotte says with a raised eyebrow.

"Yes, I'll be fine. Thanks. Now go before Betty has a meltdown."

Marilee feels like she is about to explode. She needs to release whatever is building up inside her. She isn't sure if it is anger or sadness. She only knows she doesn't like it. In her head she trusts Jamie and in her head she said she would let it go, but she can't. She needs to run. After telling security and her dad she heads for the trails. She runs for miles before she stops to take a breather. She wants to scream, but she knows she can't. Someone would think something bad was happening to her. She also knows if she don't let these feelings out it will only hurt more. So she leans on a nearby tree and slides down to the ground and cries. Though she wants to believe Jamie, everything is telling her that he is cheating. After a few minutes of crying and the weird feeling that someone is watching her, she heads back toward the lodge. She spends the rest of the day with Celia and it is probably the only thing that helps soothe the pain. They watch princess movies and fall asleep on the couch.

Jamie comes home late to find Marilee and Celia on the couch. It makes him smile. His phone buzzes and his smile fades. He ignores it, erases it, and falls asleep next to them.

Waking up to the smell of Jamie's cologne brings tears to Marilee's eyes. She gets up, but he grabs her hand as she passes over him. "Where are you going?"

"To the bathroom," she says.

"Hurry back," he says, squeezing her hand. As his hand slips out of hers, she quickly runs to the bathroom and breaks down. Jamie senses something is wrong so he puts Celia to bed and goes to check on Marilee. Before he can knock on the door he hears her sobbing. He quickly enters and sees her on the floor. Her eyes widen. She didn't want him to see her crying. She thought she could hide her feelings from him, but now what is the point. "What is it?" he says, kneeling down to her.

She decides to let all of it out. "I'm not stupid, Jamie," she cries. "I saw the message from Ruby.

Just tell me if you're cheating. I can't take it anymore."

"Hey," he says, pushing the hair out of her face. "Stop that, I told you nothing is going on with me and Ruby. I haven't seen her since that last kiss. I've been texting her information and sending some through Vanessa."

"But the text."

"I never said that she hasn't been trying to persuade me," he says. Marilee stops crying, realizing she may have acted a bit silly. Hope feels her up.

"So, you're not cheating?"

"Of course not," he says. "She keeps texting me, but I've said no a hundred times and I will keep saying no, I promise." He tilts her chin up to look at him. She hugs him, feeling stupid.

"I'm sorry that I doubted you," she says.

"I would have doubted too after everything. Let's just forget Ruby, okay."

"Deal," Marilee says, drying her eyes.

"The good news is that the house is done so no reason to even see her again."

"It is?"

"Yep, you ready to move in?"

"Ah, yeah," Marilee says. "There is so much to pack!"

"We'll get to that in a minute," Jamie says. "We have a little catching up to do first."

She giggles as he picks her up and carries her to bed.

~

Marilee is packing up boxes as Jamie gets their clothes together. "Are we leaving security here for Betty and Charley?"

"We can if you want," Jamie says.

"I'd feel better knowing someone is looking out for them."

"Then say no more. I'll get some more to guard our house." Marilee closes the box and tapes it shut. "Is that the last of it?"

"I think so."

"Great," he says.

"The fun part is unpacking," Marilee says as their friends walk in.

"You know you guys could have hired someone to do all of this for you," Vanessa says.

"But then we couldn't have spent this quality time together," Jamie says.

"Is that what this is?" Charlotte says, carrying another box out the door.

"By the way, how many suites do you own?" Betty says.

"Ha, ha," Jamie says. "By the way, how was class yesterday?"

"Intimidating," Betty says.

Vanessa laughs. "It will get better. Mr. Saunders is very easy to get along with."

"Who?" Jamie asks.

"Mr. Saunders, one of my professors from college. He's awesome. He said he'd help get Betty to where she needs to before fall."

Jamie's forehead crinkles. "Something wrong?" Dylan asks.

"No," Jamie says, feeling that the name is familiar, but he just can't figure out from where. He forgets his thoughts when he picks up a box and clothes spill out everywhere. "Oh, come on!" Everyone laughs, but comes to help clean the mess. "I really appreciate all of you guys."

"That is what Family is for," Vanessa says.

"Okay then," Charley says to break the silence. "Let's get these guys out of my new apartment."

"Can we lend a hand," Bryce asks as him and Scott walks through the door.

"Oh my God!" Marilee shouts as she sees Scott. Everyone rushes to hug him.

Bryce laughs. "I know y'all see me every day and everything, but don't I get a hello at least."

"Hello, Bryce," they all say with a hint of laughter. They all gather and give Bryce a hug too.

"Okay, okay," he says. "Let's get you kids moved in. Vanessa, do you have all your things packed?"

"Yeah, I paid someone days ago when I knew the house was going to be ready."

"Okay," Bryce says. "What about Dylan and Charlotte?"

"Yep, all ready to go," Dylan says.

"Alright, then. Time to start a new chapter. Are you all ready for this?"

"I think we are," Jamie says as he smiles at Marilee.

23

As Marilee settles in the new house she gets a feeling in the pit of her stomach. “What was I thinking?” She begins to worry about everything that is supposed to happen tonight. The whole Family will be here for the housewarming party and Celia’s birthday party she feels there is still so much to do. The caterers arrive to get set up. Marilee shows them to the kitchen. “You can follow the driveway to the back entrance. It will be a lot easier to set up.”

“Thanks,” Chasity, the caterer says. “It is such an honor to cater for your Family.”

“Well, thank you,” Marilee says.

“Hey, sis!” Charley comes in with his suite on followed by her dad and brothers.

“Wow,” she says. “Y’all look awesome, so dashing.” Charley looks toward the caterer who is still staring at them.

“Hello,” Charley says with a smile.

“Oh, sorry,” she says snapping out of her thoughts. “I’ll go get everything, the food.”

“Alrighty then,” Marilee says with a laugh.

Charley shrugs his shoulders. “Betty is meeting us here.”

“Great.”

“Can we help with anything?” Bryce says giving his daughter a hug.

“No, I think we are good.” Tommy comes up to her and gives her a hug. “Tom, tom.”

“Don’t call me that, Marilee,” he sighs.

“Sorry,” she says, ruffling his hair. “I have to go get ready, but there is a game room down the hall if you guys—

"Awesome!" Jimmy says as he runs out of the kitchen.

"Okay, I will see you guys in a bit," she says with a laugh. On her way upstairs she notices Arianna, Will, and Devin come through the door. "Guys!" she says as she runs to them. "I'm so glad you made it."

"Of course," Arianna says, giving her a hug.

"I'm running behind as usual so make yourself at home. The bar is to the right." She hurries to her bathroom to get ready. As she is getting ready, Jamie comes in and kisses her neck.

"You're not ready yet?" he says.

"No and if you keep kissing my neck we are both going to be late."

"So be it," he says and kisses her neck again.

"No," she says with a giggle. "Go away so I can finish getting ready."

"Fine," he says. "Later." He smiles and takes a look out the window. "Oh, shit."

"What?" She hurries to the window to see.

"Tyler and Ruby? What the hell?" he says, grinding his teeth. "I forgot to revoke their invitation. The invite was for the entire Family. Don't worry, I'll take care of it."

"No, don't cause a scene. Let them stay."

"Are you sure?" he narrows his eyes.

"Yes, I suppose. Just behave." Jamie rushes downstairs to greet his guests, but finds Vanessa already talking to them.

"Hello," Jamie says, trying to avoid eye contact with Ruby.

"I'm trying to explain to them the many reasons for them to not be here," Vanessa says with her hand on her hip. "And Celia's birthday too..."

"It is okay," Jamie says, placing his hand on Vanessa's shoulder to calm her down. "They can stay." Her forehead creases. "They are Family after all. I trust they can behave themselves." Jamie gives Tyler a glare.

"Of course," Tyler says. "All is good here."

"Then enjoy the party." Jamie watches Tyler carefully as he enters the house. "Keep an eye on them," he says. Vanessa nods and they separate. He spots his dad and Missy walk in so he greets them. "Oh my God!" he shouts as he embraces them both. "Missy, you're walking!"

"Well, barely," she says, acknowledging her crutches. "I also have to wear braces on my legs. I can't walk without them."

"But we are getting there," Scott says.

"Well, it is definitely a good start," Jamie says. "I'm so glad you guys are here. Charlotte is in the bar with the rest of the gang. She will be so excited to see you." Jamie stops talking as Marilee comes down the stairs. "Wow," he says. Scott and Missy laugh at him.

"She is stunning son. Go meet her at the bottom of the stairs and tell her." Scott pushes him to snap him out of his stare. As he reaches the stairs he grabs her hand. "You look, breathtaking doesn't even cover it," he says. "I don't have the words to describe how beautiful you are."

"I think you are doing pretty well," she says with a giggle. "Oh my God," she says as she spots Scott and Missy. "Is Missy walking?"

"Yeah, want to go catch up?"

"Yeah." He pulls her toward the bar, but two men stop them.

"Mr. Garrison, we would love to have a word in private, if we could?"

Jamie sighs. "Sure," he says.

"John and Conner, I'd like for you to meet my fiancé, Marilee."

"A pleasure," Marilee says.

"Likewise," the man nods, shaking her hand. "You are a vision Miss..."

"Oh, Marilee, please."

"Marilee, you have a beautiful home."

"Thank you."

"I'll meet up with you in a bit," Jamie says, kissing her cheek and motions for the men to follow him to the office.

"So, gentlemen," Jamie says as he shuts the double doors to the office. "Would you like a drink?" he asks as he pours himself one.

"Sure," John says and Conner nods. He hands them their drinks and leans up against his desk. "So, how may I help you? This isn't about your sons is it, John? Because I went pretty easy on them."

"No, no and thank you for going so easy on them," John says. "But they did give me some information to pass to you."

"And what is that?" Jamie says taking a sip of his drink.

"This man they were working for, Jason Saunders—

"I knew that name sounded familiar!" Jamie says as it comes to him.

"What?"

"Oh, nothing. What about him?

"He is trying to take over the weapons distribution. He is already got most of the north."

"Why am I just now hearing about this?"

"The reports, sir," Conner says with obvious tension in his voice. "They have been coming in consistent. We assumed everything was fine."

"Well, who is in charge of the reports?"

"Tyler Brown, sir," John says. Jamie puts his drink down on the desk and takes a breath.

"You two stay here." He rushes out of the office to look for Tyler and runs into Vanessa. "Where is Tyler?"

"He went to the bathroom. Why? What is going on?" she says, noticing his anger growing.

"We may be fucked, that's what," he says. "Where is my dad?"

"Bar." She follows him. He goes straight up to his dad and whispers in his ear.

"We have a situation. I need everyone in the office. I'll meet y'all there after I find Tyler." He looks around the bar. "Where is Marilee?"

"I'm not sure," Scott says, looking toward Missy.

"She went to check on Celia," Missy says.

"Alright, if any of you see her, send her to the office and don't lose sight of her." He leaves the bar to go and find Tyler. Passing by Ruby, he grabs her by the arm and pulls her in another room. "Where is Tyler?"

"How should I know?" she says. "Did you know about him forging documents?"

"What?" she gasps. "No, honest." He narrows his eyes at her. "I would have told you and you know that." She grabs hold of his shirt, but he pushes her hand away.

"I don't have time for this, Ruby. I need to find Tyler."

"I've missed you," she says.

He sighs. "Ruby, you have to stop this."

"Just one more kiss." She leans in taunting him, but he walks away to go find Tyler. When he walks out of the room, he pushes his hair back with frustration. His phone rings and he quickly picks it up.

"Marilee, where are you?" She doesn't answer. "Hello?"

"Hello, Jamie," Tyler says. Jamie's eyes widen with rage. He can hear Marilee crying in the background. "Can you hear her?"

"If you touch her–

"Oh," Tyler laughs. "It's too late for that."

"Please stop," Marilee says. It brings tears to Jamie's eyes.

"I want to hear her scream my name, asshole. You fuck mine, I fuck yours."

He hears the phone fall to the floor and Marilee screaming for him to stop. Jamie knows he will not get to her in time. "You're dead!" he shouts as loud as he can through the phone. Everyone turns to stare at him as Scott runs up to him.

"What is it?" Scott says grabbing him by the shoulders. Jamie wants to punch everything in his sight, but everyone is staring at him. He looks to Vanessa.

"Handle the crowd, please."

"Of course," she says. She walks toward the curious crowd and walks them to the bar. Jamie turns back to Scott.

"Tyler has her, we need to find her now. Dylan, track her phone."

"We'll find her son. Let's go to the office." They drag Jamie to the office as he talks to security.

"Sweep every inch of this estate. Find her!"

"Her phone is still here. It looks like it is in the base–

The hidden door of the office slides open before Dylan can finish his sentence. Marilee stands there staring at them. Her beautiful white gown is tattered with blood dripping from her hands. "Oh God!" Jamie says, running to her. "Are you okay? Tell me you are okay, baby." He picks her up and carries her to the couch. "Find him!" he screams, making Will, Dylan, and Charley run to hunt Tyler down. He looks back down to Marilee and strokes her hair back. "Hey, talk to me, tell me...he searches her body for wounds, but finds none.

"I'm fine," Marilee finally says. When she notices how upset he is she grabs his face. "Hey, I'm fine."

"I'm sorry," Jamie says with tears in his eyes. "I will kill him for doing that to you."

"Jamie," she says. "Look at me." He opens his eyes and she can tell he is holding back tears. "He never got a chance, okay." He pulls her in for a hug.

"Thank God. But the blood."

"It's not mine," she says, pulling out her knife. "You told me to keep it on me at all times," she says, giving Charlotte a smirk.

"That's my girl," Jamie says. As he pulls her toward him again, they bring in Tyler and place him on his knees. He can barely walk on his own and blood is seeping for his wound, courtesy of Marilee. Jamie goes for the kill, but Scott pulls him back.

"We need answers first, Jamie," he says.

Grinding his teeth at his father, Jamie holds off. "Fine." Walking back to Marilee, he grabs her hands to pull her up off the couch. "Are you sure you are okay?"

"Yes," she says.

"I still want Vanessa to take a look at you," Jamie says. "Girls will you take her upstairs and help her get cleaned up. I'll send Vanessa up when we are done here." Charlotte and Arianna nod and grab Marilee by the hand to lead her out. As she walks by Tyler he gives her a smirk and blows her a kiss. She smirks back and kicks him in the jaw. "Damn," Dylan shouts as the girls walk her out. Before leaving the room she turns back and Jamie gives her a wink.

"Never a dull moment in a Garrison household," John says.

Scott pulls up a chair and sits down to talk to Tyler. "So why work for this Saunders guy? I know he isn't paying more than I do?"

"Ask him," Tyler says, nodding toward Jamie. Scott rolls his eyes at Tyler's immaturity and punches him in the face.

"Oh shit," Jamie says, jumping with surprise.

Scott stands up irritated. "I should have never put him in charge of finance. This is on me."

"Enough of this," Jamie says, rushing towards Tyler, standing him up, and pushing him up against the wall.

"Jamie we need him alive," Devin says.

"I know and he is going to tell us everything we need to know about this Saunders guy." His eyes widen quickly remembering and he drops Tyler to the floor. "Shit, Charley, quick, call Betty."

"No need," a man says from the doorway. They all turn to see a man with dark hair, in his thirties. "I think we may need to have a chat."

"Mr. Saunders?" Vanessa gasps.

24

Everyone in the room is silent for a moment, even Jamie. When it finally hits him that Betty is next to this man, he quickly grabs her arm and pulls her into the office. She runs to Charley. "Let me start by saying that I wasn't a part of his plan." He points toward Tyler.

"And you think that makes you safe," Jamie says.

"Come in, Mr. Saunders," Scott says, placing his hand on his back and leading him to the chair to sit. Jamie shuts the door and gives Charley a nod. After whispering in Betty's ear he shows her out the door.

"Call me Jason, please."

"Well, Jason," Jamie says. "Since I have you, I guess that means I don't need this one." He reaches down, pulls Tyler up off the floor, and places a blade to his throat.

Tyler gives him a crooked smile. "But you don't kill Family, remember." He laughs.

"That damn rule keeps coming to bite me in the ass," Jamie says, releasing Tyler.

Devin walks forward and scratches his forehead. "I think it's about time to change that."

"That's great, but how? I can't go back on a law that I created," Jamie says, throwing his arms in the air.

"Any law made by a high king has to be written and sent to me for approval," Devin says, giving Tyler a cocky grin. "I don't remember approving such a law."

"I see," Jamie says, giving Tyler a raised brow. "So the law is void." He starts walking toward Tyler, but Tyler shows no hint of being scared. He looks around the room and knows he is going to be killed. He sighs and gives Jamie a smile. "Well, you know what...she was worth it." Jamie takes a breath and with a quick, solid motion slices Tyler's throat. He enjoys watching him fall to the ground.

"Okay," Devin says walking toward Jason. "Now that we have that issue taken care of."

"I never wanted any trouble," Jason says. "I'm just a business man."

"A very smart business man," Scott says as Dylan hands him a file.

"Maybe we can help each other out here," Devin continues.

"I'm listening," Jason replies, his eyes wandering around the room.

"You snagged our Northern weapons distribution in a matter of months. Very impressive. How do you think you could handle our drug distribution?"

"Actually, Devin, I'm taking care of that," Jamie says.

Devin turns to him and sighs. "Yes, Jamie, and I know how you are taking care of that, but some things have changed. We will talk on that matter later." Dylan's eyes widen along with Jamie's. Dylan quickly comes to stand beside him so he doesn't do anything stupid. Biting his jaw, Jamie pours himself a drink. "Now, Mr. Saunders, do you have some morals against drug distribution?"

"No, not really," Jason says.

"We could use your expertise. Drugs make a hell of a lot more money than weapons."

"I don't believe I have choice in the matter," Jason says.

"On one condition," Jamie says. "Betty gets to graduate early."

Jason laughs. “How early? She still has a lot to learn.”

“Charley, what do you think?” Jamie says with his arms crossed. Devin shoots him a glare.

“Take off two years,” Charley says, making Jason laugh harder.

“Two years! That is ridiculous. I could speed up her basics a bit, but–

“You can do it Mr. Saunders,” Vanessa says. “Just help her like you helped me.”

“You had all your basics completed in high school.” He sighs, giving in. “Fine, I’ll do my best. But she has to put in the work. It will be all day sessions and sometimes nights, given my new job and everything.”

“Okay, that is settled. Let’s go enjoy the party.”

“Um, Devin, a word,” Jamie says as everyone else leaves. As soon as the door shuts he lashes out on Devin. “What the hell, Devin. You knew my plans for shutting down the drug distribution part of this.”

“I know, but now this guy can be our fall guy,” Devin says. “You won’t have to worry about it now.”

“I’m not worried about that,” Jamie says. “I’m worried about selling drugs.”

“Don’t worry, Jamie, you won’t have to deal with it anymore.”

“But I will still know, Devin.”

Devin notices the fire in Jamie’s eyes when he speaks on the subject. He can tell Jamie is passionate about getting rid of his part in the drug distribution. “We are not going to agree on the subject tonight so let’s just go enjoy the party. We can talk about this issue later. Go be with Marilee.” Jamie sighs, frustrated as Devin walks out. All his planning to end the drug distribution may have all been for nothing.

"Shit," he says, pulling his hair back and gulping the last of his drink. As he goes to check in on Marilee, he runs into Scott.

"Hey, what are we to do about her?" Scott says pointing to Ruby.

"Damnit," Jamie says. "I'll take care of it."

"Are you sure?"

"I'm the one that killed him."

"Well, go check on Marilee first. I'll make sure she doesn't leave."

"Thanks, Dad."

Jamie storms into their bedroom. "Marilee!" he shouts.

"I'm here," she says from the bathroom. She comes in with a robe on and wet hair. "I had to take another shower." He pulls her toward him quickly, making her gasp a bit.

"I'm so sorry," he says.

She breaks away from his grasp. "It's not your fault, Jamie. Stop blaming yourself." She places her hand on his cheek. "You can't keep blaming yourself for every bad thing that happens to me. The only one at fault is Tyler." She bites her lip. "Did you kill him?"

"Of course," Jamie says.

"Good," she says, giving him a kiss. "Thank you."

"No problem, I quite enjoyed it," he says with a hint of laughter. "But now," he sighs. "I have to go and tell Ruby that I killed her husband."

"Oh, crap," she says. "Nobody has told her yet?"

"No, she is just waiting downstairs like nothing is wrong."

"Oh, God, well, go ahead. I'll be fine up here. I don't want to go downstairs until she is gone."

"Okay, I'll put a guard at your door. Please don't leave until I return."

"You have my word." She smiles.

As Jamie comes down the stairs he spots Ruby. He takes a deep breath, wishing he had another drink. "Ruby," he says. "Can I have a word?"

"Sure," she says as he grabs her arm and pulls her into another room.

"We need to talk."

"Okay," she says. "What is the matter?"

"Tyler was falsifying documents for months," he says, noticing her disinterest. "He took Marilee."

"Oh, shit," she says. "Jamie, I swear, I didn't know."

"I know that, it's just..."

"You found them then? She's okay?"

"Yes," Jamie says. "She's fine, but..."

"So he is dead?" Ruby asks. "You killed him, didn't you?"

"I had to Ruby—

"No, I understand, but what about your rule?"

"Devin voided it."

"I see," Ruby says. "Well, I guess I should be going."

"Ruby," Jamie says, pulling her back to him. "I am sorry." He gives her a quick hug so he doesn't lead her on. "You will always be part of this Family."

"Thanks, Jamie," she says with her eyes starting to gloss over. "I know he was a bastard, but I did love him at one point."

"Let me get you a car to take you home."

"Thanks."

Scott walks to Jamie as soon as he sees Ruby leave. "How did she take it?"

"Okay, I guess." Jamie brushes his hair back and sighs. "Did we get the mess taken care of?"

"Clean-up is here now," Scott says. "Son, I know you are concerned with the drug distribution, but try not to let it get to you. Devin will come around. If you can find a way to produce money elsewhere."

"I know," Jamie says. "I'm going to go and check on Marilee. She should be about ready to come downstairs. Can you make sure Bryce and the boys are good?"

Scott nods, but knows this whole thing is taking a toll on Jamie.

~

As Jamie enters the bathroom, Marilee is putting on her makeup. She smiles when she sees him come in. Every time they are apart she has a pit in her stomach until she sees him again. Now she knows he is safe, she takes a breath. "Hey," she says. "How did it go?"

"Okay," he says, wrapping his arms around her.

"What's wrong?" she says. "Besides the obvious."

"Devin," he says, letting go of his embrace and scratching his head. "He has put someone else in charge of our drug distribution."

"Well, that's good, right?" she gives him a glance and continues to put on her makeup. "You never really liked that part anyway."

"Yes, but now it will be even harder to phase out. Especially, with this Mr. Saunders guy. He seems to be very smart."

"Yeah, Betty told me he was here. Do you trust this guy?"

"Not at all, but if he can help Betty, I'm willing to try. It's just Devin knows my plans and I don't think he wants me to go through with them now."

"I thought y'all all came to the agreement together."

"We did, but now that he is the boss, I don't know. It's just a punch in the gut; along with other things."

"Okay, well," Marilee says, standing up not knowing how to make him feel better about everything that has happened tonight. "Let's go spend some time with our family. We can focus on the not so pleasant later."

"Good idea," he says, giving her a kiss. "You know, you are becoming quite the bad ass."

"Oh, yeah?"

"Yeah. Promise me that you will keep that knife on you at all times."

"I will." She wants to tell him it was sheer luck that she stabbed Tyler, but she wants him to think she can defend herself. "I have a few more finishing touches to do so I'll meet you downstairs."

As soon as he walks down the stairs he knows the news has spread. All eyes are on him. He sits down at the bar and rolls his eyes and raises a finger to the bartender. "Make it a double please."

"Yes, sir." The bartender nods and brings him the bottle. "You look as if you could use the bottle sir."

Jamie smiles. "Thanks."

Betty comes to sit beside him. "Oh, Betty." He gives her a hug. "I'm so glad you are okay."

"I'm fine," she says. "You know, Mr. Saunders really is a nice guy. He told me everything before I came."

"I hope you're right," Jamie says. "Betty, did Charley tell you—

"About how you negotiated my future for me?" she says with a smile. "Yes, you didn't have to do that, Jamie. I want to get this on my own, okay."

"Okay, but are you ready for all the work you will have to put in? You don't have to become a doctor you know."

"Are you kidding me?" she says. "Jamie, this is a dream come true for me."

He smiles. "I just want you to do this for you and not the Family."

"Don't worry, big brother," she says, making him laugh. "This is my dream."

"Awesome, I'm glad you get to live it then."

"How is Marilee?"

"Good, she will be down in a few minutes. Betty, I don't know what I would've done if–

"Hey," Betty says putting her arm around him. "She's good and he's dead so all is how it should be."

"Right." He smiles and pours her a drink. The whole family joins them at the bar. The bartender gives them each a glass.

"We need a bigger bar, guys," Vanessa says.

"I told them that," Charlotte says.

"Hold that thought," Jamie says, spotting Marilee coming down the stairs. He rushes to her. "Breathtaking as always." He grabs her hand and walks her to the bar.

"Just in time for a toast," he says giving her his seat next to Betty.

"Great," she says.

"Dad, you mind?"

"Sure," Scott says. He raises his glass and looks around at everyone he holds dear. "To family," he says. "And I'm not talking about the Family." He speaks in a quieter tone and motions around the house at the other people. "I'm talking about this right here." Acknowledging them all with his free hand, smiling. "This is family and we will always be family, friends, and allies. Nobody will ever come between us or try to divide us. This is a pact I want us to make, here and now. No matter what is thrown at us, no matter how much we disagree on something, no matter what...we never hurt, or plot against each other. This unit right here, it stays as one and it stays true, do we all agree?"

"Agreed," Dylan says to start it off. Soon everyone follows his lead and agrees. They raise their glasses and drink. They all feel at this moment that nothing could ever tear them apart.

25

Marilee gives Celia a bath and as she washes her she starts to think about tonight. How she thought Tyler was going to kill her, how he touched her, how she thought she would never see Celia, Jamie, or her friends ever again. She tries to hold in the tears so she doesn't scare Celia, but they come anyway. "Miss," Sasha says, coming in the bathroom to see if she needs anything. "I can take care of this, please. This is why I am here. You have had a trying day...go."

Marilee dries her eyes. "Thank you, Sasha," she says. "And you are here because you are family."

"Yes, ma'am, but family helps each other, so go, please."

Marilee smiles and decides to take Sasha's help. She walks around the now empty house and spots the library. She hasn't seen the collection of books Jamie has purchased so she takes a look. The library is pretty awesome with floor to ceiling book shelves, comfy couches to read at, and a wall-to-wall sliding glass door that opens to a huge courtyard with even more seating. She scans the books and among them are some of her favorite reads. She smiles. As she scans more she notices a book on Ireland. She misses it dearly. She loved the land, the castles, and the peacefulness. She keeps looking and spots a book on Ireland families. Intrigued, she pulls it off the shelf and begins to read aloud. "You won't read much about us in that book, if that is what you are looking for," Jamie says, sitting down next to her.

"Why not?" she asks.

"Well, once upon a time the Families came to the United States. When things got bad for them, they changed their names and laid low. Some went back to Ireland and some stayed. We were the ones that stayed. My great-great grandfather was among them. He was ran out of New Orleans, but changed his name to Garrison and started his own business. Years later he became one of the richest men in real estate. He still had ties to Ireland, friends he could trust so they decided to keep him here as long as he could stay under the FBI's radar. All the other factions were getting arrested because they wanted people to know who they were. They wanted to be feared and that led to their downfall. We were able to come back to New Orleans because nobody knew who we were. Hopefully, we can keep that going. We have thrived on keeping our secret." He looks through the pages of the book and points to a young man. "There he is."

"Wow," Marilee says. "He is so young."

"Yeah, that was when he took over for his dad. The competing families moved back to Ireland, but he stayed. He was stubborn and hell bent on his Family taking New Orleans back one day, so the story goes."

"Sounds familiar."

He laughs. "Come on," he says. "I'm starving. Let's see what is in the kitchen."

As he looks through the refrigerator he wonders about Marilee. Is she really okay? Will she want to talk about what happened? Should he ask her? He closes the fridge and looks at her. "What?" she says. He rubs her cheek softly. "Are you okay? You can talk to me."

She sighs. She was hoping she could avoid talking about it for a while. "No, Jamie, I'm not okay. That was the worst thing I've ever been through, even worse than when I was beat into a coma. He violated me. Even though he didn't accomplish his goal, I can still feel his breath on my neck and it sends unnerving chills down my spine." She begins to tear up, but thinks better of it. "So no, I am not okay, but I will be."

"I just want you to know that I'm here, okay."

"I know, thank you," she says, squeezing his hand. "You know, I'm a bit tired. I think I'll go on to bed. Is that okay?"

"Of course," he says, knowing he has upset her. "I'll be up in a bit." When she is up the stairs, he curses himself for bringing it up. Feeling his emotions getting the best of him, he walks out the back door and into the woods. Sitting down beside his favorite childhood stream, he cries. He cries for her, for betraying her, and for not saving her. A twig snaps behind him and he jumps.

"Jamie?" Dylan says. "Are you alright?" Jamie quickly wipes the tears away and laughs.

"Not really," he says abruptly.

"Well, then, let's have it. Is it Marilee? Because she seems fine."

"She is just trying to be brave," Jamie says with pain in his eyes. "She just don't want me to blame myself." He stands up, and throws a rock as hard as he can into the woods, hoping to release a little of his anger. "Ah! In my own house!" he screams.

"This isn't your fault, Jamie. It's Tyler's and you killed him."

"That is where you are wrong."

"What do you mean?" Dylan laughs. "How could this possibly be your fault? Tyler was obsessed with thinking you slept with Ruby. He was looking for revenge for something that never happened." Jamie turns and faces his brother with more tears filling his eyes. "What?" Dylan asks, confused of why his brother is about to cry again. He sighs as it hits him. "Tell me you didn't!"

Jamie takes a breath. "It was the night she left. I thought she was gone for good."

"Shit, Jamie!" Dylan says, pacing.

"I know—

Dylan grabs Jamie by the shirt and punches him in the face. "No, you don't know! You fucking ass! Jamie doesn't try to stop him so Dylan decides to take the opportunity to keep punching him a few more times. Jamie falls down and Dylan climbs on top of him and continues punching him, until someone pulls him off.

"What in the hell is wrong with you guys?" Vanessa says. Dylan takes a breath, stands up, and straightens himself.

"Just letting off some steam," Dylan says, reaching down to help Jamie off the ground. "I might have got a little carried away." He looks down at as he realizes he just beat the crap out of his brother. Jamie's nose and lip are bleeding and swollen.

"You think?" Vanessa says. "Come on, help me get him inside so I can clean him up." They help Jamie inside and take him to the office. "Stay here and I'll go get my bag. Can you two behave while I'm gone?" They both give her a nod.

Jamie looks around the room, squinting a bit as he regains his vision. "They cleaned up fast."

"Yep," Dylan says. "Man, I'm sorry."

"No," Jamie says. "I deserved it. I deserve much worse."

"You just made a mistake, a stupid, beyond stupid mistake." Dylan says. "One you will not make again, right?"

"Of course not," Jamie says, holding his face toward the ceiling to get his nose from bleeding on him.

"Good. Then you must learn to deal until fight night and then you can let it out." Jamie smirks at Dylan's comment and Vanessa comes back into the room.

"Alright, are you going to tell me what happened or can I just guess?" Vanessa says. Dylan and Jamie are both silent. "Very well. Dylan, you found out about the very stupid blunder your brother got himself into. Is that about right?"

"How the hell did you know?" Jamie asks.

"Oh, please," she says with a laugh. "I knew you would eventually." She rolls her eyes at them as they glare at her. "Alright, I followed you that night to the Michaelson Hotel. I wanted to make sure you were okay."

"And you didn't stop me?" Jamie asks.

"Really, are you looking for someone to blame? I am not your keeper, James Garrison, and you are a big boy! You made your decision, not me." She presses down on his nose a bit too hard as she wipes the blood off.

"Ouch, sorry," Jamie says. "I know."

"Why were you out in the woods anyway?" Vanessa says.

"I was just trying to clear my head."

"You think it was your fault," Vanessa says with pity.

"Yeah." Jamie says about to lose control again.

"No," she says, slapping him in the face. "You bury that shit, James Garrison. We have other messed up shit to focus on." Jamie's eyes widen in shock. He can't believe she just slapped him. He looks to Dylan and they both laugh.

"That hurt a bit," he says, rubbing his face.

"I'm glad I could give you guys a laugh, but I'm serious."

"What are you worried about?" Dylan asks.

"Hello, getting our weapons distribution back on track."

"Well, if Saunders backs down, they should come right back to us," Dylan says.

"She's right. What if they don't want to come back? What if Tyler already got to them." Jamie says. "Time to get back to work." He stands up and pours himself a drink. "We have to go visit the locations and do some damage control. Dylan can you come with us on this?"

"Of course. I'll need tomorrow to take care of some things, but then I should be good."

"Okay, then Vanessa make arrangements."

"Got it," she says. "We'll talk tomorrow. You guys should get some sleep."

Dylan and Vanessa leave, but Jamie stays to think about what they can do about their weapons situation. He really doesn't want to leave Marilee alone right now, but if he doesn't work fast they could lose clients. He picks up the phone. "Dad?" he says.

"Yeah," Scott answers. "Is everything okay?"

"Yeah, sorry. Are you still in town?"

"Of course. We are staying at the lodge," Scott says. "What is going on?"

"I just need to talk, can you meet me in the bar?"

"Yes, what is this about, son?"

"I just need to talk, Dad," Jamie says with a sigh. "Can you give me about fifteen minutes?"

His dad is waiting at the bar when he walks in. A glass is ready with whiskey as he sits down. "So, what is this about?" Scott asks.

"I'm just all messed up, Dad," Jamie says pulling at his hair and gulping the whiskey. He closes his eyes and welcomes the satisfying burn that usually makes everything better.

He lifts Jamie's chin, seeing Dylan's handy work and sighs. "Is this about Marilee?" Scott says, joining his son in a drink. Jamie nods. "Is she upset?"

"Not too much," Jamie says.

"Then leave it alone," Scott says, grabbing his shoulder. "If she wants to talk about it, she will."

"I don't want to leave her alone," Jamie says.

"I know and I get it, but you need to take care of this weapons issue fast."

"I know." Jamie swallows hard and refills his glass.

"Just go and get it done quickly so you can get back for her. We will keep her occupied if that will make you feel better."

"Will you stay until I return?"

"Of course," Scott says. "If that will help."

Thanks, Dad," he says, shoving his emotions down along with the rest of his drink. "Thanks for listening. Sorry I woke you up."

"I can't imagine what you must be going through. The thoughts in your mind are your enemy, son. Don't let them get the better of you. Marilee is the bravest, strongest, and most capable young woman I have ever met, besides your mother. She is going to be just fine and she will understand that you have to leave."

"You're right," Jamie says.

"Get some rest, son. You will need it."

"Bye, Dad," Jamie gives his dad a hug and heads back home. He don't know why he thought he would feel better after talking to his dad. At least they will keep an eye on Marilee for him. Back at his office he watches the sun come up.

26

Marilee wakes up to breakfast in bed. "What is this?" she says.

"I just wanted to suck up a bit," Jamie says with a grin as he climbs in bed with her.

"Well done," she says. "What are you doing today?"

"Getting married, if you will have me?" Marilee gasps with surprise.

"Are you serious?" she says. "Today?"

"Why not?" he asks, preparing himself for a long line of excuses.

"We can't get married...we have to..."

"There is nothing to do today except get married, the only thing stopping us is you. Please, say you will." He grabs her hand and places it over his heart. She hesitates, but looks into his eyes and realizes there is only one thing she needs to ask herself. Is he worth it?

"Yes," she says. "Why not? Let's just do it." She giggles as she sees his eyes light up. He kisses her and goes to the closet to pack. He scrambles about in the closet for a moment and then comes back to kiss her again.

"Oh my God, we are getting married," he says, going back to the closet. "We need suitcases."

"Should we call the guys and tell them?" she says. He stops running around and bites his lip. "You know they will be mad if we don't."

"Yeah, but they are going to want me to go to this meeting tomorrow."

"Is it important?"

"Very, I suppose," he says.

"Then, we can wait–

"We've waited long enough," he says. "I finally convinced you."

"Jamie," she says softly as she walks over to him. She places her hand on his cheek. "A few more days isn't going to change my mind. I promise, I will marry you. Take care of business first."

"Fine, but I'm going to take care of this today. You girls meet us in Vegas."

"Okay, I'll call the girls. We had planned to do this anyway."

"Really?" he laughs. "Wait," he says stopping her from dialing. "Let me let the guys tell them. You go and tell Sasha and your dad."

Marilee has to admit she feels a bit more excited than she thought she would. Jamie smiles and realizes that all his dreams are finally coming true.

~

Betty and Charlotte come running into Marilee's room. "I can't believe you are finally getting married!" Betty squeals.

"I can't believe you're not. How could you turn my brother down?" Marilee says.

"I didn't turn him down. You know I love Charley," Betty says. "I just want the whole extravagant wedding; the white gown, the big cake, and all our family and friends. Besides, one of us better have a wedding for Dad. He will want to walk one of us down the aisle."

Marilee's smile fades. "I didn't think about that."

"Shit," Charlotte says. "Betty, why would you say that."

"I'm sorry," Betty says. "I wasn't thinking."

"It's okay, I just never thought of what I won't have at the wedding. I just thought of what I didn't want. I didn't want all the fuss, but I wanted my dad."

"I'll talk to him. He will be fine with it."

Marilee nods, but she isn't so sure how she feels about it yet. "So, Arianna, Will, and Devin will meet us there tomorrow."

"Great," Charlotte says. "Why don't we get a head start?"

~

Marilee tilts her head up at the extraordinary ceiling décor of their hotel. "This is amazing," she says. Betty and Charlotte are just as stunned. "I'd have never thought in a million years that I would get to come to Las Vegas, much less getting married at *The Venetian Resort*." She holds her queasy stomach. "That plane ride did not do me good."

"Me either," Charlotte says. "I know what will make us feel better. Drinks, anyone?"

"Y'all go ahead," Marilee says. "I want to call Jamie."

"Well, we need to get settled in first anyway," Betty says. "Are rooms are close by so let's meet in the hallway in an hour."

"Sounds good," Charlotte says as they exit the elevator.

"Here is mine," Betty says. They walk in together and Charlotte takes a look around, making sure everything looks safe.

"Looks good," Charlotte says.

"Wow," Betty says. "They do go all out, don't they?"

"Always," Charlotte says with a laugh. After they check out all the rooms, Charlotte leaves Marilee to call Jamie.

"Hey," he says as he answers the phone. Her heart melts at his voice.

"Hey," she says. "How is everything going?"

"Fine," he says. "We should have everything taken care of by tomorrow."

"Great. We made it to Vegas and these rooms are amazing."

"Good. I can't wait to get there."

"Me too," she says. "I called to check on Celia and she is having a blast with our dads. They are going to take her fishing tomorrow with Sasha."

"I got some men coming to keep an eye out, but for now stay safe. Did Charlotte check the rooms?"

"Yes, and all is good."

"I can't believe they are taking Celia fishing. That would be something interesting to see," Jamie laughs. "Shit."

"What is it?"

"Oh nothing, sorry," Jamie says. "Our meeting is starting. I got to go. Love you."

"Love you too, bye." As she hangs up the phone she lies on the bed to get her nervous stomach under control. She hears a knock at the door. Getting a bit nervous, she takes out her knife. "Who is it?" she says, thinking it may be the girls. Nobody answers. She looks through the peep hole, but nothing. As she is looking through the hole, someone knocks on the door again making her jump backwards. "Shit." She hears laughing behind the door so she opens it to see Arianna, Devin, and Will laughing. "Not funny guys." She slaps Will on the arm.

"Sorry," Arianna says. "It was their idea."

"Well, I guess you can have a hug then." She laughs and gives her a hug. "I thought you guys weren't coming until tomorrow night?"

"Well, you know Arianna," Will says. "And I thought Jamie would be going a bit crazy at the thought of you three in Vegas alone."

"I'm glad y'all came early," Marilee says. "Just in time we were going to go for drinks."

"Great," Arianna says. "Give us a bit to freshen up."

"We were planning on meeting up in about an hour anyway. Go and do that door thing with the others too."

"Consider it done," Will says.

~

They go downstairs to the hotel bar and order drinks and laugh about scaring each other. It gets late and they lose track of time. Around midnight, they decide to go to bed. "We are going to have to get up early and go shopping for the wedding," Arianna says, walking by the dress shop in the lobby. "I want to do a bit of window shopping before we go upstairs, though."

"I will as soon as I talk to Jamie," Marilee says, getting her phone out.

"Yeah, I want to talk to Dylan too," Charlotte says.

"Fine, but hurry up," Arianna and Betty starts looking in the window at some dresses.

"Actually," Marilee says. "I think I will go on up to the room." Walking toward the elevator, Marilee holds her stomach, feeling nauseated again. "I'll see y'all tomorrow."

Devin sighs. "Something is wrong with her."

"What?" Arianna says. "She seemed fine to me."

"No, he's right," Betty says. "She is worried."

"About what?" Arianna says.

"The wedding...duh," Charlotte says.

"No, it's more than that," Devin says.

"How do you know?" Arianna asks.

"Trust me," Devin says. "I'm going to go talk to her. I'll be back."

He runs to catch her before the elevator door closes. She notices him coming so she holds the door. A man behind her in the elevator grabs her hand. She gasps as the door closes and Devin runs faster. He reaches the doors just as they close. “Damnit!” he says, hitting the doors with his fist. He runs to the stairs and climbs as fast as he can, actually beating the elevator up. He waits for the light to light up and make the ding sound, but after a minute he realizes he may have screwed up. “Shit, he took her to another floor!” Before he can run to the stairs, the elevator finally dings and he readies himself for a fight. As the door opens, Marilee appears as pale as ever with blood covering her hands. “Oh my God, Marilee, are you okay?” he asks, grabbing her shoulders. She looks at him with a blank stare and quivering lips. She drops her knife and passes out in his arms. Devin looks at the man in the corner of the elevator. He has been stabbed in the gut and in the neck. He quickly dials for backup and stops the elevator. They arrive within a minute.

“What happened?” Will asks.

“Questions later,” Devin says. “We have to clean up this mess quickly before someone comes by. I’m going to take Marilee to her room. Girls come with me.” Devin puts Marilee in her bed. “Get a washcloth and wash the blood off of her. Girls, keep Marilee in her room. I’ll be back shortly. Don’t call Jamie. I will take care of it.” They nod reluctantly. “Okay,” he says as he reaches the elevator again. He sighs. “We have less than ten minutes before they call someone to fix this elevator. Take it to the roof and call for cleanup. Got it.”

“What about security cameras?” Dylan says.

"Shit. I'll take care of that. You guys cut the wire to the feed and I'll take care of the rest."

"Got it," Will says as he shoots out the camera.

"Will!" Devin says, looking around for witnesses.

"What? I had the silencer on."

"Just go." Devin gets on his phone to find the closest person to handle the situation for him. Luckily, there is someone in security to help. "Thanks so much. I owe you one, Kyle. Anything you need, let the Family know."

He is able to go back to check on Marilee after he makes a quick stop at the store downstairs. "That was a close call," he says. "Luck is definitely on our side tonight. How is she?"

"She's in the bathroom cleaning up," Arianna says.

"Can you guys give us a minute alone?" Arianna narrows her eyes. "Trust me, Arianna. I'll explain in a minute. I just need to talk to her about something first."

She nods. "Come on girls. We will be at the bar when you are done," she says. "I can't sleep now."

Devin knocks on the bathroom door. "Marilee, are you alright?"

"Yes," she says. "I don't know why I passed out like that."

"Well, after I took care of the mess you left, I went down to the store to get some things for your upset stomach."

"Oh, thanks," she says, opening the door. "That was sweet. You didn't have to do that. You have other things to worry about than an upset stomach."

"It was no trouble. I want you to know that you can talk to me if you ever nee—

He stops and holds his finger up as his phone rings. "Hold on, it's Jamie." He sighs before answering. "Jamie, how's it going?" He takes the phone away from his ear and Marilee can hear Jamie screaming. She bites her lip and laughs. "Maybe you should take it," Devin says, handing her the phone. I guess the girls couldn't keep a secret for longer than five minutes.

"Sorry," Marilee says.

"I'll leave you to it, then. Please, for both our sakes, don't leave the room."

She laughs. "I promise."

~

"Really?" Devin says sitting down next to Arianna. "You couldn't wait five minutes before you outed me." Arianna and Charlotte point at Betty and she smiles. "Well, the reason I didn't want him to know is because he was about finished with things up. He was scheduled to call me in ten minutes with an update. I was going to tell him then."

"Sorry," Betty says.

"Hopefully, he finished before he went completely mental." He raises his hand to the bartender. "I'll take a double of something, I don't care what." He strokes his hair back and Arianna rubs his back as her phone rings.

"Hey, Jamie," she says. "Okay." She hands Devin the phone.

"I have a man at her door, Jamie," Devin says, exhausted.

"I know," Jamie says. "Sorry I went off before."

"Really? Are you okay?" Devin laughs.

"Yes," Jamie says with a laugh too. "What about you? Everything good?"

"Yes, we got everything taken care of. Did you get the job done?"

"Right before Betty's call. Perfect timing. Tying up some loose ends and then we will be on a plane."

"Great, see you soon." He narrows his eyes when he hangs up the phone. "That was odd."

"What?" Arianna says.

"Jamie was just nice to me."

"Well, that is odd," Charlotte says with a chuckle. "I'm going to keep an eye on Marilee. Anyone else want to come?"

Devin chugs the last of his drink. "Let's all go," he says. "I don't want to leave anyone else alone. Bartender, can I have the bottle to go please?"

27

Jamie dials Marilee's phone, hoping she answers this early. She picks up and he can tell he woke her. "Hey, sorry. Did I wake you?"

"Maybe," she says with a yawn. "Everything okay? Are y'all on your way back?"

"Yeah," he says. "I can't wait to see you." Hearing a knock at the door, Marilee sighs. "Who is that this late?"

"Probably just one of the girls," she says. Opening the door without thinking, she squeals as Jamie pushes her back inside the room.

"You should never open the door without looking," he says. Kissing her, he takes her away. "God, I missed you."

"I missed you too," she says before he starts kissing her again.

The sun comes up with them tangled up together and someone knocking at the door. "Marilee!" Arianna yells. "I know you hear me. I told you it would be early."

"I'll meet y'all downstairs for breakfast," Marilee shouts. Jamie laughs and pulls the covers back over their heads. "I guess I need to get ready."

"Okay," he says. "We will have men following y'all. The usual bunch. Try not to go too far."

"Well, tonight we have the bachelorette thing and we will be crazy busy tomorrow. I don't think I will see you again before the wedding."

"Oh, you will see me before, trust me," Jamie says.

"Okay," she says with a sigh, hoping he is right.

"Is something bothering you?" he asks. "Are you having second thoughts?"

"No, nothing like that. I'm just tired. I'll be fine."

He knows she is lying, but he don't want to press his luck. "You better get ready," he says as her phone beeps for the hundredth time. "Or Arianna will have both our heads." She laughs, but quickly gets out of bed.

~

"Marilee?" Betty asks. "Are you alright?"

"Yeah, why?"

"You've been sitting there for five minutes staring at the wall," Betty says.

"Oh, sorry. Just daydreaming."

"What do y'all think about this dress?" Charlotte asks. "I want to look elegant, but sexy."

"Nice," Arianna says, feeling the beaded work on the dress.

"That is so you, Charlotte. I love it," Marilee says.

"Are you going to pick something out today, Marilee?" Arianna says. "Just start trying stuff on. Something will speak to you."

Marilee goes into the dressing room after picking out a few dresses. She sits for a moment thinking. She doesn't want to be doing this right now, but if she doesn't her friends will start to wonder what is wrong and she really doesn't want to open that conversation with them right now. "Marilee?" Betty says knocking on the door. She looks at the time and jumps up from the bench. She has been daydreaming for thirty minutes. "Are you okay?"

"Yeah, I just can't decide between these dresses."

"Well, let us see," Arianna says. Marilee plays along and comes out to show them the dresses one by one. While she is trying on dresses, a woman walks into the dressing room waiting area with some mimosas.

"You all look as though you could use a break," she says.

"Yes, thank you," Marilee says. "As she takes a sip of her drink, she sees a dress that catches her eye. "Excuse me," she says. "That dress over there." Marilee walks over to the dress. "This one." She looks back to the clerk. "Does it belong to anyone?"

"No, ma'am," the clerk says. "I believe that just arrived today. It is from an Irish designer."

Marilee's eyes widen and sparkle. She never knew what she truly wanted until this moment. Hearing the lady say Irish sparked something inside her. She would have loved to have an Irish wedding. A traditional Irish wedding at the castle she had come to love. Now, she will never have it, but at least she can have her Irish dress. "May I try it on?"

She stares into the mirror at herself. The dress is light blue, with corset strings in the front. The dress has a medieval Celtic vibe that Marilee loves. It is simple, yet the beading makes it a bit more elegant. She smiles, knowing that she has finally found the one. She steps out of the dressing room and everyone gasps, even the clerk.

"Marilee, tell me that is the one you are getting," Arianna says. "It is breathtaking."

"I believe it is," Marilee says.

~

They finish the day out at the spa and back to the hotel to get ready for their night out. As she is getting ready, Jamie comes in. "God, Jamie!" she says.

"Sorry," he says with a snicker. "I told you I would be back to see you."

"I'm glad you did," she says.

"Did you find a dress?"

"I did," she says. "But don't go getting any ideas. You can't see it until the wedding."

"I'd much rather see you in nothing at all," he says. She giggles as he starts undressing her.

~

The girls go out dancing and the guys go to an exclusive bar for Family members only. They are bombarded with women and after an hour of it, Jamie is ready to go. "Can we go now, guys?"

"What time is it?" Devin asks. Jamie looks down at his watch.

"Almost nine," Jamie says.

"Shit," Devin says. "We're late. Let's go."

"Where?" Jamie asks, jumping out of his chair to follow them.

"You'll see," Devin says, giving Jamie a smirk. They walk to the back of the club to where a bouncer stands in front of a set of massive wooden doors. They show their rings. "Mr. Macleary," the bouncer nods. "An honor to have you with us."

"Thank you," Devin says. "These are the Garrison boys and of course Will, the king of London."

"Oh, it's a pleasure to finally get to meet the infamous Garrison's," the bouncer says. "And, the King of London. Wow, it is going to be a great night."

"Guys, what is going on?" Jamie asks with a crease in his forehead. The bouncer smiles and opens the doors.

"Come on," Devin says with a laugh. "You'll see." They pull him down a long hallway that leads to another door and another bouncer. He gives Devin a nod and opens the door. As soon as the door opens Jamie hears the shouting, and the music. He smells the smoke, liquor, blood, and sweat.

"Oh man, are you serious!" Jamie says with a grin and shaking Dylan's shoulders, excited. "Fight Night? This is awesome, guys, thanks."

"Not just any Fight Night," Dylan says. "The Fight Night. The one where only one man in each Faction fights for the title."

"Awesome." Jamie looks down at the cage and sneers.

"Well, it was Charley's idea," Devin says. "Him and Will wanted to surprise us all for our bachelor party, but didn't know who to contact. Dylan overheard us talking about it so we figured someone should be surprised."

"Thanks guys," Jamie says, patting them both on the back. "Do we have seats?"

"Yes, of course," Devin says. "The best." Jamie follows ready to get the night started. They get their beer and snacks and settle in their seats. As soon as they get comfortable Jamie's phone buzzes. His smile fades.

"What is it?" Dylan asks.

"Probably nothing," he says standing up. "I'll be right back." He walks to the bathroom where it is a bit quieter. Someone has sent him a video. He pushes play and his breath is taken away. The video is of him and Ruby at the Michaelson Hotel the night Marilee left him. "Shit!" he says, fast-forwarding to see if it caught all the footage and it does. "Damnit!" he says. With his mouth going dry, he reads the next text: *Call off the wedding or else.* He immediately assumes it is Ruby so he tries her number, but she doesn't answer. "Shit!" he yells again. Jamie texts Dylan to meet him in the bathroom and not to tell anyone. He leans up against the wall and pulls his hair in frustration.

"I'm so stupid," he says, realizing that his dream of marrying Marilee may just go up in smoke. Dylan rushes in the door, noticing Jamie's expression.

"What happened?" Jamie swallows hard with shame, but shows him the video anyways. "Shit, Jamie. Who sent this?"

"I don't know. I called Ruby, but...Damnit!" Jamie hits the mirror and breaks it. Luckily, he doesn't cut himself. "Dylan, if she sees this..."

"Relax, they could be bluffing," Dylan says, trying to calm him down.

"Should I go through with the wedding?"

"Don't be ridiculous," Dylan says. "Of course you should. This is probably just Ruby messing with you. I'd be surprised if she didn't try to stop you one last time."

Jamie calms down at the thought. "It does sound like something she would do." He sighs. "Okay, I'm sure that is all it is. She wouldn't dare show Marilee this, you're right. Over-reacting," he says with a sigh. "I'm good now."

"Good, let's go enjoy the fights."

"I can't just watch now," Jamie says. "I have to get in there and fight."

"Jamie, this is your bachelor party. You can't fight the night before your wedding."

"I have to, Dylan," Jamie says with rage filling his eyes. Dylan sighs knowing it is the only thing that will calm him down.

"Damn you, Jamie, just go sit down and I will come get you."

"Thanks, man," Jamie says. "I owe you."

"Yes, and then two more." Dylan says. Jamie goes back to his seat and waits for Dylan.

"What is wrong with you?" Charley asks, noticing him fidgeting. "You look a bit anxious."

"No, I'm fine. Just ready for another drink."

After about two fights, Dylan returns. "Where have you been?" Devin asks.

"We have a problem," Dylan says. "The guy representing our faction is ill. We either find a new fighter or we forfeit."

"Well, we sure as hell aren't going to forfeit." Jamie says, standing up.

"Jamie, it is the night before you're wedding, you can't fight," Will says.

"I'll do it," Charley says, standing. Jamie pushes him back down in his chair.

"No," he says. "Marilee would have all our heads. Besides, I don't plan on getting beat up."

"Jamie, I know you can handle yourself," Devin says with a sigh. "But these fights are not like the fights back in New Orleans. These are the best of the best."

"Don't worry," Jamie says. "I can handle it." They all shake their heads, doubting him, but know he will not listen to reason.

"Marilee will be pissed at you for doing this too," Charley says.

"Better me than you, little brother," Jamie says, tapping Charley on the cheek.

"Well, I guess you better go and get ready then," Devin says. Jamie smiles and starts toward the dressing room. "But Jamie," Devin shouts. "Be careful with Dublin, he's a beast."

"Got it," Jamie says.

~

After the first few fights, Jamie is wore out, but he gets to rest now for about thirty minutes. He has won every fight so far. After freshening up a bit, he goes to grab a drink. "What do you think you are doing?" Marilee says from behind him. He flinches at her voice and spits out his whiskey. "Shit, Marilee, what are you doing here?"

"Vanessa got a text about the fights," she says with her arms folded. He slams his glass down on the counter.

"Damnit, Vanessa, why did you bring her here?"

"She didn't bring me here!" Marilee shouts. "What's the big deal? Do you not want me here?"

"No, it's not that I don't want you here," Jamie says, taking a breath as he strokes her cheek. "I'm...fighting."

"Oh, since when are you a professional fighter," Marilee says, sitting next to him at the bar.

"I've done it a few times," Jamie says, brushing her hair out of her eyes. "It helps me relax." He notices the creases in her forehead starting to form. "See this is why I didn't want you to know. That, and the fact you will distract me if you're here. You look to damn good to be here tonight. I will lose for sure." He gives her a smirk making her laugh. He pushes her hair off her shoulder and kisses her neck.

"Alright, you win. Just please be careful. Don't go and get too sore for the honeymoon." She gives him a wink.

"I will be careful," he says. She gives him a kiss and goes back toward Vanessa and the girls.

Jamie waits a few minutes after he sees the girls walk out the door and he tries to call Ruby again. She still isn't picking up. Just as he puts the phone down it buzzes. The text reads: *Are you going through with the wedding*? This time the text is from Ruby. Jamie bites his jaw in irritation as he texts her back: *Yes, and nothing will stop me from marrying her. If you show that video to her so help me, Ruby*!

Goodbye, Jamie.

Ruby, don't do anything stupid.

He quickly calls his men to check on her at home. "She isn't there, sir." He calls her again. "Damnit, Ruby, pick up!"

"Jamie, they are ready for you," the cage attendant shouts. Jamie holds up five fingers to get more time. The man nods so Jamie texts Dylan to meet him in the locker room.

"Man, this chick has it bad," Dylan says.

"I'm worried about her," Jamie says.

Dylan sighs at Jamie. "Okay, give me your phone and go fight. If I hear anything, I'll let you know, but stay focused. I don't want you getting hurt in there."

"Okay," Jamie says. "Thanks."

"The next two you got for sure. Just put them down quickly. The sooner you get this done, the sooner we can find out what is going on." Dylan pushes him out toward the cage.

He stays focused and ends all the fights the same way. He rushes in and punches them as if they were trying to hurt his Family. It doesn't take long before the ref stops the fight. He doesn't show off as the crowd screams. He goes to his corner where Dylan is waiting with some water. "She's not home and not answering her phone."

"Have you traced it?"

"In the process now," Dylan says.

"Who's next?"

"One more and then, Dublin," Dylan says. "Are you up for that?"

"We'll see, I guess," Jamie says, taking another swig of his water.

"You'll get a ten minute break after this one."

"Marilee came to see me earlier, did you see the girls?"

"Yeah, who do you think got them out of here so quick?"

"Thanks," Jamie says.

"Always got your back, brother, but you really do need to stop doing stupid shit." Jamie laughs as Dylan pushes him up to go fight. "Now go kick some ass."

28

"Okay, that was fast," Dylan says, stepping back into the cage. They pick up Jamie's opponent and carry him off.

"I'm just ready to be done with this," Jamie says, grabbing the water bottle from Dylan.

"Hey, this was your bright idea," Dylan says.

"I know," Jamie says trying to catch his breath. "This isn't helping as much as I thought it would. Any word?"

"No," Dylan replies, checking his phone. "Wait, they traced her phone."

"What?" Jamie says, standing up. "Where?"

"Here, in Vegas," Dylan says with a hint of laughter. "Can you handle a drink before the last fight?"

"I think it would be stupid not to," Jamie says.

As they go to the bar, the Dublin fighter comes up to them. "I would go easy on drinks," he says.

"And why on earth would I want to do that?" Jamie says, glancing at the huge man standing beside him leaned over the bar.

Dublin shrugs his shoulders. "I just don't want you to get vomit all over the cage or me."

Jamie smirks at the comment. He knows the man is just trying to get a rise out of him. "Thanks, but I think I can manage my drinks."

"Suite yourself." Dublin walks off and Dylan takes his place at the bar.

"He has a point. Go easy until after the fights," Dylan says as his phone goes off again.

"What?" Jamie asks, noticing Dylan's nose crinkle with confusion.

"She's here. Ruby is here," Dylan says, jumping up to look around. "It tracked her in the bathroom?"

"Shit," Jamie says, jumping up. "I got to go talk to her."

"Your fight is about to start," Dylan says.

"I'll only be a minute. Come with me and wait outside so nobody comes in." They both walk quickly to the bathrooms and Jamie enters while Dylan waits at the door.

"Ruby?" Jamie says. "Are you in here?" He goes to the stalls. "Ruby?" he asks again, but no answer. He opens each stall as he gets a very bad feeling. As he gets to the last stall, he takes a deep breath. When he opens the door, he sees her dead eyes staring at him. "No, no, Ruby." He goes to inspect the body. She has no wounds that he can see, but he notice a bottle on the floor. "Damn Ruby, why would you do that?" Then he sees a card next to her body. "Shit."

"They are ready for you, Jamie," Dylan yells into the cracked door.

"Get in here," Jamie says.

"What is it?" Dylan runs in the bathroom. Jamie looks down at the floor and points to the stall. As Dylan peeks into the stall he gasps. "Oh shit, Jamie."

"We need to get her out of here before someone sees her," Jamie says. "He hands Dylan the card.

"What the hell? The ladies of Louisiana? That can't be a coincidence."

"Call Devin and tell him to bring a blanket," Jamie says as he strokes his hair back. "We will carry her out the back door."

"Jamie you still have one more fight and you can't not show. You're a king. How would that look?"

Jamie bites his lip. “Fine,” he says, slicking his hair back into a ponytail. “I’ll meet y’all in back in ten minutes.”

“Jamie, no offense, but you saw Dublin, right? He isn’t going to be as easy as the others.”

“Thanks for the confidence, Dylan, but don’t worry, I got a plan. Just get her out of here before anyone sees her like that.” He looks at her one last time, sighs, and walks out. He enters the ring with his heart pounding. He isn’t sure if it is because of what just happened or because he is fixing to fight someone who looks like a lumber jack. Knowing he isn’t a professional fighter, he doesn’t show off any special moves. He just knows he has to get the job done fast. The announcer starts the fight and he runs at Dublin as fast as he can, jumping in the air to get his momentum. He comes down on him with an elbow to the temple, sending Dublin down to the floor. The crowd is stunned in silence as they wait for the referee’s call. After the referee’s shock wears off, he raises Jamie’s hand and the crowd cheers. Making his way out of the cage, he fights his way out of the crowded arena. Finally, he makes it to the exit and runs to meet the guys in the back. Seeing the car running, he jumps inside. “Where is Ruby?”

“It’s taken care of,” Devin says.

“What did you do?” Jamie says, hitting the back of Devin’s seat. Devin’s head turns and his eyes glare at Jamie for being defiant. “She deserves better than being tossed into the river,” Jamie says, his eyes glossy.

Devin sighs at Jamie’s usual temper tantrum. “That is why I had my men take her back home. Her husband just went missing, the cops will be convinced it was suicide.” Devin notices Dylan and Jamie exchange glances. “Am I missing something?”

"No," Jamie says. "Giving Dylan a pleading glare not to say anything about the video yet. He doesn't want Charley and Will to know. He knows that they will never forgive him.

"So, did you win?" Charley asks to lighten the mood. The rest laugh and as Jamie gives him a little chuckle they pull under the hotel awning.

"Yes, Charley, I won. Did you have doubts?"

"Hotel bar?" Dylan asks.

"Yes, please."

Charley and Will call it a night as Dylan, Devin, and Jamie go to the bar. Devin sits in the middle of the two. "So, what is it that I should know?" As Jamie waves his hand to the bartender for a drink. He places the phone in front of Devin. Picking up the phone, Devin watches the video for about two seconds and throws the phone back down on the counter. "How much of it was caught on camera?"

"All of it," Jamie says, sliding the phone back into his pocket.

"This was when Marilee left you that night?"

"Yes," Jamie says with his hands covering his face.

"Shit, Jamie," Devin says with irritation.

"We found this card beside the body." Dylan slides the card to Devin.

"Jamie," Devin says, rubbing his forehead. "I will leave this in your hands. You know what you have to do."

"Yes, sir," Jamie says.

"Now," Devin says as he stands up and removes his sleek grey jacket and places it neatly on his seat. "Stand up." Jamie takes a sip of his drink and closes his eyes and sighs, knowing what has to happen now." He places his drink down on the counter. “I said stand up.” Devin growls through gritted teeth and fists clenched to his side.

“Guys—

“Stay out of this, Dylan,” Devin says. Jamie stands up to face Devin with slumped shoulders. “Marilee is a remarkable woman,” Devin says with assertion. “She deserves better than that, better than...this. He points at Jamie with disgust.

“I agree,” Jamie says.

“But yet,” Devin says, biting his lip in anger. “She wants you.” Without warning, Devin punches Jamie in the stomach. Dylan shoots his head around the bar to make sure nobody is watching, but it is empty and the bartender is minding his own business. Jamie hunches over, trying to catch his breath and Devin bends down to whisper in his ear. “Don’t let her find out about this and don’t slip up again. If you do, it will be you lying on the bathroom floor.” He pats him on the shoulder to end their conversation and grabs his jacket. “Meet back in our room in twenty minutes.”

Twenty minutes later they all meet up in Devin’s room. Everyone sits in the living area waiting on the girls to come join them. As they walk in, Jamie’s heart jumps at seeing Marilee smile at him. She walks over and kisses him. “Hey, I heard you won,” she says.

“Yeah,” he says with a weak smile.

“So, now that the girls are here we can update them on what is going on. Devin explains what unfolded earlier with Ruby, leaving out the video crisis.

“Oh, God,” Marilee says, grabbing Jamie’s arm. “I’m so sorry, Jamie.” He gives her a half smile, feeling the most guilt of his life. He wonders if she knew, would she still marry him? He strokes his hair in irritation at his thoughts. He is fairly certain that there is no way in hell that would happen.

"So, where are the Ladies of Louisiana and how can we kill them?" Charlotte asks.

"Well, we are looking into it," Devin says. "You girls don't worry about it. We have a wedding tomorrow. Everyone get some rest."

Marilee follows Jamie out the door. "I thought you were staying with the girls tonight." He says.

"Considering recent events, I really don't want to leave you alone tonight," she says.

"Well," Jamie sighs. "That absolutely works for me." He picks her up and she giggles with her skin tingling just as it always does when he touches her. He carries through the doorway.

"You know you don't have to do that until tomorrow," she says, biting her lip.

"Practice," he says, closing the door with his foot. He throws her on the bed and locks the door. "I need to shower. Don't go anywhere." He gives her a wink and takes his shirt off. "You can always join me."

She smiles. "Okay, I'll be in there in a second. As she grabs some clothes from her suitcase, her phone buzzes. She sighs, but grabs it and starts to open the text as she gets to the bathroom.

"Who is it?" Jamie asks, seeing her on her phone.

"Not sure," she says, her eyebrow raising. "It's a video."

"No!" Jamie shouts, trying to get out of the shower in time to stop her. "Don't open it—

"Oh my God," she says, placing her hand over her mouth. She drops her phone on the floor and holds her stomach, trying not to vomit. "You slept with her, you bastard. She looks up at him with disgust, crying. He places a towel around his waist and sighs.

"I was drunk," he says, aggravated that she found out. "It was the night you left, I was angry."

"So was I!" she shouts. "But I didn't go and have sex with someone else because of it."

"I'm sorry," he says, upsetting her even more and she slaps him across the face.

"Get out!" she yells.

"Maril—

"Get out," she says, slapping him again. She starts throwing things at him until he leaves the bathroom. When he is finally gone, she locks the door and falls to the ground, feeling like she is going to die.

"Shit." Jamie sighs and hurries to get dressed. "I'm going to kill those bitches." He grabs the card from his pocket and dials the number.

"Hello, Mr. Garrison," a woman says.

"Who is this?" Jamie growls. "Is this Haley? Whoever it is you have my attention so what the hell do you want?"

"To ruin your life, just like the Garrisons ruined mine."

"Well, congratulations," he says.

"Oh," she says with a laugh. "That is only the tip of the iceberg, Mr. Garrison. I plan on making you all suffer a great deal more."

Jamie laughs. "Well, I suggest you hurry because you will be dead soon and I promise you it will be me that kills you." Haley is quiet and he knows he has her scared. "Have I got your attention now? See you soon, Haley."

Marilee decides to get off the floor and wash her face with some cold water. She sees the bag Devin got her for her upset stomach. She is so beyond hurt, she can't think straight and her stomach is in all sorts of knots. She spreads the contents from the paper bag out on the counter. She sorts through the antacids and a little box. She reaches in and pulls out a stick that reads pregnant. As she cries again, not knowing what she is supposed to do next, Jamie lightly knocks on the door.

"Marilee," he says. "I'm going to go tell Devin to call off the wedding. I'm so sorry." She struggles with her thoughts for a moment. She takes a look at herself in the mirror and back at the pregnancy test in her hand. Quickly putting all the items back in the paper bag she yells, "No!"

"What?" Jamie says, confused as she opens the door. "What do you mean?" Jamie feels like his heart has been torn out of his chest as he sees her red swollen eyes. "What do you mean, no?" he asks again, hopeful.

Folding her arms across her chest she exhales. "Who else knows about this?" she asks, trying to avoid more tears.

"Just Dylan and Devin," he looks down ashamed.

"Good," she says. "Don't tell anyone else." He narrows his eyes at her. "It never happened. I never saw that video. Just leave it as it was before."

"Marilee, I—

"Jamie, I can't," she says as more tears fall down her cheek. "I just can't, not right now."

"Okay, okay," he says pulling her close and waiting for her to shove him away, but she never does. He takes her to the bed and she cries herself to sleep on his chest. When she is asleep he texts his men to start looking for Haley and any accomplices. Soon, he falls asleep with his arms around her.

~

They wake up to the sound of knocking and Jamie is thankful she is still with him. "Marilee!" Arianna shouts at the door. "Let's go!"

"Crap," Marilee says. "I forgot she wanted to get an early start."

"It's six in the morning," Jamie says. "What could possibly take ten hours to do?"

"She's Arianna, remember, she is crazy."

"Oh, yeah," Jamie says, brushing the hair out of her eyes. She quickly remembers last night's events and looks away from him.

"Give me a few minutes," she shouts back to Arianna and then back to Jamie. "I got to go." She starts to get up out of bed.

"Hey," he pulls her back to him stroking her cheek. "So, I will see you at the altar then?" She wants to fall apart, but she can't, not now.

"Yeah, I'll be there," she says quickly getting up and going to the bathroom, hoping Jamie doesn't follow.

Jamie decides not to follow her and give her some space. He goes down and grabs some coffee for her and runs into Devin. "Hey," Devin says, placing his hand on Jamie's chest to make him stop. "I'm sorry about last night. I may have gotten a bit carried away."

Jamie sighs. "No, you didn't. I deserved more so maybe another time." Devin gives him a smirk. "I called the number on the card."

"And," Devin says with his eyes widened in interest.

"Haley answered."

"Really? So where is she? I assume you are hunting as we speak?"

"Yes, we should know something soon."

"Good," Devin says glancing at the coffee. "We have nine hours before the wedding. Let's get it taken care of shall we. Is that for Marilee?"

"Yeah," Jamie says. "I'll meet you back—

"I'll take it to her," Devin says, taking the coffee from his hand. "I forgot something upstairs anyway."

"Sure," Jamie says, a bit disappointed. He wanted to see her one more time, but he does want to get this Haley thing taken care of quickly.

~

Knocking on the door, Devin feels a bit nervous. He's not sure if he wants to be right about her or not. He definitely understands Jamie's urges, he gets them too, but he also feels immensely protective of Marilee. She opens the door as she brushes her hair. "Hey," she says. "I know, I'm hurrying."

"Don't worry, Arianna said she would meet you downstairs. "I brought coffee."

"Oh, thanks," she says. "You didn't have too."

"Well, Jamie got it. I just brought it, but would you be needing decaf?" Devin closes the door behind him. She fidgets with her fingers for a moment trying to decide if she should tell the truth. He places the coffee down on the bedside table and as he looks back up she begins to cry. "Oh, shit," he says. "Marilee, it's going to be okay." He pulls her to his chest.

"No," she cries. "It won't. Everything is different now."

"How is everything different?"

"I saw the video, Devin," she says.

"Damnit," he says. He curses Jamie in his head. He told him never to let her see that video. "I'm so sorry. I just saw him and he didn't say anything to me."

"I told him not to," she says pushing away from him and wiping her eyes.

"You're still going through with the wedding," he says. "I'm impressed."

She narrows her eyes. "Impressed?"

"I just mean that most women would have ran off by now."

"How could I not marry him, Devin?" She paces back and forth. "I'm about to have his baby, again. I can't raise two babies by myself and there is my dad, the lodge, my brothers...oh my God, Betty—

"Hey, stop," he says, noticing she is going into a rant. He takes her shoulders and steadies her to look into her eyes. "You will never be alone. Nothing will change if you don't go through with the wedding. You will always and forever be Family. Everyone will understand—

"No," she says, shaking her head. "They can't know about this. Charley already has issues with Jamie. I don't want to make it worse. Promise me that you won't tell anyone."

Devin sighs. "I promise. Are you sure this is what you want to do?"

"Yes." She turns back to the mirror and straightens her hair.

"Okay then, if it helps," Devin says. "He was pretty messed up over you when you left. He didn't think you were coming back."

She stares at him, not wanting to waste any more tears on the subject. "You can go now, Devin."

"Look, I'm not taking up for him," he says. "And I did punch his dumbass in the gut last night for it." Marilee cracks a smile. "If you want to hold on to something today, just know that any other man would have given in to Ruby as soon as she made the advance. Jamie didn't." He opens the door to leave. "He loves you more than you could possibly know, despite his stupidity." He turns to leave.

"Devin, wait," she says. "How did you know to get me a test? I didn't have a clue, how did you?" He comes back in and closes the door back, shrugging his shoulders with a grin. "I remember when you were pregnant with Celia. You had the same pale look on your face and you couldn't keep anything down."

"Oh, yeah," she says, tickled that he remembered. "Not really looking forward to that part."

"Well, at least Jamie will be with you this time. I remember back then, all you wanted was him to be there with you."

"Yes, but I had you there. Thanks for that."

"It was my pleasure," he says. "When are you going to tell him?"

"Probably after we talk about the other thing, after the wedding. If I tell him now, he will probably think I'm marrying him because I'm pregnant."

"Aren't you?" Devin says, just to be sure she knows what she is doing.

"No," she says. "I love him, despite of his stupidity."

"We all do," Devin says with a laugh.

"I'm just angry and it is going to take some time to forgive him for this."

"Well, you're secret is safe with me," Devin says, kissing her cheek. "For now." He gives her a wink and opens the door to leave. "See you at the altar."

~

Marilee finally heads out the door to meet the others downstairs for their big day of beauty. She gives the guard at the door a nod and smile as she shuts the door behind her. He follows as she walks to the elevator. Before she enters, he checks to see if it is secure. They ride down in silence stopping to pick up a couple of ladies along the way. Marilee gives them a polite nod without making eye contact. She really isn't up for small talk. As the elevator music plays, one of the ladies hums along. She stops when she drops her purse and everything spills out. "Oh my," she says, bending down to retrieve the items.

"Oh let me help you," Marilee says. Her guard sighs in irritation, but bends down to help as well. As he does, the woman stabs him in the neck. Marilee starts to scream, but the other woman puts her finger to her lips.

"I wouldn't do that, darling," the woman says. Before Marilee can say anything the other woman hits her in the back of the head.

Marilee wakes up in a hotel room alone with her head feeling like it has been sliced open. Her wrists are tied to the side of the bed. She starts to panic, but the more she wiggles the more the ropes burn her wrists. As the tears start to form in her eyes, she notices the name of the hotel on the nightstand. *The Venetian* insignia fills her with hope. Arianna will be looking for her by now and if they left the body in the elevator, it is only an amount of time. She gasps as she hears the keycard unlocks the door. The two woman from the elevator walk in. Marilee narrows her eyes as she remembers who they are. "You are the Ladies of Louisiana." They smile, but say nothing to her. After grabbing a few things, they whisper in a young man's ear and then leave again. He gives Marilee a smirk and moves toward her.

~

Devin meets the guys downstairs. "So," he says to get an update.

"She is here in Vegas," Jamie says. "At least her phone is. She might have high-tailed it out by now though. We are waiting to get an exact location."

"Do you still have men with the girls?"

"Yes," Jamie replies. "Always."

"Good, this could be a diversion," Devin says, leaning closer to Jamie so nobody else can hear. "She told me she saw the video."

Jamie bites his jaw. "How is she?"

"Confused, but good," Devin says. "I assured her of your condition that night."

Jamie smirks. "I can't believe she still wants to marry me after what I did."

"Yep," Devin says, dying to tell him Marilee's secret, but he promised he wouldn't. He pats Jamie on the back. "You're a lucky man. Let's get this bitch Haley taken care of. She almost took everything away from you."

They start to walk off when Jamie's phone buzzes. "Yeah," he answers. "Really?" He notices Devin's forehead fold. "They got all three of them." He looks back to Devin. "Do we want to kill them now or meet and greet." Devin looks at the time on his watch.

"We have time, let's meet and greet." Devin says with a smile.

"Meet and greet it is," Jamie says. "I'll text you an address within the hour." He hangs up and starts suggesting places. There are a few abandoned warehouses near here."

"Let's go find one and let's do this one alone. We can meet up with the others later."

~

The warehouse is empty and secluded, a good location for a kill. Devin nods his head in agreement. "Make the call." Jamie gets a sensation down his spine, one he gets when he's about to get revenge.

Ten minutes later he is staring Haley in the eyes. Their men tie the three Ladies of Louisiana to chairs in the darkened warehouse. Devin and Jamie walk around them like vultures. "So which one of you are the one causing so much trouble?" Devin asks in his usual sarcastic, Irish tone. Haley's eyes widen when she hears his accent.

"You are Devin," she says, swallowing hard. "The head of Ireland?"

"Yes, and something tells me that you are Haley."

"I never wanted to involve you," she says. "We just wanted revenge for what the Garrison's did to our families."

"I totally understand," he says. "Revenge is sweet, and when someone makes a vicious attempt to harm your family, there is no better feeling after getting justice."

"Exactly," she says, glaring at Jamie.

"Hey, I didn't kill your family, my grandfather did."

"And I know, giving your obsession with getting even, that you will understand what has to happen now," Devin says as he pulls his gun and shoots her two accomplices. As she gasps, Devin hands Jamie the gun. Aiming it at Haley, Jamie is ready for his revenge.

"Wait," Haley says. "You'll never find her if you kill me," she cries. Jamie pauses and looks to Devin. Quickly, Devin gets out his phone and calls Arianna and confirms their fear. He gives Jamie a nod and Haley gives a smirk.

"Where is she?" Jamie shouts.

“Promise to let me go and I will tell you.” Jamie bites his lip thinking. He stops and smiles at Devin. Jamie slowly lowers his gun and Haley let’s out a gasp of relief.

“Oh, no need to smile,” he says. “You’ve only postponed the inevitable.” He calls the hotel. “Yes, this is Jamie Garrison. Can you tell me which room the Ladies of Louisiana is staying in, please?” He waits for a moment and gives Haley a wink. She starts to cry again. “Thank you.” He hangs up with the hotel and calls Will. “Room 1042, quickly. Kill whoever gets in your way. Call me when you have her.” Haley begs for her life as they wait for the call. Five minutes later his phone rings. Jamie gives a sigh and Devin can tell something is wrong.

“What is it?” he asks. Jamie hands him the phone. Haley tries to apologize, but Jamie doesn’t want to listen.

“You failed,” he says, pointing the gun at her head. “I told you that you would die soon.” He shoots and just like that revenge washes over him as he stares at her body.

“Clean this up,” Devin says to the men who accompanied them. He comes to stand beside Jamie. “You feel bad for her?”

“I did,” Jamie says. “Not anymore.”

“Good,” Devin says, making Jamie’s eyes squint with confusion. “I’m just thinking it is a good thing you still have some sort of conscience.”

“Okay, you’ve been talking to Dad, haven’t you?” Jamie says.

Devin laughs. “Let’s get you back to Marilee.”

~

Marilee tries to scream, but the man quickly covers her mouth with one hand and unties her with the other. Thinking to herself that he is helping her, she stops squirming. He points to the door and smiles. Hastily, she jumps off the bed toward the door. He grabs her arm and laughs. "Sorry," he says. "I'm just teasing you. I can't let you go. My orders are to kill you."

She struggles out of his grip and pulls her knife from her ankle holster. His smile fades. "Do you really think you could take me?" he asks.

"Come at me and we will find out," she says with her heart pounding. As the man comes at her, she slices his hand. Backing away a bit, he growls, but comes at her again grinding his teeth. She lunges at him as he comes forward, but this time she misses. "Nice try," he says with a laugh. Squeezing the knife tighter as he grabs her from behind, she slices at his arm. This time she slices him pretty deep. He quickly lets her go. "Enough of this!" he shouts and pulls out his gun. "Get on your knees," he says, taking a quick glance at his arm.

"Please," Marilee pleads. "You don't have to do this."

"On your knees!" he shouts louder, placing the gun to her temple. She cries as he forces her to her knees and takes the knife from her grasp. "Now, let's see how you like it." He takes her knife and slices her arm. Her eyes widen as the knife cuts into her skin and she screams out in pain. He kicks her in the stomach to shut her up. "Doesn't feel so good, does it?" He kicks her in the stomach over and over until she can't breathe. She gasps for air. "Alright," he says. "Get up." Coughing, she tries to get up, but she can't. "I said, get up!" he snaps. Pulling her by her hair, he drags her up to her knees again. She pleads again, but he ignores her and kicks her again. As she falls to the floor, the door flings open and Will and Charley come running in. Will doesn't hesitate to shoot the man and Charley swoops Marilee up in his arms. His heart sinks as he sees the blood.

“Charley?” she says.

“Yeah, it’s me. Let’s get you out of here.”

29

Marilee stares at herself in the mirror. It is six o' clock and they are waiting to be called down the aisle. Her arms are sore and bandaged, but she still plans on walking down the aisle. "Marilee, are you okay?" Betty asks. "You look a bit pale."

"Yeah, I'm fine," she says, holding her stomach. Vanessa assured her that the baby was fine, but she wonders if he done any damage. "Just a bit light-headed." Betty retrieves her purse and pulls out a pack of crackers.

"Here," she says. "Eat these. You've barely had anything to eat today."

"Thanks," Marilee says, taking one of the crackers and putting the whole thing in her mouth. A little old lady peeks in the room.

"Girls, they are ready for you," she says.

Marilee's eyes widen as she tries to swallow the cracker. Betty laughs. "Here, take some water." She swishes and checks her teeth.

"Come on ladies," the woman says hurrying them out the door. Marilee stops and puts some lipstick on. Thinking about her decision. Vanessa comes back to hurry her and notices her hesitation.

"Remember what I said, just ask yourself that one question." She leans in to whisper in her ear. "Is he worth it?" Marilee pauses and bites her lip, but Vanessa pushes her out the door. "And stop worrying about the baby, she or he is going to be just fine." She was worried about telling Vanessa her secret, but she needed to know if the baby was alright. Marilee is the last to enter the doorway. Everyone is waiting on her to walk down the aisle. She begins to walk slowly contemplating the question, *is he worth it*?" Her thoughts take her back to when she first fell in love with him, back when he was just James Riley. She thinks about how much they have went through together. As she glances up at him, he smiles. She turns to Devin and he gives her a wink. Thinking about all the pain that Jamie has put her through in the past, she stands next to Charlotte. The wedding officiant begins and she considers running out the door, but as her feet move slightly she remembers Jamie going through some pain as well. She isn't the only one who has suffered loss and heartbreak. Though he has done something almost unforgivable, she asks herself another question. If she had to do it all over again...would she? Is he worth doing it over again? "Do you ladies take these men to be your husbands?"

Charlotte and Arianna immediately say yes and turn to Marilee for her answer. Jamie closes his eyes, waiting for her to say no. He can't even believe that she has made it this far. He never thought he would have the opportunity to marry her and when he got it, he messed it up. He can only hope that she forgives him.

"Absolutely," Marilee says. Jamie opens his eyes in shock. He doesn't understand why she would marry him after what he has put her through, but he doesn't care at the moment. He grabs her and without waiting for the officiant to finish, he kisses her like he hasn't kissed her in years. After the kiss, he leans in to whisper in her ear. "I'm so sorry," he says.

"I know," she says.

~

Considering how important the guys are they didn't get much of a honeymoon before they had to head back home. Marilee and Jamie hasn't talked about what happened nor has she told him she is pregnant. She knows she has to tell him before Devin does, or Vanessa. Closing her eyes as she lays down beside Celia, she wishes she could just forget. It would be so much easier to just forget. Jamie peeks in to check on Celia. Marilee quickly closes her eyes and pretends to be asleep so she doesn't have to talk about anything. She can't stop picturing Ruby and him together. He has confirmed her worst fear. She will just never be good enough.

Jamie closes the door and sighs. Marilee hasn't said anything about what happened in Vegas and he's not sure if he should bring it up or not. They haven't slept in the same bed since they've been home. She falls asleep next to Celia every night. He has to find a way to fix it, but he's not even sure if it can be fixed.

"Jamie," Vanessa says, snapping her fingers in his face. "What's up?" She leans on his office desk as he stares at his drink.

"Nothing," he says as he strokes his hair back.

"Still worried about Marilee, aren't you?"

He give her a side-ways glance. "Yes," he says. "Vanessa, how can I fix this?" He looks up to her for some hope.

"Time, Jamie," she says with sympathy. He sighs because that isn't the advice that he wanted. "She has to learn to trust you again. Nothing you can do will speed up the process. Just deal with your punishment."

"I hate the fact that she hates me," he says, taking a sip of his drink. "She won't even look at me."

"So no honeymoon then," Vanessa makes a pouting face.

"What do you think?" he says, not even giving her an eye roll.

"Sorry," she says. "You need to take your mind off of it. Go find some trouble to get into."

Jamie cracks a smile. "What did you have in mind?"

"You, Dylan, and I could take a trip to Georgia."

"Why? What is in Georgia?" he asks as she hands him some papers.

"An opportunity has presented itself and I say we take action."

"What are you talking about?" he says reading the papers she has put in front of him. "Why am I looking at land?"

"Dear lord, you are losing it, James Garrison." She sighs. We should take this opportunity to up our presence in Georgia. We need to start planting seeds there if we want more control."

"I see," he says. "And what am I supposed to build?"

She looks toward the ceiling and sighs. "Hotel, another lodge, restaurant, a flipping mall, I don't know, but something, anything."

He bites his lip. "It would help our presence in Georgia a bit," he says.

"Well, what a splendid idea you have, my king," she says. "You're welcome."

She walks out the door. "We can leave tomorrow, set it up."

"Already taken care of," she says.

Jamie closes the door to his office, lies down on the couch, and sighs. Pondering the thought of how he can show Marilee that she can trust him again.

~

Everyone is busy today which means Marilee is left alone with her thoughts. "I need to work," she says. "Sasha," she yells down the hallway.

"Yes, ma'am," Sasha yells back.

"I'm going to the restaurant. I'll be back this afternoon."

"Yes, ma'am." Sasha says. "Be safe."

"I'm taking Shane with me." A stalky man comes to follow her out.

"Good," Sasha says. "I'll let Mr. Garrison know."

She pulls up to the lodge and smiles. She misses this place a bit and she misses her boat. Looking down towards the dock, she sees it. After a moment of thought, she starts walking down to it. As she gets closer, her heart starts to hurt thinking of all the time her and Jamie has spent on it. She stops and turns away, but she hears something. She climbs onboard and sees Jamie sitting on the floor of the boat, his eyes red and an empty bottle of whiskey lying next to him. He jumps when he sees her. "Hey," he says.

"Sorry," she says. "I'll go—

"No, please," he begs as he stumbles to his feet. "Marilee, I can't take this. I know I am in the wrong here, but I can't stand us not talking to each other." She arches her eyebrow, but knows it's killing both of them.

"Fine, you want to talk?" she says, walking over to the wheel. "You raise the anchor and I'll drive." He swallows hard at the fact he got his way, but now he doesn't know where to start. She takes the boat down the bayou for about a mile and he still hasn't figured out what to say. "Are you going to talk or can I turn this thing around?"

"I'm trying to figure out what to say," he says.

"I don't think there is anything you can say, Jamie. Nothing will make it better. I just need time."

"That is what everyone keeps saying," he says with a sigh. "Well, we have the rest of our lives now."

"Yes, we do," she says. "You know, I knew." She laughs. "I didn't want to think it was possible, but I knew you cheated. The worst of it is I gave you an out and you still lied...right to my face."

"Would you have still married me if I told you the truth?" he asks.

"I did marry you, Jamie. I knew the truth and I still married you."

He bites his lip with exhaustion. "I hate that you hate me."

"Jamie," she says, turning off the engine. She turns around to face him with her arms folded. "I don't hate you. I'm just pissed, okay. If you were so upset that night, why not try and get me back?"

"I don't know. I was upset, but also angry too." She narrows her eyes. "You called me a monster, the one thing that I never wanted to become. I believed you, I guess."

She tilts her head down with shame. She knew that hurt him, but she didn't realize how bad.

"People say things they don't mean when they are angry, Jamie."

"I know," he says. "I'm just explaining my thoughts at the time. After that, everyone was trying to make it better and I had to get away. I went to the Michaelson and drank until I couldn't no more. On my way, I ran into Ruby." He sees Marilee flinch at her name. "I barely remember any of it. I was very drunk. I would have never if I hadn't been."

"But you did," she says, shaking her head in disbelief still.

He strokes his hair back. "When I saw you were back, I was so happy but miserable at what I had done. I was scared to lose you and that is why I lied."

"I just can't help feel like..." She fiddles with her nails so she doesn't have to look at him. Tears start to run down her face, but she quickly wipes them away.

"Like what?" he says. "Tell me."

"Like I am never going to be good enough."

"What?" he stands up, making her jump a bit and she backs away. "What are you talking about?"

"Maybe that is why you wanted her so bad. I'm not good enough for you. I don't think I ever will be."

"Listen to me carefully," he says, he grabs her shoulders and looks her in the eyes. She doesn't try to back away anymore. "You are too good for me. This had nothing to do with that. This happened because I was upset, angry, and stupidly drunk. And because the reason I thought you wouldn't come back to me is because you are too good for me. I have always known that." He grabs her face. "I will never do anything like that again, please believe me." She nods her head. "I will try to be the man that you deserve from now on." As he strokes his thumb across her cheek, she cries harder and he pulls her to his chest. "I love you so much, Marilee."

"I love you too, Jamie."

"Now, what?"

"I don't know, time, still. I will get passed this eventually."

"Would it make me a total jackass if I left you for a few days?"

"No, actually, it may help," she says. The comment hurts, but he sucks it up.

"Oh, okay, then. We have some property we need to go look at in Georgia."

"Are you buying it?" she asks a bit curious.

"We are thinking about it," he says. "We need to up our presence in Georgia so building something may help."

"What are you going to build?"

"Not sure yet, why?" he smiles. "Any ideas?"

"Well, a few. What would you think about expanding the lodge?"

"It has crossed my mind," he says as he starts the boat back up. "Is that something you would want?"

"I think so," she says, thinking about how good of a distraction that would be. "Eventually, maybe we could have one in Ireland." She smiles and that is all he has ever wanted lately, to see her smile.

"Maybe," he says, giving her a wink. "Come on, let's get home."

30

"So," Vanessa says as she walks over to Jamie. She places her hands on her hips, waiting for him to finish surveying the land. "What do you think?"

"It's a good location, but not for a lodge," he says, with displeasure on his face.

"Well," Dylan says. "Do we want to pass up snagging such a good location? It would be fantastic for another Michaelson." Jamie kicks at the dirt, thinking. "It is right in the middle of everything. What more could you ask for?"

"I really wanted another location for a lodge," Jamie says.

"Well, hell," Vanessa says. "Is there any reason you can't do both?"

"That is a good question?" Dylan says as they both look at Jamie waiting for an answer.

He smiles, seeing that they are eager for this property. "Call Dad and see if it seems good financially."

"Yes," Vanessa and Dylan say as they give each other a high-five. He laughs at their excitement. "Let's go," Jamie says. "More to survey."

"What do you mean?" Vanessa says. "I only scheduled this one."

"Well, you gave me an idea so I ran with it." He says as they walk to the car. "I think we need to go big. We need hotels in the north as well. Our weapons distribution is getting back on track. We can't afford to lose it."

"So we are building in the North too?" Dylan says.

"We can't afford that, but I think if we find something that fits our ideas we can renovate or buy someone out. Call Dad and see if he can meet us in Boston. I already have a couple of places in mind."

~

Marilee wakes up sick to her stomach. She hates this part of the pregnancy. Her doctor's appointment is today. She is nervous, but excited to see how far along she is. Betty knocks on the door of her bedroom. "Are you ready yet?" Betty says, eager to find out herself.

"Almost," she says. "Are you sure that you have time to go with me, Betty? I know you have a lot going on at school."

"Are you kidding?" she says. "I wouldn't miss it. I'm just glad you let me in on your secret. I'm all caught up this week at school anyway."

"Great," she says. As the trees whip past the window, Marilee wonders if she can handle another baby right now. Will Celia be jealous of her or him? She doesn't realize how long they have been driving as they pull in the parking lot of the doctor's office.

"Here we are," Betty says. "I really hope this is safe?" she says.

"I know," Marilee says. "I didn't want to tell anyone though. I did use a false name so we should be okay."

"Alright," Betty says. "Well, I did call someone about it."

"Betty," Marilee sighs, "what did you do?"

"Don't be mad, he already knew anyway. I just thought it would be safer if we had someone to come with us."

Someone knocks on her window, making her jump. She smiles as Devin waves at her. She jumps out of the car and gives him a hug. "What are you doing?" she says. "You are way too busy to be worrying about me."

"Wouldn't miss it," Devin says.

"Thanks, Betty," Marilee says. "Good call."

As they wait, Devin notices a woman walk out of the waiting room. "Excuse me," he says. "I'll be right back." He follows her out to the parking lot. Somehow he knows this woman, but he can't put his finger on it. "Excuse me, Miss," Devin says. "Can I speak to you for a moment?"

She stops and turns. "Yes, can I help you?" she says.

"I'm sorry," he says with a smile. "You just look so familiar. Do I know you?"

"I don't believe so. Somehow, I think I would remember you," she says. He smiles at the compliment.

"Sorry to have bothered you," he says, but still has this feeling that he has seen this woman somewhere before." He goes back inside just as the nurse calls Marilee back, using the name Betty Jackson. "Well, you put a lot of thought into that," Devin says.

"Shut up," she says, walking back with the nurse. She turns back to them. "Guys? Are you coming?"

"Are you sure?" Devin says, looking around the room, jumbled. Marilee laughs. She isn't used to seeing Devin unsure of anything.

"Yes," she says. "Please." Devin smiles and follows Betty.

Betty and Devin sit down on the couch reserved for guests as Marilee goes to change into her gown. The nurse comes in to set up as Marilee comes out of the bathroom. "Have a seat on the bed," she says. "It will only take me a moment." The nurse sets everything up and tells Marilee to lie back. Marilee does as she is told and feels her stomach jump as the cold wand touches her stomach. The nurse glides it around on her belly for a few minutes, but stops and bites her lip. "What is it?" Marilee asks.

"Let me try again," the nurse says with a sigh. She glides the wand again as Marilee looks toward Devin and Betty. She wasn't sure this is what she wanted, but now she knows she did want it and she's scared. "I'm sorry," the nurse says. "I can't seem to find a heartbeat."

"What does that mean?" Marilee asks, knowing already.

"At some point the baby's heart stopped. I'm sorry." Marilee thinks back to Vegas when the kidnapper kicked her over and over again. "The doctor will be in to talk to you shortly."

The nurse leaves and Devin and Betty quickly come to her side. "Marilee," Betty says.

"No, it's fine," Marilee says. "I wasn't sure this is what I wanted anyway, right." She notices Devin's vein popping out of his neck as he grinds his teeth. "Hey, I'm fine." She wants to reassure them both. "I'm going to go get dressed." As she shuts the door in the bathroom, she slides down the wall and breaks down. She isn't fine. She wanted this, but someone has taken it away from her and she is beyond devastated.

Jamie arrives back home excited to see Celia and Marilee. He starts to run up the stairs, but sees Betty sitting on the bottom step. "Hey," he says. "What's up?" He sits down next to her and notices her sulking. Grabbing her hand, he squeezes it. "Betty, what is wrong?"

"Jamie, I'm not supposed to tell you something, but I'm worried about Marilee. She says she is alright, but I'm not buying it."

"What is it?" Jamie asks as tears fall down Betty's face. "I won't say that you told me, I promise. But if it is about Marilee, I need to know."

Betty struggles with her thoughts for a moment. "Back in Vegas..." Betty begins.

"No," Marilee says as she comes down the stairs. "Betty, how could you?"

"I'm sorry," Betty cries. "I was worried and I don't buy this version of you that is fine. You need to tell him. He has a right to know."

Marilee sighs. "Fine, Betty. Just go." Betty wipes her eyes and gives Marilee a hurt expression. "Wait," Marilee says. "I'm sorry that I made you worry. Thanks for being there for me. Come here." She gives her a hug. "I'll talk to him. I promise."

Betty gives Jamie a smile before she leaves. "So," Jamie says, standing to meet her as she walks to the bottom of the stairs. "Something on your mind? Should I be as worried as Betty?"

"Okay, here it is," Marilee says, not wanting to get emotional about it. "Let's go take this to the bar." Jamie follows her and when she has a seat he goes behind the bar he pours them a couple of drinks. She takes a sip and looks at him. "Back in Vegas, I found out something. I didn't tell you because we were dealing with other issues."

"Well, what is it?" he asks.

"I found out..." she wills herself not to cry. "I found out that I was pregnant."

"Oh my God!" he says, his eyes lighting up. "Why didn't you tell me?"

"I lost it, Jamie," she says, taking another sip of her drink. She closes her eyes not wanting to see the disappointment on his face. "When I was kidnapped, I guess he kicked me too many times." Jamie grinds his teeth. She waits for him to throw a glass or a bottle at the wall, but he only sighs.

"Marilee, I'm so sorry." He says as he grabs her hand. "I know there is a lot going on between us, but I wish you would have told me. I could have been there for you."

"I know...I just...I was excited..." She begins to cry and he comes to comfort her. Vanessa comes in and Jamie gives her a nod to leave. Marilee cries into his chest for about an hour and he lets her without any interruptions, until Betty comes in with everyone standing behind her.

"Don't be mad," she says. "We all just want to be here for you."

Marilee laughs as she sees all her friends standing in the doorway. "It's okay," she says. "I would have told you all eventually."

"We totally understand," Charlotte says. Charley gives her a hug.

"We are all here for you, sis."

"Thanks, guys," Marilee says. "I appreciate it, I do, but all I want right now is to take a bath. I'll be fine, really." She walks out wishing she would have never said a word to Betty." Jamie curses under his breath when Marilee leaves the room.

"Jamie, she doesn't need you throwing a tantrum right now," Devin says.

Jamie laughs. "Why are you even here?" Jamie says, trying to calm his voice as he pours another drink. "You knew about this, didn't you?"

Devin looks down at his hands and sits down at the bar in front of Jamie. "She didn't have to tell me, Jamie. I knew it before she did."

"Of course you did," Jamie says with a laugh. He downs a shot of Fireball. "You could have told me."

"I wanted to give her the chance to tell you. It wasn't my place and you are forgetting that the people responsible for this is already dead." Jamie closes his eyes and pictures himself shooting Haley and gets a lot of satisfaction out of it, but he is still angry. "Betty called me yesterday and told me about the doctor's appointment. Marilee didn't want anyone to know, but Betty was afraid to go on an outing alone so naturally, I went."

"Every time," Jamie says. "I am the husband, I am supposed to be there for her when she needs me! Not you!"

"Then be there for her now and stop trying to find someone to blame for your screw-ups!" Devin pulls Jamie across the bar by the shirt. "Be the man she deserves you jackass." He pushes back and they exchange scowls.

"Okay," Dylan says. "This isn't helping anyone."

"Dylan is right," Vanessa says. "I think we need to give Marilee time to grieve, as well as Jamie. Marilee isn't the only one who lost something today."

Devin sighs. "Damnit, I didn't think," he says. "Jamie, my apologies. I was only thinking of Marilee. Can you forgive me?"

Jamie nods, but takes another sip and walks off. "I'll be in my office."

"I'm such an ass," Devin says.

"Yes," Vanessa says. "But in your defense, Jamie doesn't usually need coddling."

"I'm going to go talk to him," Dylan says.

"I'll come too," Devin says as he follows. "I'll need to go back home tonight."

"Jamie," Dylan knocks on the door. "Can we come in?"

"Sure, why not?" he says.

"Jamie, I really am sorry for my outburst," Devin apologizes again.

"It's fine. I'm just so angry."

"And you have reason to be, but you need to go and speak to her."

"She doesn't want to speak to me right now, Devin, I am sure of it."

"Why should you let that stop you?" Dylan says. "You are her husband and this was your child too. You both should be able to grieve together. If she doesn't want to talk to you, then you make her listen. As soon as she understands that you aren't going anywhere until she talks to you, the sooner she will back down."

"Would you do the same if it were Charlotte or Arianna? What would the two of you do?"

"I would talk until she knocked me unconscious," Dylan says.

"Same," Devin says with a laugh. With a jolt, Devin turns his head quickly to a picture on the shelf. He goes to grab it. "Who is this woman?" Devin says.

"That was my mother." Jamie says. "This is Celia Riley?"

"Yes," Jamie says, noticing Devin's face go pale. "Why?"

"Jamie, I saw her today."

"Not funny, Devin," Jamie says, grabbing the picture from him. He places it back on the shelf.

"I'm serious, at the doctor's office. I swear it was her."

"Devin, my Mom died when I was fourteen. I saw her die myself."

"I'm sorry," Devin says. "I know the story, but I swear the woman in that picture looks exactly like the woman at the doctor's office."

"People look like other people sometimes," Jamie says.

"You're probably right, sorry," Devin says, realizing this is a bad time to bring up his mother.

"I better get back home. Call me if you need me and Jamie don't hesitate to call next time. I am your friend first, always." Jamie looks shocked at his comment. "I won't admit it again." Devin smiles.

"Thanks, Devin," Jamie says, raising his glass to him.

"So, what are you waiting for," Dylan says. "Go talk to her."

~

Jamie walks upstairs wondering how this is going to go. Marilee is stubborn and when she doesn't want to talk, she runs. But she is in the bathtub so maybe he may have a shot to talk. He walks into the bedroom. It is quiet so she must still be in the bath. "Marilee?" he says, so he doesn't scare her. She doesn't answer. "Marilee?" he opens the bathroom door and she isn't there. "Shit!" He runs down the stairs to get everyone. "She's gone!" he yells. "Sasha!"

"Yes, sir?" she yells, running into the room.

"Celia, is she with you?"

"Yes, she is in the kitchen eating, why?"

"No reason," Jamie says, taking a breath. "I'm over-reacting, thanks Sasha."

"Jamie, what the hell?" Vanessa comes to calm him down.

"Marilee isn't upstairs," Jamie says. "She said she was going to take a bath."

"This is a big house, Jamie, don't freak out. She is probably here somewhere. God, you are getting paranoid."

"Do you blame me?" Jamie says. "Every time I turn around someone is trying to kidnap her."

"Good point," Vanessa says. "Maybe we need to put a tracking device on her."

Her phone is still in the bathroom. "Wait, I know, sorry guys. I know where she is. Stay here just in case though." He goes back upstairs to the bathroom closet. Pressing the hidden button, the door opens. He follows the hallway that leads to the tunnel and then out to the woods. As he opens the door, he enters the woods and walks to the stream where he used to go as a child. He sees Marilee sitting near it with a blanket wrapped around her.

"How did you find me?" she says, not even turning around.

"It took me a minute," Jamie says. "Why make us worry?"

"I'm sorry, I just needed some alone time."

"You could have had that in the bath."

"I just needed some time to myself, Jamie, somewhere besides the house."

"I get it, but we need to talk, Marilee. I know what I did makes you not want to talk to me. If I could go back and change things, I would. You don't have to deal with this alone."

"I just want to be angry, Jamie. I don't want to try and deal with it. If I think about it too long, I may not come back from it. I'm dealing the best way I know how."

"Do you blame me?" he asks. "Is that why you don't want to be alone with me?"

"No, of course not," she says. "Why would—

"What else am I supposed to think?" he says, trying not to sound too harsh. "I mean, you call Devin instead of me and it's been over a month since we have had any kind of real conversation, not even a kiss."

"I've kissed you, Jamie," she says.

"No, you haven't, not really and not like you used to."

"What do you want from me?" she says. "You want to know the truth. The truth is that if I let myself get too close to you, I'm afraid I'll fall apart. I don't want to feel that part of me right now."

"What part of you?" he asks, pushing her hair out of her face.

"Passion, love, the way you make me feel like you'd die for me."

"Why not?"

She sighs with annoyance. "I...don't know," she says. I can't explain it. I just want to be angry."

"Alright, you can be angry, but so can I. I just want to say one thing about it."

"What?" she says.

"I love you, Marilee and I always will. I will never leave you. Do you understand?"

"Yes," she says as she looks at the stream.

"And we can always try again."

"What?" her head swings back around to look up at him.

"We can try again. If you want another baby, I am on board with that." She gives him a smile. "I mean it. We can do it right here if you want."

She pushes him and laughs. "Thanks," she says. "And I'm sorry. I didn't think about your feelings in this. I know I'm not the only one who has lost something." He kisses her cheek.

"Let's get through this together then, okay."

"Deal," she says. "I'm still going to be a bit angry though."

"Me too." Jamie says, as thunder bangs overhead and makes them both jump. "Shit, we better get inside." As they get to the door that leads inside, it begins to storm. He closes the door and turns on the light so they can see their way through the now darkened staircase. He looks down at her and strokes her cheek. She closes her eyes and he kisses her. It seems like forever since their last kiss.

Marilee decides to hold off on being angry for a bit and enjoy the moment.

~

"We have to go back to Boston," Jamie says as he peeks in at Marilee in the shower, making her jump.

"Again?" she asks, turning off the water and wrapping a towel around her.

"Yes, sorry," he says. "They need me to approve the new warehouse."

"It's alright," she says. "I just wish we could spend some time together, you know, after last night. I finally think it's time we had some alone time."

"Really?" he says. "Well, you can come with us if you want."

"I don't think I want to spend all day alone while you are in meetings. It's okay, I can wait."

"Well, I'm glad you can," he says, making her laugh. He grabs her and takes her towel off. Kissing her lips, he picks her up and carries her to bed.

~

It has been a while since Jamie has been in such a good mood. He is on top of his work and making money. His family is getting back to normal and his wife is trusting him again. Things are looking up and he is showing it. "What is up with you?" Scott asks. "You are just a ray of sunshine today."

"Well, thanks," he says with a laugh.

"Marilee and him are doing a lot better," Dylan says. "It's pretty disgusting."

"We are getting there. I'm just glad she is finally talking to me...among other things." He smiles.

"Getting disgusting again," Dylan says.

"Alright, so we have a meeting with a man named Carl Yeager," Vanessa says, getting right to business. "He is the head honcho in Boston. If you want something done, he is the man to see. He deals in real estate, advertising, mergers, and he was forced to retire in the military. This man isn't someone to piss off so let's make this quick."

"Does he have any information on us?" Scott says.

"Just that we are in real estate," Vanessa says. "That is all I am aware of anyway."

"Who are we competing with here?" Dylan asks. "Families, I mean."

"A lot," she says. She gets the headshots out and puts them on the table. "You have the Massey Family which pulled from our lot and changed their name. Not sure which Family they came from, but are very much still in play here." She points at the first picture. "This is the main guy, his name is Neal Massey. He has two sons." She points to the other two pictures. "This one is Caine, the oldest. He is said to be a real charming businessman. No real trouble with him. But this one," She points to the other picture. "This one has been arrested on several occasions; petty theft, breaking and entering, and several assault charges. This loose cannon's name is Brian. He is very dangerous, but I hear he is real stupid."

"Who are these guys?" Jamie asks.

"These are the Roman Brothers. They stay on the north side. Hopefully, we won't have to worry about them. As long as we stay off their turf. Jack is the oldest and the brightest, and John is more worried about women than anything else. They are usually into it. Jack runs most things and this Family," she says, pointing at the last set of pictures "They want to run it all. They are in constant feuds with the other Families. They are the Lambert Family. They own just about everything downtown. Three sisters, two brothers, and father and mother still leading the way. They are a very prominent Family in this town. Bert, the father is even on the city council. The ones we have to worry about are the Masseys. They will find us, I am sure of it."

"Alright, then," Scott says. "I guess we are all caught up. Stay out of trouble and I will see y'all at the meeting tomorrow morning."

Vanessa starts clearing the table off as they leave. "Good work, Vanessa," Scott calls back. "Thank you, sir," she replies. "I don't know where these two would be without you," he says.

"Dead," she says with a smirk. "I'm sure of it."

"Ha, ha," Jamie says.

Dylan shrugs his shoulders. "It's true."

As Scott leaves, Vanessa turns to them. "Okay," she says. "Let's get ready."

"Oh, no," Jamie says. "You aren't getting us out tonight."

"Oh, come on," she says. "I'm in total need of a drunken night out."

"Vanessa, we need to be sharp for tomorrow, not hung over."

"Just one drink out then, please," she says. "I promise, one drink downstairs at the bar."

Dylan shrugs his shoulders again. "Why are you even here?" Jamie asks him with a sigh. "Fine," Jamie says. "One drink."

They sit at the bar and order their drinks. As Vanessa sits down, a man comes over to sit beside her. "Hey, there," he says. "What brings such a pretty little thing to Boston?" She looks up and realizes the man is Brian Massey.

"Business," she says, trying to play it nice. "And you?"

"Oh, I'm a local," he says. I just like this bar." He slides closer over to her to whisper in her ear. "How about me and you get out of here?"

"No, thanks," she says. "I'm here with my brothers." She glances their way.

"I see," he says. "Well, maybe some other time, then," he says with a smile and walks away. She gets a bad vibe about him, but assumes all is good. They finish their drinks and decide to go upstairs and turn in for the night. "Thanks for having a drink with me guys," she says, shutting her door. Going to the bathroom, she starts to get undressed. She stops when she smells a familiar cologne. She gasps as the bathroom door shuts and Brian is standing there. "Hello, pretty little thing," he says. She tries to scream out to Jamie and Dylan, but he covers her mouth. She bites his hand, turns around quickly, and punches him in the face. She runs to get away from him, but he catches her leg and pulls her back toward him. She kicks and fights him off again. "Damn, girl," he says. "You're a scrapper." He slaps her across the face and she goes down to the floor. "Sorry, sweetheart, but nobody turns down Brian Massey." He picks her up and throws her against the shower wall and turns on the water. "How about a nice shower?" he says, ripping off her dress the rest of the way. "No," she says, as he laughs.

"Oh, come on," he says. "I just can't resist that accent of yours."

She stops resisting. "Is that right?" she says. "Okay, love, in that case do what you must." He smiles.

"Well, that's more like it," he says. As he kisses her neck, she reaches behind her and pulls her knife. She stabs him in the neck and he falls on the tile floor.

She catches her breath for a moment and then it sinks in that she has just killed a member of the Massey Family. “Shit.” She calls Jamie and Dylan as quick as she can.

“What the hell?” Dylan says. “This is why we stay in the same room.”

“What the hell are we going to do, guys?” she says. “This can’t get out that we killed him. If anyone finds out this could mean war for us.”

“Shit, shit, shit!” Jamie says, pacing back and forth. “Okay, listen, this is what is going to happen. “Vanessa, you are going to go to my room and get some sleep. Dylan and I will take care of this.”

“Jamie—

“Just do what I say!” he shouts. “We’ll be at the meeting tomorrow, I promise.”

“Okay,” she says. “Please, just be smart about this. If anyone sees you...”

“I know,” he says. “War.”

After Vanessa leaves, Jamie and Dylan start to think. “How are we getting out of this one?” Dylan asks, leaning up against the wall.

“Got to go old school,” Jamie says.

“Oh, hell no,” Dylan says. “Come on. There has to be another way.”

“There is no way we are getting this body out of here without someone seeing us,” Jamie says. “We can’t burn it in the bathroom. Do you have a better plan?”

Dylan rolls his eyes. “I’ll go get something sharp.”

“It’s got to be quiet,” Jamie says.

“Got it,” Dylan says with a sigh. About thirty minutes later, Dylan comes back with some knives, tree trimmers, and some butcher knives.

“Alright,” Jamie says. “Let’s get started.”

“I really don’t want to do this,” Dylan says, looking down at the body.

“I know, but we do what we have to do, right?” Jamie says, bending down to cut first. He takes one of the butcher knives and slams it down on Brian’s arm until it separates from the body. Throwing it under the running water, they continue until Brian is in pieces. They take the pieces and dry them the best they can, places them in garbage bags, and then puts them in suitcases. They walk out the door and to the car without anyone giving them a second glance. They drive until they reach an alligator farm. “This will have to do,” Jamie says. “I miss Louisiana.” They dump the pieces and watch as the alligators have their fill. “Alright, let’s get back.”

The next day at the meeting they give Vanessa a nod that everything is okay. They get through the meeting and say nothing else about what had happened. “That went well,” Scott says after the meeting. He can tell something is off with the kids. “Am I missing something?” he asks. They all nod.

“Everything is fine, Dad, don’t worry.”

“Okay, then,” he says. “We got everything we need to move forward. Just go by the warehouse and sign the papers and we can head back home.”

“Sounds good,” Jamie says. “We’ll meet you there.”

They get in the car and Vanessa has to ask. “What did you do?” she asks. “I couldn’t sleep at all last night. I was worried sick.”

“Jamie went old school,” Dylan says.

“What do you...oh, God,” Vanessa says, realizing what they had to do. “Guys, I’m so sorry you had to do that.”

“We should be okay,” Jamie says. “Nobody gave us a second glance.”

"Good," Vanessa says. "Bastard got what was coming to him though."

"That he did," Jamie says, giving her a wink in the rear view mirror.

31

Not saying a word about what had happened over the weekend, Jamie is back to work trying to keep their faction the most powerful one in the United States. The morning begins with a phone call.
"Hello," Jamie says.

"Hello, Jamie," William says. "Long time."

"Yes, sir," Jamie says. "It's been a while." Even though Jamie is King of the US factions, he still respects William enough to call him sir and William admires that about Jamie.

"I just wanted to take this time to let you know that three more leaders will be retiring at the end of the year."

"That is great," Jamie says. "Which leaders?"

"Texas, California, and Washington."

"Oh, wow," Jamie says. "Those are our biggest. Washington only has the one daughter, who does he plan on appointing?"

"Well, that is just it. He wants her to take his place."

"What?" Jamie laughs. "A woman to head the whole faction?"

"Yes, and that is the only way he will retire so the choice is yours. If you agree, you will have to go to Washington to make it official."

"Well, I'll have to think about that one," Jamie says. "No woman has ever lead a whole faction before."

"Yes, but I hear she is well trained."

"Okay, I'll set it up. I would like your opinion on it though, William. I trust you. What would you do?"

"I would give her a trial period and if she performs well then I'd go with it."

"Thanks, William."

"No problem, Jamie. Another thing I wanted to talk to you about. I heard you all went up to Boston this weekend?"

"Yes, sir," Jamie says. "What about it?" Jamie curses to himself, hoping it has nothing to do with Brian.

"Well, I have a friend in Boston. He runs the hotel on Main Street. I think I may be able to convince him to sell."

"Wow, that would be wonderful, actually," Jamie says. "Thank you, sir."

"No problem. I will contact him and let you know. One other thing."

"Yes, sir?"

"Well, just a heads up, Neal Massey's son, Brian has went missing. He was last seen at the hotel you lot were at. If Neal finds out that you may have something to do with this...I'll just say that Frank was a puppy dog compared to this guy. Especially, when it comes to his sons."

"I understand, sir. I assure you, it will not be an issue," Jamie says. He doesn't deny it, but he doesn't come clean either. He knows William probably already knows anyway. He has to make sure that nobody can link the three of them with Brian at the hotel bar. That is the only time they can be associated with him.

Jamie takes a breath as he hangs up with William, and calls in some favors to quickly take care of the problem in Boston. He calls in Vanessa. "We may have a problem," he says.

"What is it?" she asks. "Do I need a drink?"

"Maybe," he says. "William just called." He continues to tell her the problem with the Massey Family.

"Do you think they will link us to him, Jamie?" She sighs. "Shit, I am so sorry."

"No, no," he says, before she starts to panic. He grabs her shoulder. "I think I took care of it. I called in a favor. We should be good."

"Damn, that's all we need is to go to war with a Family right now. I mean, we would win but still."

"William said that Massey made Frank look like a puppy dog," Jamie says with a hint of laughter.

"That isn't good," she says, scrunching her nose.

"Well, let's just hope my guy comes through. Right now, let's worry about Washington." He gets his notes out and starts researching.

~

As everyone eats dinner, Marilee turns to Jamie and gives him a raised eyebrow because everyone is eating and not talking. "Okay," she says. "What is going on?"

"Nothing," Jamie says. "Why?"

"Everyone is just too quiet."

"Good food," Dylan says.

"You have to go out of town again, don't you?" Marilee says with a sigh.

"I'm sorry," he says.

"No, no," she says. "It's fine, I just hate the timing."

"I know and if it wasn't an emergency..."

Marilee smiles. "I know. Just hurry back."

~

Jamie boards their private plane and as the door shuts, he gets a feeling in his gut. "Something isn't right," he says.

"What?" Charley asks. "Don't freak me out, this is my first big trip with you guys."
"Sorry," Jamie says as the corner of his lip turns upward. "I need to make a call before we get in the air." Jamie dials the hotel in Boston to make sure they are still needed. "Is the issue resolved?" Jamie asks as one of his new recruits answers the phone. He is a young man by the name Heath.
"Ah..." Heath mumbles.
Jamie narrows his eyes at the phone. "Heath is there something I should know?"
"No, sir...I..."
"Heath, I will kill you if you lie to me," Jamie says with a stern tone.
"Sir," Heath whispers. "It's a trap, get home now."
~

As Marilee goes over in her head that her family is back to normal, she smiles. She is happy she could get passed all the drama and get back to being happy again. But just as they are getting normal again, he has to leave. Brushing her hair, she sighs. "It's only a couple of days," she says as she looks at herself in the mirror. As she turns to walk out of the bathroom, she sees an older man standing in the doorway. She jumps, startled. "Who are you?" She asks as she backs away slightly.

The man smiles. "Sorry to scare you," he says. "I did knock, but you didn't answer. My name is Neal Massey. I have a problem I'm hoping can be sorted out." He motions for her to take his hand.

"What is this about?" She refuses his hand and walks by him into the bedroom.

"If you would come with me, my dear, I think we can straighten everything out." He walks to the doorway and motions for her to go before him. She obeys. As she begins to walk down the stairs, she notices Betty, Sasha, and Charlotte all in a line.

"What is going on?" she asks, stopping midway down the stairs. "Where is—

"Your daughter is fine," he says. "She playing in her room."

"Well, I would really appreciate it if you could let the nanny go up with her. I don't like her being up there alone." Marilee glares at him until he finally complies.

"Very well," he says, waving for Sasha to go upstairs. Marilee gives her a nod as she passes them on the stairs. "Billy, go stand at the door. Will that suffice, my lady," he says, gesturing for her to comply with his wishes. "If you would join your Family downstairs now." Biting her lip, she has no other choice but to obey his command.

As she joins the girls, she turns to him. "Would it be alright if we took the conversation into the bar?"

Massey and his men laugh. "Not at all, my dear."

Marilee goes behind the bar to make them some drinks. "Okay, so what is it that we need to straighten out?" she says, pouring the girls some shots. "We like to drink Fireball here. Would you and your men like a shot?"

"You are very hospitable," he says narrowing his eyes. "That's either brave or clever." He smells the shot of whiskey.

"I like to think of myself as both sometimes, but I still don't know if you are a threat to me. Do I need to worry?"

"I'm afraid so," he says. Marilee swallows hard as the burn of the Fireball helps her from being to panicky.

"What did he do?" she asks pouring another shot and guzzles it wondering what Jamie has gotten them into this time.

"His other girl seems to have had a chat with my youngest son and now he has gone missing."

"Is that all?" Marilee laughs.

"I don't find my son missing amusing and neither is your predicament. I would think you'd be a bit more alarmed with all your guards dead and all your friends about to be." He points his gun at Charlotte.

"Just because your son is missing doesn't mean Jamie had anything to do with it!" She shouts a bit desperate.

"That is more like it," he says with a smirk. Marilee makes him and herself another drink. They drink at the same time never losing eye contact with each other.

"So, what's the plan, then?" Marilee says.

"I'm trying to figure out which one of you to kill."

"For me to kill," the man next to him says.

"Oh, I forgot to introduce my oldest, Caine."

Marilee looks to Charlotte and Betty for some reassurance, but she gets none. They look just as frightened as she does. She pours another shot for his oldest. "Well, then you get one too." She pours herself another as well. Caine doesn't even pick up the glass.

"You better take it easy on those," Massey says. After all, you are in the presence of monsters."

"I've dealt with my share of monsters," Marilee says.

"Not like me." He smirks. Don't you have a daughter upstairs?" He notices Marilee's catch her breath and he laughs. "Don't worry." He rolls his eyes.

"Though it would be fair, a kid for a kid." Caine says.

"Why do you assume he is dead?" Charlotte finally speaks to get them to stop talking about Celia.

Massey sighs. "Marilee knows. If anything was to happen to your little girl, do you think you would know? Do you think you would already feel the pain before you knew for sure?" He says staring at his glass with anger. When Marilee doesn't answer he snaps. He pulls her over the bar by the shirt and points his gun to her head. "I asked you a question!"

"Yes!" She cries. "I would already know."

He looks at Charlotte. "And there is your answer. Plus, we have a man inside the hotel that said Brian went to the lady's room, but somehow he never came out. A trace of blood was found in the room where she was staying. Shall I go on?"

"Father, just pick one and let's be done with this!"

"Fine," Massey says picking up his gun. "Sorry, sweetheart." He points his gun at Marilee. Betty runs at him to stop him.

"No!" she yells, just as the shot is fired. She turns to Marilee who is gasping for air. "Sorry," Betty cries as she sees Marilee's face and realizing what she has just done. She smiles to comfort Marilee, but it quickly fades away. As she falls to the floor, Marilee and Charlotte fall with her.

"Betty, no!" They both cry. "Why did you do that? Marilee asks.

"This isn't happening," Charlotte says. "She's going to be fine."

Marilee looks up to Massey and his oldest. "You will die for this," she cries. "I will make sure of it."

"I'm sure you will try," he says. "Until then." He backs away to leave, but stops as he begins to cough. Marilee holds her head high as he bends over in pain. "What the hell did you do?" He takes the shot glass and throws it at her. She ducks as it flies over her head. "I'm going to kill you," he shouts.

"I'm sure you'll try," she says.

Dad, we got to get you to the hospital," Caine says. "The men will take care of them." Neal Massy gives her a look of shear hatred as he is dragged out by his son. "Kill them all!" Caine shouts.

Charlotte quickly grabs Marilee and runs behind the bar as gunshots are fired. She quickly grabs the gun from behind the bar and Marilee curses herself for not knowing it was there earlier. Charlotte runs out in the gunfire and starts shooting and it doesn't take long before all Massey's men are dead. Charlotte falls into the chair bleeding.

"Oh my God!" Marilee says.

"I'm fine," she says as she falls in the floor next to Betty. "I'll be fine." Marilee cries as she hovers over the bodies of her best friends.

"The guys come in a few minutes later to the chaos. It is like life in slow motion to Marilee as Charley and Dylan come in to see their soul mates lying on the floor, their bodies covered in blood. All she can hear are screams and cries and she knows it is all because of her. She tries to comfort Charley, but he throws her off of him. Jamie comes to comfort her, but he feels broken inside himself.

~

As the storms get worse, the Family gather around by the fire in the living room. Sasha makes them some coffee and decides to take Celia upstairs and give everyone some grieving time. “I can’t believe she is gone,” Marilee says as she cries on Bryce’s shoulder. “Why did she do that? This is all my—

“No,” Bryce says. “We aren’t doing that.” He places his arm around her. “We aren’t placing blame. This was her decision.”

“She was stupid!” Charley says, shoving the coffee table towards them with his foot. He stands up and walks to the bar.

Dylan comes in with Vanessa. “How is Charlotte?” Marilee says.

“She will make it,” Vanessa says. “It looked a lot worse than it was.” Marilee nods and puts her head back on Bryce’s shoulder.

“He will hate me forever,” Marilee says. “She died to save me. He will never forgive me. I will never forgive myself.” She continues to cry wondering if Neal Massey survived the poison she gave him. Jamie stands up to go and talk to Charley.

“That may not be the best idea,” Bryce says.

“I’ll risk it,” Jamie says. As he walks into the bar, he grabs two beers from the fridge and sits down beside Charley. He slides him the other one and doesn’t say anything. About half-way through the beer Charley decides to talk.

“I just don’t understand,” he says. “Why her? Out of everyone, why her? She was the good one.”

Jamie doesn’t take offense, because he knows Charley is right. All Betty wanted to do was help people all the time. She always wanted to do the right thing, ever since he can remember. “She was.” Jamie continues to drink his beer. “Charley...”

“Don’t,” Charley says. “I don’t need a speech.”

“I wasn’t going to give you one. I just know I felt this way once. When I thought Marilee was dead and all I wanted was revenge.”

"Yeah, well," Charley says with a laugh. "She came back, Betty isn't."

"No, but just know that when you are ready, I will be too. All you need to do is say the word and we are gone."

Charley nods and bites his lip trying not to cry. "Thanks, man. I know I give you a hard time because of Marilee, but Betty really loved you. Thank you for loving her back." He sniffs and wipes his nose on his sleeve.

Jamie coughs, but can't contain his tears. "Damnit," he says.

"Bury it, son," Scott says as he sees his son about to lose control. "Bury that shit and use it when the time comes." The Family join them both in the bar and gather around. "We will find the son-of-a-bitch and kill him, but we need to do this right. He is clever, but so are we. He will join his father soon. So everything else will have to go as scheduled. All meetings, plans, builds, and deals will continue."

"Dad..."

"You have until the weekend, son...that is all. I will not let him live any longer than that."

"Agreed," Bryce says.

"When we hurt, work helps," Scott says looking to Charley. "Trust me, hold it in until the time comes. It will give you more satisfaction."

"Okay, let's get to work," Jamie says, giving Charley a glance for an agreement. Charley nods and continues to drink his beer. Scott starts to leave the room, helping Missy walk out with her crutches. "We will stay at the lodge. I will be here to help you get business taken care of. Meet me in the morning for breakfast."

"Dad, the storm is too bad outside. Everyone needs to stay here tonight."

Scott sighs. “Alright, where do we sleep?”

“Take your pick,” Jamie says. “There are two guest suites down here and two upstairs.”

“We’ll take one down here. It will be easier for Missy.”

“Thanks, sweetie,” Missy says as she bends down and gives Jamie a kiss on the cheek and gives Charley a sympathetic smile. “If you need to talk, I’m here.” They both nod with a forced smile as they walk out.

The phone rings and Jamie sees Williams face on the screen. “Hello, William,” Jamie says.

“Jamie, I am so sorry to hear about Betty. We are on our way. Anything we can do, we will do it.”

“Thanks, William,” Jamie says. “We could use you soon. We may be starting a war.”

~

32

After Betty's funeral, they have a reception at the house for the Family. Everyone loved Betty. Jason Saunders comes to give his condolences. "I loved her spirit," he says. "She would have been the best doctor."

"Thanks for coming," Jamie says with a hint of anger in his voice. He doesn't need to feel right now because all he can feel is anger. "Excuse me," he says as he walks away. Marilee gives Jason a half-hearted smile and continues greeting people as they walk in.

The weekend has come. All their work is caught up and they are ready to start planning their revenge. Jamie goes to his office and William, Scott, and the rest of the men follow.

"So, where are we doing this?" Charley says, anxious and a bit twitchy.

"It needs to be private," William says. "Maybe even remote."

"This is their domain, William," Scott says. "I don't want to get caught up in a trap. We need a surprise attack."

"We need to know where they are going to be at the time of attack," Jamie says. "We have a guy on the inside. I can get him to find out." He sends a quick text.

"So, what about weapons?" Bryce asks.

"Well, we have no shortage on weapons," Scott says. "But we need to do this as quiet as possible. We don't want to alert the police."

"We also need to do it as quickly as possible," William says. "In and out."

Jamie's phone buzzes and he smiles. "Well, I guess we will be going to a party at the Ritz-Carlton. He will be there and get this, Neal...not dead."

"What?" Charley says. "How?"

"I guess Marilee didn't give him enough poison. They got him at Mass General."

"Well, easy target, right?" Charley says. "Let's go."

"Maybe," Jamie says. "But there will be a lot of people there."

"I can get you in," William says. "As long as you can get in and out quickly."

"Done," Jamie says. "You ready, Charley?"

"Hell yeah," Charley says.

"We still have to figure the party out," Dylan says. "Do we want to take men with us or go solo?"

"Let's take a few with," Scott says. "You never know when things may go bad."

"Alright, research mode for a bit and then plan," Jamie says. "We need floor plans, names of employees, people we can pay off, and the loyal ones we need to kill. What is his favorite food, women, drinks, and what we can do to get him alone? I want him to suffer, but I don't want anyone around when Charley kills him." Jamie notices Charley's reaction to his comment. "Are you sure you want to do this, Charley? I can—

"No, I got this," Charley says. "It should be me."

"Okay," Jamie says. "Then we do it tomorrow night. We can hit the hospital first and then go to the Hotel. Let's get to work." Jamie claps his hands and everyone goes their separate ways to get to work.

"Let me get Missy to her room and I will be back to help," Scott says. They work all night on the plan to kill Neal, Caine, and anyone else who get in their way.

Around two in the morning they fall asleep on the couch. Everyone piled on top of one another and the doorbell wakes Jamie up. He sees Sasha start to run down the stairs. “I got it Sasha, you can go back to sleep.”

“Thank you, sir,” she says.

The loud cracks of thunder still rumbles through the house. Lightning shines through the floor to ceiling windows in the living room. The storm isn’t showing any mercy tonight. Jamie walks up the foyer steps and opens the door. A familiar face stares at him. “Hello, Jamie,” she says. His heart stops for a moment and he is taken back in time. As the thunder sounds and lightning strikes, it snaps him back to the present. “Mom?”

A Garrison Family Saga

Book One: *Monstrous Men*

Book Two: *Vicious*

Book Three: **Title Coming Soon**

Made in the USA
Columbia, SC
07 November 2020

24091958R00186